Journey's Revenge:

A #1544 Novel

Journey's Revenge:

A #1544 Novel

Simone Kelly

www.urbanbooks.net

Urban Books, LLC
300 Farmingdale Road, NY-Route 109
Farmingdale, NY 11735

Journey's Revenge: A #1544 Novel

ISBN 13: 978-1-64556-594-9

First Mass Market Printing June 2024
First Trade Paperback Printing November 2023
Printed in the United States of America

10 9 8 7 6 5 4 3 2 1

Distributed by Kensington Publishing Corp.
Submit Orders to:
Customer Service
400 Hahn Road
Westminster, MD 21157-4627
Phone: 1-800-733-3000
Fax: 1-800-659-2436

Acknowledgments

Wooohooo! This was definitely a wild ride completing this book. To think this all started because several of my coaching clients were considering getting a sperm donor. It sparked an outlandish idea that launched this new supernatural series, and now I can't stop.

I'm grateful to the Urban Books family: Carl Weber, Martha Weber, Jasmine Weber, and Karen Mitchell. To the editors, Diane Taber and Alanna Boutin for their amazing feedback.

A heartfelt thanks to my literary coach, who I named the "book psychologist," Coach Emily Claudette Freeman.

Thanks to all that helped me with my research:

Marjorie Bernard, Dr. Angela Brinson-Brown, Dr. Cybele Pacheco, Tina Coppens, NYPD Detective 2nd Grade David Cherry, Mama Myriam, and Kenny Belizaire.

Special thanks to my brainstorming pals and beta readers who let me call them with my crazy ideas:

Acknowledgments

Monica Gonzalez, Opal Pabarue, Delilah Garcia aka my Spanish translator, Cheryl Kendrick, and a special big shout out to Tesha Sylvester, who is always down to hear the spoilers. She's great at giving me feedback on who I should kill—in my books, of course. ~insert evil laugh~

I'm so grateful for the Own Your Power's Writer's Lab who joins me every Sunday online, so we can crush our writing goals and hold one another accountable:

NORM! AKA Latrice Scott, who was there every Sunday rain or shine, so I call her Norm from Cheers. LOL Also, the most consistent members are Laron Henderson, Lora Mitchell, Rolande Vantaire, Sheryl Singletary, and Yali Giovanni. I'm so proud of you all for staying true to your passion for becoming an author, and I'm grateful for our little FB community that's over 100 members and counting.

Congratulations to the You're Making a Scene Content Winners: Warrington Etienne, Delilah Garcia, and Lena Marie.

Last but not least, Johnny A. Thank you for your patience, your love, your support and for being my voice of reason to keep me calm. You are appreciated beyond measure. Love ya, babe.

A huge hug and kiss to the readers who have supported me throughout the years. I hope to continue my growth as an author and bring you many more adventures. See ya in the next novel.

Also by Simone Kelly:

Jack of All Trades, Master of None?

At Second Glance

Like a Fly on the Wall

Whispers from the Past

#1544

Chapter 1

Journey

Journey felt like she had been heavily sedated. Tick tock. Tick tock. Her body felt so weary. Tick tock . . . tick tock. The clock's ticking sound was so loud in Journey's ears. Her mouth was dry and felt sticky as if pasted with rubber cement glue. Journey slowly struggled to open her eyes that felt sealed shut.

Then she heard a soft whisper of a girl's voice say, "Wake up. You're missing out on life, sugar."

Was she dreaming? She wondered where the hell she was. Her eyes slowly focused on a teenage girl, maybe about 17 years old, lying in the bed across from her. The room was white and light blue. Journey was freezing. Her vision was blurred. She could make out a girl sitting across from her. The young girl had sickly pale skin. She pushed her long, fluffy auburn curls behind her ears.

"Heeeey, Sleeping Beauty." The girl's blue eyes sparkled, and she smiled wide, revealing a small gap.

Although her skin was pale, Journey could see she was so full of energy. Journey wanted to reply, but her mouth refused to open. Her eyes followed the girl as she jumped out of her twin-sized bed and sat on the edge of Journey's. She felt so lost. She wondered if she and the stranger were friends. She also wondered if she had finally gone crazy and ended up in a mental ward.

"I'm Francesca." Her face was sprinkled with honey-colored freckles to compliment her hair. She pointed to the whiteboard near the edge of Journey's bed that revealed her name.

Journey Salazar

"I see that you're Journey. What a bad-ass name." Her accent was strong, definitely not a city girl. Francesca had a serious twang when she spoke, a real Southern belle.

Journey's brows crinkled as she struggled to speak.

"Take your time, girl." Francesca encouraged her. "You probably just need some water, sugar."

Journey glanced down at her body. She had bandages on her arm and neck. Francesca pointed to the water bottle near Journey's bed.

Her voice was a raspy low whisper. "Thank you." Journey took her time to move her arm. It felt weighed down with a sandbag. She couldn't do it. She searched her unfamiliar surroundings, and a cyclone of fear enveloped her. Journey's heart beat faster as the panic set in.

The chart on the door.

The intrusive beeping sounds from the machines.

The *Get Well* balloons.

The sterile smell of rubbing alcohol was smacking her in the face, alerting her that something terrible had happened to her. She felt like she just came out of the desert after walking for miles. "Hey, Fran . . . Fran . . . cesca. Where . . . Where are we?"

"Emory. Emory Hospital. We were in the ICU together and now, we've been moved. You're stable now after your operations and all. Helloooooo . . . So wait, you don't remember anything, huh?"

"No." She looked at her wrist and noticed the hospital bracelet. Journey tried to move her arm again, but the IV restricted her. She also realized how her nails were longer than she kept them and painted a beautiful aqua color. The beautiful peacock tattoo sleeve on her arm was wrapped in bandages and peeking out at her. The peacock used to seem fuller and almost alive, but now it stared back at her, almost mocking her. Her arm had much less muscle tone as well.

Francesca slapped the hard mattress. "Girl, you are lucky to be alive! It was not your time, that's all. You must have a lot of living left to do." She had an old soul, sounding like someone's Black grandma. Francesca lowered her voice. "I heard the nurses gossiping about you when they thought I was asleep. They said you tried to take yourself out."

Journey examined the IV hooked up to her. Francesca's hand brushed against her arm.

"You had a laahhht of broken bones, internal bleeding, brain injuries. . . . You a miracle, girl. You better thank God and baby Jesus." She fell back and laughed. "You got a second chance. Them angels ain't finna take you with them just yet." She narrowed her eyes and whispered closely, "Suicide is a sin, Journey."

A shiver ran through Journey's body. She nodded slowly. "What? Suicide? I . . . didn't . . . didn't try to kill myself." Her memory was foggy, but she knew that could not be right. She would never try to kill herself. Journey loved her life. She searched her mind for clues but had none. She had no idea how long she had been in this hospital.

"Well, it was all over the Atlanta news channels. You didn't land on the bottom floor like you planned, or you would have definitely been dead. Splat!" She slapped her hands together. "You only fell a couple floors down on someone's patio." She laughed. "Them angels caught you, sugar! They said, nope not today, Satan!"

Journey was not amused by Francesca's callus way of describing her near-death experience. A chill came across her body, and she felt an intense fear come back to her. It was a faint memory that she needed to escape to somewhere fast. Was she being chased? Did someone attack her? Journey swallowed as she felt chills go down her back. A burning house. She heard the roaring flames.

"Fiiiiire," she mumbled. The fear of being trapped in a burning building resurfaced. "Fire. In the news, did they . . . did they mention the fire? Did anyone die?"

"Fire? Um, no chile. They said you were fighting with the people in the apartment. Causing a whole commotion. Arguing and stuff." Her speech was rapid. "You was acting crazy, got mad, and jumped. I pray you get help, 'cause they might put you in the crazy house when you get outta here, so you better act normal and apologize. They said you kinda snapped. A psychotic episode. Do you take meds?"

Journey said, "What? No . . . no, that can't be right. I remember seeing the flames. I felt the heat from the fire and all. I remember . . ."

Francesca gave her a look of pity and shook her head. "Journey, Journey . . . just feel your head. Was you high?"

Her arm was so stiff, as if she hadn't moved it in years. She took her time to raise it and felt her forehead. She slowly slid her hand across her cold scalp. The hairs on Journey's forearms rose. "Where's my hair? My hair! Are you serious? Who did this to me?" She teared up as she felt a short buzz cut. Although it was gentle to the touch, soft like velvet, she felt violated. "Who the fuck cut off all my hair off?" Her heart raced.

"Relaaaaax. Hair grows back! They had to shave it for your brain surgery. You had two of them. You dived off of a damn building, girl. Would you rather have a lot of hair and be brain dead, or be bald now and heal later? They said you had swelling of the brain or something. If you could have seen how many doctors came in here to study your ass like a lab rat. I told you; you are a miracle. They even had med students in here learning. I could barely get any sleep myself. Like them raggedy li'l' curtains block out the noise. Tuh!" She shook her head. "It was like you were a celebrity. You had a lot of visitors too."

As she pointed around the room, Journey noticed the cards and flowers on the counters and shelves. Her eyes gazed up at the colorful *Get Well Soon* balloons in the corner of the room.

"It was hard to get some privacy. I'm so happy you woke up, though. Now, I can finally have some company. It's been lonely up in here." She shook her head. "But let me stop complaining." Francesca slapped Journey's leg and laughed. "Oops, sorry."

Journey didn't feel anything. Not one thing. She looked down and noticed her legs were like long poles under the white sheet. She looked malnourished. She used to have nice legs, not these long poles. This had to be a nightmare. She wanted to wake up from this terrible dream.

Francesca said, "Oh, yeah, you probably can't feel that. Your spinal cord took a beating in that fall, they said."

Journey tried to move her legs. Fear gripped at her heart. "What? Am I . . ."

"Paralyzed? I don't think so. They been testing your reflexes and stuff. I heard them say you weren't. You might be able to walk again. It's just gonna take some time. You got enough fight in you, Journey."

Footsteps were approaching. Francesca looked toward the door. "Oh, shit. He coming." Francesca jumped back into her bed and pretended to be asleep.

A tall Latino man with sky-blue scrubs walked in. No, he glided in. His long strides were smooth and graceful. He had a low haircut and very neat goatee. Journey thought he had the most beautiful eyebrows and alluring hazel eyes. They opened wide when he saw Journey. He stopped in his tracks when their eyes met.

He came close to her and said in a soft voice, "You're awake? Oh my God. You're awake? Journey?"

He put his fingers in front of her eyes, and Journey's eyes followed them as he moved them from left to right. He laughed and then yelled toward the door. "She's awake!" He ran out, and Journey thought he was the doctor or a nurse or something. He got some more people to enter the room, and everyone started cheering and clapping.

She looked to her left and saw Francesca lying in her bed, smiling, peeking from under her covers like a child who was up way past her bedtime.

He sat down next to her. "Hi, Journey. I'm Dominick, your medical assistant. Can you hear me? Can you understand me? Squeeze my hand if you can understand me."

She tried to squeeze but was so weak. She felt a light twitch. That was the most that she could do.

"That's it. Good job, Journey."

She thought he was so fine. Not really her type, but fine nonetheless. His long, dark lashes drew her in to examine his handsome face. Dominick's right hand had a dramatic tattoo on the fingers that extended all the way up to his forearm. They were streaks of lightning bolts in hues of purple, red, and black. She stared at it, amazed by the detail. He had a work of art on his body.

"I'm so glad to have you back." His voice was so soothing. It was deep and calming. She knew that voice. She remembered hearing him in her dreams. Dominick. *Yes,* she thought, *he tells me stories. He talks to me. He plays me music. In my dreams? Or was it real? Dominick*. Just hearing his name made her feel safe. She relaxed, realizing that he was one of the people who took care of her. Journey tried to smile.

"Oh my. What's that?" He banged on the tray table over her bed. "Is that a smirk, Journey? Are you smiling? I feel your hand squeezing. It's gentle, but I felt you. You're doing great, mama. That's it." He almost looked like he was tearing up.

More people entered the room. He looked up. "Dr. Amadi! Thank God you're here. She's awake!"

The doctor came in with two nurses. Dominick quickly got out of the way. Dr. Amadi was a short man, stocky, with deep chocolate skin with glasses. He had a soft African accent. "Is it easier to blink? Just blink twice for yes."

Journey opened her mouth slightly. For some reason now, when she tried to speak, nothing came out. Francesca had heard her just fine, but nothing worked with them. She blinked twice, but felt so helpless. She felt so lost not being able to put the pieces of her memories together.

Who are all of these people?

After all of the clapping and cheering, the doctor said, "I'm going to alert her mother."

Journey just wondered, *Why isn't she here? Why would she leave me here with these strangers?*

A female doctor came in, cheesing so hard. "Hi, Journey. I'm Dr. Alexander." She was a slender, tall black woman with cat-rimmed glasses. She had a beautiful pyrite crystal around her neck, hanging from a gold chain that looked like a big gold nugget. It sparkled when the light shined on her. She had style. Journey liked her energy a lot. She started to shine a tiny flashlight in Journey's eyes and started examining her.

"We're just checking your vitals to make sure you are okay. You've been asleep for a long time, my dear." Journey could hear a slight Southern twang in her voice, but it sounded as if she were trying to cover it with a more proper accent.

The doctor put the stethoscope to Journey's heart. "My, my, you're just as excited as we are. Can you take a few deep breaths with me, Journey?" Dr. Alexander then took a dramatic deep breath. Her chest heaved as she tried to show Journey what she wanted her to do.

Journey tried to copy her but could not fill up her lungs as powerfully as Dr. Alexander had.

"That's it, that's good. You're doing it." The doctor encouraged her as she patted her hand.

There was an audience of the medical team behind her. Journey was so confused and afraid, but the doctor had a motherly energy that soothed her. She couldn't believe this was happening. Journey felt all these eyes on her, and this sudden shame came crashing down on her. They were judging her. They were pitying her. She was furious, since she would never try to kill herself. A psychotic episode? That was not her!

There is nothing wrong with me, she thought. She had so many questions. Who did this to her? How long had she been there? She had to remember. She wanted her life back.

Journey fell into a deep sleep and woke up to a warm hand holding hers. She heard soft sniffling and crying. "Jesus! Thank God you're really awake. Nini, my baby. I thought you slipped back into a coma. You had us so worried." The woman kissed her on her forehead and caressed her face. "Thank you, God!"

Her mother looked different from how Journey remembered her. She had gained some weight in her face. Her normal black bob had streaks of silver as if she had forgotten to dye her hair.

She thought, *How long have I been here?* Journey felt like she had been transported into a damn time machine. She wondered why she couldn't speak. She could blink, but nothing would come out of her mouth. She had this sudden urgency to leave but felt so trapped.

Journey looked behind her mother to see Francesca making eye contact. Maybe she could ask for her help in translating, since Francesca could hear her loud and clear, but her curtain was closed now. Maybe she was sleeping.

Her mom rubbed Journey's legs, and she felt something brush against her. It was a very light sensation. Her legs still couldn't move. She blinked rapidly to let her know she was fully awake.

"Can you try to speak? Can you say something, Nini?"

She tried to open her mouth slowly, but nothing came out.

Dominick came back in. He said softly to her mother, "Como es ella?" He leaned over Journey. "How are you doing, mama? Are you in any pain? Blink twice for yes, once for no."

She blinked once.

"Do you know why you are here?" her mother asked.

She blinked once.

"You were with Ty. Your father. You had us all worried you fell from—"

Dominick touched her shoulder softly and whispered, "Maybe don't go there just yet."

Her head snapped back. "Can you please give me some time alone with my daughter, Dominick?"

Journey knew that tone all too well.

He nodded quickly. "Sure, sure." He left quietly, looking back with a smirk.

Her memories were blurry but coming back slowly. She remembered going to Ty's apartment. That's where the fire was. Tyler Carter, sperm donor #1544. Her father. She remembered there was a scuffle, a bad fight. Journey blinked, trying to wash the memory away.

Was I the cause of the fight?

Her mom interrupted her thoughts. "I don't know why on Earth you'd want to hurt yourself. You have a wonderful life that any girl would dream of. I gave you everything you ever wanted, Nini. I'm so glad you didn't succeed." Her eyes got misty. "You almost left me alone. You better never try this shit again." She started to blow her nose. "I'm going to get you top-notch therapy and help you get back to your old self again. I might even hire Dominick to help us when we bring you home. You'll see. It will all work out." She sounded as if she were trying to convince herself.

"Maybe your sister Elizabeth can come back to visit longer and stay with us for a bit. She did mention she would be willing to help since she does her schooling virtually. I think her doing Reiki on you last week is what woke you up. She is very talented. That was her birthday gift to you. She's such a kind soul."

Her sister Elizabeth? Journey suddenly got excited at the thought of her sister. She was amazed that Elizabeth had come all the way from Cali to see her. She was disappointed that she didn't even get to meet her in person after all this time video chatting. They had met through the sibling registry for the New Life Fertility Group.

She thought that Elizabeth was still mad at her. Journey had withheld the truth about meeting their father Ty for over a month. Elizabeth was very upset with her secrecy and felt Journey was hogging Ty all to herself. Journey had to admit it that she was being selfish. She had wanted to build the strongest relationship with Ty and be his favorite. Journey had been the first to contact him, so in her mind, she deserved to foster the closest relationship with their father. After all, it was only fair since out of the siblings that she knew, she was the only one without a stepdad in her life. However, her greediness had backfired, and now she felt that all of her plans had failed.

Her mom's voice was hopeful, as if she were trying to convince herself. "You'll be teaching yoga again in no time. And you'll register again for college, so you can finish your degree." Her mom rubbed Journey's bony knee while she looked up at the ceiling and squinted as if trying to hold back more tears.

Journey screamed in her mother's mind.

"I did not try to kill myself. I didn't do this to myself, Mommy. I don't need help."

Her mom jerked back as if she had heard her telepathic message, but she didn't say anything.

Journey still didn't know how long she had been in that bed and was frustrated. She wanted to scream until the entire hospital heard her. Her chest heaved in frustration.

Her mom stroked Journey's soft peach fuzz on her head and stared at her. Journey closed her eyes, and a tear cascaded down her cheek. "Oh, don't worry, Nini. Oh, my poor baby. You will heal, my love." She wiped her tears. "You will be able to speak and walk again soon with therapy. The doctors are hopeful. You passed many tests so far. Everyone has been rooting for you these last two months."

These last two months.

These last . . . *two months?*

She was frozen with that new revelation. Two months? She couldn't believe it had been that long. That freaking long? Her eyes scanned the room and noticed some Christmas decorations pinned up over the whiteboard. A Santa and some reindeer cut-out designs were on the door. Last she remembered, it was September. She missed her twenty-third birthday. Sadness took over. Her chest felt heavy.

Her mother rambled on. "You are sooooo loved." She waved her hand across the room, and Journey's eyes followed the display of flowers and cards on the windowsill once again. She showed Journey a photo on her phone. There was a beautiful Latino girl that stood out first. She had shiny ebony curls and wore a hoody with baggy pants. Her honey-colored eyes and lashes were long, just like Journey's. Two boys embraced the girl in a loving sandwich. One was very tall and lanky with deep chocolate skin and a low haircut, almost bald. The other boy was a little shorter and stockier with long blond dreads and very pale skin, almost a little sunburned on his nose. Although they all had different skin tones, they resembled one another. The eyes and lips were similar: almond-shaped eyes and curvaceous lips. Their eyes lit up, exuding so much joy.

"See, your sister and brothers came to see you. Do you remember them?"

Journey blinked twice, realizing who they were. *OMG, THE FANTASTIC FOUR!* Her crew, her siblings. She'd only met them on video. She was so sad that she had missed them in person. Robbie, Zack, and Elizabeth.

Her throat got tight, trying to hold back the roar of sadness from missing everything. Tears came down uncontrollably now. Journey's cries were loud, like a tortured animal. The loud sound frightened her mother. A nurse peeked in the room to make sure everything was okay. Her mother waved her away to let her know everything was fine.

"Oh, it's okay, baby. Yes, they were so happy to see you too. You are so loved."

She kissed her daughter's hand. "Elizabeth worked on you daily, doing Reiki and other interesting stuff. She had crystals on you. Was ringing bells and rattles. The nurses thought she was a *bruja*! It was hysterical." She laughed. "But that magic works. Look at you, you're up. You're up! Some people are in a coma for years. We are so blessed. God gave you a second chance, my love. I'm going to let you rest some more."

Journey knew she had unfinished business to handle, but it was still a bit foggy to her. For now, she would milk this time for what it was worth until she could plan her next move. She knew one thing; she had to get better and fast. This bedridden life was not for her.

Chapter 2

Ty

To Ty's surprise, Journey had survived her tragic jump from his building. He knew for sure now—she had to be a witch. No wonder Papa was so concerned about her being a danger to the family. It was a miracle to have fallen two floors and not be totally brain dead or paralyzed. Eyewitnesses saw her dive off the balcony as if jumping into a pool. He still couldn't believe it.

It had been two months since his world was flipped upside down. There had been a few rumors and lots of speculation about what really went down, but Ty has tried his best to stay away from it all. He figured it would just go away because he really didn't think she was ever going to wake up from her coma. That was, until he got the call today.

Claudia yelled ecstatically, "Ty! Ty! She's awake. She's awake!"

"Wow, she is? That's . . . uh, that's great news, Claudia." He pulled up the collar on his jacket to shield his neck from the winter chill. He was happy that it wasn't a video call, since his face couldn't hide his disappointment. Ty saw his reflection in the building's glass door, and it was a look of pure fear in his eyes. He fidgeted with his construction hat and took a deep breath to hear the full story. He was at work observing the updates on his latest building in downtown Atlanta.

"Is she alert? Talking yet?" There was something deep down in him, telling him that she would deny everything that had occurred or just straight up lie. Journey was the type to twist things and not take responsibility for her actions. A real manipulator. He thought she probably woke up with an evil vengeance. She was probably just as obsessed as the day she had caused all that havoc in his penthouse apartment.

Claudia rambled, almost out of breath. "Yes, the doctors say her vital signs are strong, and it's amazing after what she's been through. She's not talking yet, but she responds by blinking or squeezing your hand. Her eyes follow you. I can tell she's struggling to talk, but it's not time yet. She's been crying a lot too."

"Oh, no, that's not good."

"I'm sure she is still in shock and depressed. It's going to be a long road to recovery, but I pray she'll be back to her spunky self again."

Ty prayed she would stay mute and not be able to use her powers for evil again, but instead, he mustered up a cheery reply. "I'm so happy for you, Claudia."

"Yes, the police were alerted and want to speak to her as soon as she's able to talk."

A knot tied around his stomach like someone had grabbed his intestines with a fist of fury. "Oh, they still want to speak to her?"

"Yes, to everyone that was there, especially since you and the nurse called 911. They have to investigate and get Journey's side."

"They took photos of my blood splatter, where the tussle took place, and questioned us all, too."

"We also have photos of the bruises on her arms," she mumbled.

"Well, I was trying to get her out of the apartment before she caused more harm and gave Papa a heart attack. I didn't hurt her, Claudia. She was fighting Papa's nurse, Jocelyn, too. I know you heard the story a million times." Ty walked down a ramp and waved to a few of the construction workers. He looked at their progress on the back of the building his company was renovating.

"Yes, I know, Ty. I knooow. They will just want to get her side of the story, is all. They want to make sure there was no foul play. You should be fine."

He clenched his jaws. "Well, you know that there absolutely was not. Both Jocelyn and I were on the floor by the time she jumped—because of her, her outburst. It turned into a crazy ruckus, Claudia." Ty took a deep breath. "I know that's your baby and all,"—his voice cracked—"but I was unconscious from her knocking me in the head."

"She's your child too."

Ty rolled his eyes. He felt emotional just recalling that tragic day. He couldn't fathom how his own flesh and blood would do that to him. "She came in with a vengeance. I'm sorry all this had to happen, but I never knew it would get so out of hand. For her to attempt suicide was—"

She took a deep breath, cutting him off. "My Journey is a handful. We just have to pray for her healing. I mentioned to you before, she struggles with depression at times. I'm not sure what else, but this time, I am going to make sure I get her therapy to really evaluate her. She needs to be on medication. She's sick. I . . . I'm just shocked she would try to kill herself when she had such a zest for living." The hesitation in her voice still sounded like a subtle accusation to Ty.

"I know—I was shocked too. I'm just happy she didn't succeed," he lied again.

My Journey is a handful? Now that's the understatement of the fucking year. He thought Claudia was as delusional as her daughter. He had to hold back a chuckle on that one. He hated how she downplayed the destruction and drama that

Journey created in everyone's lives when she didn't get her way.

"Well, if you want to visit her, maybe in a week or so. I'll keep you posted on how she's doing. I'm just so overjoyed! I thought we lost her for good when she had to have those brain surgeries. There was only a forty percent chance of survival. But we aren't out of the forest yet."

Ty asked, "What does therapy look like to help her get back to normal?"

"The doctors are saying if she continues improving, they will discharge her from the hospital to Peachtree Long Term Care Facility that covers everything from physical therapy, occupational therapy, speech therapy, and also tests her cognitive functions. It can take another six weeks or longer depending on her progress. *Hay que vaina*. So much to handle. I may have to take off work, but I have so many cases coming up for court."

"Can't you get help?"

"Oh, yes, I plan to. She has such an excellent Medical Assistant. She had several so far, but Dominick is by far the best. He's the most attentive, and he's into a lot of holistic practices, which I know Journey loves. I've seen him use essential oils and use other things to soothe her. I'm thinking of hiring him as a caretaker for her until she gets back to normal."

Ty said flatly, "Great. Great."

"Look, I know your last encounter with Journey was not the greatest, but she's family, Ty." Her voice softened. "She's your blood. Families fight, but families can also heal."

Ty shook his head. A sperm donor is what he was and what he planned on staying. *I never wanted to be Daddy.*

Sure, families fight, but he never hit his dad in the back of the head with a glass trophy where he needed ten stitches, much less left a scar to remind him for life. Although, growing up in the Carter house was not like a happy sitcom, since Ty did have to peel his dad off of his mother a few times. He even had to punch him once, but with good reason. He was not making excuses for Journey. Ty didn't want to bust Claudia's bubble with the truth. He just wanted to get off the phone at this point.

"Will you visit her?"

Ty took a deep, exaggerated breath, exhausted from her rambling. "Claudia, I'll think about it, okay? I just don't know if my face will be the face she wants to see right now. Maybe it may trigger something and create a relapse."

"We'll just see about that. I'll ask her. If she blinks yes, then it should be okay."

"No rush. Let her heal up. Listen, I gotta get back to the site. My guys are calling me."

"Oh, wait. I'll be quick, I promise. The other reason I was calling you is that I'm arranging for her other siblings—at least the ones you know of—to come visit again soon now that she's awake. Maybe their presence will help her perk up."

"See, now that's an idea. I wouldn't mind Elizabeth coming back. She was such a help to Papa. She's a sweet kid. Smart too. Seems to have a good head on her shoulders."

"Yes, she was. The boys were adorable too. I could see some of you in them. I know you weren't able to meet up with them before they left. Do you think you want to meet the rest of them this time? I'm sure they will be so excited to meet you in person."

His stomach squirmed as he took a deep breath. "It shouldn't be a problem."

He was nervous to meet them all at once. Would they be looking at him like he was the guilty one that threw their dear sweet sister onto the balcony below? But Ty realized his imagination was getting the best of him.

Elizabeth had given him more insight on Journey. She felt that Journey was holding him back from them. She hinted in so many words that she and her brothers had no idea that Journey had even met him yet. Elizabeth said they were pretty upset with her for stringing them along because she wanted to spend most of the time with Ty.

She said the guys were afraid of her power. Her obsession with Ty made him feel like he was a piece of property.

The real reason Journey had jumped was a secret that Ty would take to his grave. The secret that no one would ever know was that Papa was behind it all, although he had no real proof of what had occurred. Ty knew he was not crazy. It was the look on Papa's face that he'd never forget. He was sure he'd seen him smiling when they thought Journey's lifeless body was on the ground. It just made the most sense, even if it was an out-of-this-world explanation. Papa was powerful beyond measure. Ty was glad to be on his good side, and even though it frightened him, he wanted to learn more.

Currently, Papa was non-verbal and had early signs of dementia. His psychic abilities might have been stronger than Ty and his nurse Jocelyn ever knew. Ty didn't even know how he could have missed the signs before. It just goes to show how you should never underestimate a person. Ty knew that he could communicate with his abuelo without speaking; however, he just thought it was his own sensitivity to his needs. He didn't think that Papa was actually sending him mind messages.

Papa had told him everything of how he tricked Journey into taking the leap without saying a word. Even though he couldn't express it as well through speech, his gift of telepathy was no doubt the messenger. Ty was still not sure how he did it. He knew Papa had the power of persuasion and had mastered it on some level. He knew how to sync with a person's thoughts and convince them to do what he wanted.

Papa had been in Ty's care since his grandmother passed. He would share a glance, a hearty laugh, and reply to a question with a little grunt or two. He could walk with the aid of his cane or walker, but his arthritis usually kept him seated in front of the television for the most part of his day. When he mustered up the strength to speak a full sentence, he would call Ty by his pet name that only family members knew—*Tylercito*.

Papa would make music requests of what Ty should play for him on the piano. Being a former pianist back in Cuba for a band, he truly appreciated hearing the melodic stroking of the keys. Ty remembered how his fingers would dance across the ebony and ivory keys, playing his favorite jazz, salsa, or pop songs of his time. Ty could see in his eyes how Papa missed the roar of the applause he used to get playing for huge crowds with his wife Mercedes, the lead singer of their band.

Papa had to live vicariously through his grandson, who was a talented pianist as well. Of course Ty would be extremely skilled, since he was trained by Papa and his mother. Papa's fingers were now more like tight claws, and he couldn't play anymore. His enlarged knuckles seemed misplaced on such a frail man. They would crack and pop when he moved them, sometimes reminding Ty of the Tin Man from the *Wizard of Oz*.

Papa's eyes misted lightly as he watched his grandson play with such ease. He should be proud, but not surprised, since that talent of being a natural musician was in their genes, just like many other traits. But music, music was what really soothed his soul. When Papa was happy listening to him play, Ty couldn't smile any wider. It was confirmation that he was still alive inside that fragile, aging body. He was still alert. He still knew what he wanted and definitely made that clear.

Ever since Elizabeth came to visit, he'd been moving about a bit more. Her healing hands seemed to do something to him. Papa definitely took a liking to Elizabeth.

Although Journey was his daughter, they only shared the same genetics, Ty thought. He was embarrassed by all of her vindictive actions that had caused havoc in his life and the lives of others around him. He was ashamed of her.

Ty had been just a number to Journey at first—sperm donor #1544. Sure, he had made some extra money in college, and in Ty's eyes, he was doing a good deed, helping women conceive with—wait for it—his exotic, ethnic sperm. He still got a little chuckle when he thought about the day he signed up to be a donor for the New Life Fertility Group. He was told that there were not that many men of color donating, and since he had Jamaican and Cuban blood, he was deemed exotic. He was okay with the compliment.

The rollercoaster of getting to know Journey went full speed ahead. She had met Ty about three months ago, and at first, he thought it was a great connection. Journey was his flesh and blood! He was excited to see what he had actually helped create. She looked like him and had the same drive for success as him. Ty was actually flattered that she wanted to meet him. He thought her bubbly energy was fun and uplifting even. Just full of personality. She had a spiritual side to her and was even a yoga teacher. At times, the knowledge she possessed even made her seem as if she were mature beyond her years. So, he figured she was grounded and had her head on straight.

He was wrong.

One thing about Journey: she was one to speak her mind—sometimes to a fault. The girl had absolutely no filter. It was even comedic at times. Ty had been so grateful to build a relationship with her in the beginning. However, as time went on, he realized something was a bit off with her. She has some special gifts like Ty, such as intuition, the power of persuasion, and the ability to read people's minds, but her gifts seemed to be more advanced than his.

She used her abilities to control others when things didn't go her way. She became obsessed with him. The one mistake Ty made that sent Journey over the edge was getting involved with her best friend, Natalia. To be fair, Ty saw her as a grown woman at 32 years old, like a big sister to Journey. Thanks to Journey's encouragement, she came on board of The Carter & Connor Investment Group as a real estate intern. That's where their bond grew into much more than a working relationship.

Natalia wanted to learn the industry, and well, Ty showed her that and then some. Their chemistry was undeniable, so they began secretly dating. But having a psychic and telepathic daughter didn't help the situation. Journey knew before they even had the chance to tell her. Her jealousy was terrifying. It got so out of control that it escalated to lying, stealing, and threats of blackmail. She even went as far as drugging and seducing Ty's best friend and business partner, Marlon. Journey would go to great lengths just to prove a point or to get you back. If Ty had known that was the risk of being a sperm donor, he would have given it a hard pass.

The last encounter, two months ago, ended up in a huge brawl between Ty, Journey, and his

nurse, Jocelyn. She was on a rampage of denial
when confronted about her evil deeds. Ty woke
up on the cold floor in a crimson puddle of blood
around his head thanks to his dear old daughter.
And to top it off, after that, she wreaked havoc on
his household, then decided to jump to escape it
all. She jumped right off his balcony—the jump
that everyone assumed was a failed suicide attempt.

As much as she was making his life a living hell,
Ty didn't want her to die. He wasn't *that* cold-
blooded. He just wanted her to learn her lesson
and leave him the hell alone after that. He wanted
her to pay the consequences in jail for stealing
over $5,000 as well as pay the company back. She
probably wouldn't have gotten more than a week
anyhow with Claudia's legal connections with the
courts.

Her mother tried to pay Ty off, but he didn't
think that was enough, and he was going to go to
the cops to report her. Journey got wind of what Ty
was going to do, so she came to the house to confront him, and it ended badly. Very badly. Before
she came, Ty had been warned by Papa, who was
screaming and crying, "No abras la puerta! Don't
open the door, don't open the door!" But he didn't
realize Papa was warning them all.

Ty waved to one of the workers and stepped
over a 2 x 4. He passed the orange cones blocking

a new walkway where decorative bricks were being laid for the entrance to the garden landscaping. Ty walked around the back to see how they were doing with the pool development. It was a little loud, but he could hear much better on this side of the building.

"Sorry to cut you short, but I *really* gotta go, Claudia."

"Okay, get back to work. Talk soon. Adios."

Elizabeth

November 2, Journey's Birthday

The Fantastic 4 had never imagined their first in-person meeting would be because of a tragic moment in their lives. Miss Claudia was instrumental in bringing them all together. She went above and beyond to make sure they were able to see their sister on her twenty-third birthday. She got their plane tickets and hotels all arranged. They were located in different states, but Miss Claudia didn't seem to mind the expense. Elizabeth came from Los Angeles, California; Zack from Colorado; and Robbie from New York City. Claudia knew that Journey had developed a strong bond with her siblings from the sperm donor website. The Fantastic Four spoke several times a week and played intuition games to test their abilities.

Miss Claudia had found Elizabeth's number in Journey's phone, so Elizabeth was able to let her brothers know about the accident. They were in touch with her weekly to see how she was doing. The idea for them all to come for her birthday sounded good, and they all were excited to finally meet.

Journey was essentially the leader of their crew. Even though Elizabeth was the same age as her, she admired Journey in many ways. At the time of the accident, all of them were upset with Journey for being so selfish by keeping her relationship with their biological father a secret. They had no idea she was meeting with Ty regularly. It was a serious betrayal, but she was still their sister after all. They learned about some of the drama that took place from Miss Claudia and the local Atlanta news. Elizabeth felt there was a lot missing from the story, but figured in time it would all be revealed.

They all met in the hospital waiting room, and it was a joyous occasion under such dreadful circumstances. The siblings had built a close friendship within less than a year of video chatting. It was such a thrill for Elizabeth to finally see her brothers in the flesh.

"Robbie!" Elizabeth screamed as she ran into her brother's arms. He hugged her so tight that he lifted her off the ground.

"What up, sis!" He looked down at her and smoothed out her hair. "You're even more beautiful in person."

"Ah, thank you, baby brother. And look at you. You're so tall and handsome." She kissed him on the cheek. She couldn't believe how much he towered over her at about six feet three inches, and he was still growing at only 20 years old. He was the youngest in the group.

"Hey, hey, we're in a hospital. What's with all the commotion?" Zack glided in the room with long strides. He toted a huge backpack hanging off of one shoulder.

Elizabeth gasped. "Zaaaack!" She squeezed him hard. His strong biceps made him look like a football jock. He was stockier and a little shorter than Robbie at about six feet.

"What's up, bro!" Their smiles illuminated with pure joy. They slapped hands and hugged.

"I love your man bun," Elizabeth teased. Zack's golden locks rested high on top of his head, wrapped in a black scarf.

"Yes, it's very elegant." Robbie teased him and slapped him lightly on the back of his head. Zack flinched and retaliated by bumping him in the shoulder with his backpack.

"Man, shut up. It's just hot as hell in Cali. My locks are down my back now."

"Cali? I thought you lived in Colorado?" Elizabeth questioned.

"Yeah, I do, but my dad has a distribution farm we deal with there, and I was just coming back from a meeting with him. We were there for a week." He leaned in closer to them both and spoke slowly and relaxed. "Honestly, I like covering my head when I'm outside and especially traveling." He put his backpack down and tightened up his head wrap. "You know I gotta protect my energy. I pick up way too much shit. You guys should try it." His eyes were heavy. Elizabeth knew it wasn't from being tired.

Robbie chimed in. "Nah, his ass just wants to remind people that he got some black in him, even though the melanin gene missed him just a bit."

"Maaan, shut up. You're always talking shit about my light skin just 'cause you got a bigger scoop of chocolate. I'm surprised you made it, since you've never even been on a plane. Buk buk buk buk ba-gawk!" Zack waved his arms like a chicken.

Elizabeth was emotional, but trying not to cry. "It's so good to see you all."

"So good to see you too, sis. You over here looking all sporty in your Converse, like you wanna go skateboarding with me later."

She looked down at her baggy cargo pants and tugged at her oversized NPR hoody. "I like to be comfortable when I travel. So, Zack, you were in Cali and didn't even tell me?"

He jerked his chin forward, being extra animated. "I was ten hours away from Downey, Elizabeth. Trust me, I thought about you, but it was too far. We were in Humboldt County, way north. That's where most of the cannabis farms we work with are located."

"Okay, okay, I'll let you slide this time. It's so good to be together for real." Her eyes got moist, and she was trying not to cry. "It's so sad that Journey couldn't see us."

She pulled them both in tight for a group hug. When they all connected, shockwaves of electricity went through them all. It was a tremendous jolt that made them all jump back.

"Woah. Did you feel that?" Zack shivered.

"What the fuck was that? I felt like I put my hand in a dang socket. Yo, shit's crazy." Robbie pointed at Elizabeth.

She put her hands up in the air in surrender. "Don't blame me. I definitely felt that! I think it was all of our energies combined."

Robbie shook his hands off as if air-drying them from water. "See, I told y'all. I'm not fucking with this magical shit no more. Too much has happened. I'm seeing and hearing things too much. At one point, I thought I was losing it. That's why I stopped practicing with y'all."

Zack reached down on the floor for his backpack. "Calm down, bro, calm down. I feel you. Trust me. It's freaking me out too, but we gotta deal with living with it. I brought us all something that might help us relax. This is how I deal."

"Oh, boy, here he go, Mr. Pusha man. You stay high." Robbie laughed and shook his head. His curiosity was piqued as he looked over Zack's shoulder while he dug into his backpack. "From your dad's dispensary?"

"And you know it. Just some strawberry gummies. Here, take one. It will calm you down. Actually, take half. They are pretty potent."

Elizabeth put her hand on Zack's shoulder. "You traveled with that? I'm glad you didn't get arrested."

"Quit being a little nerd. It's not a big deal. I got my medicinal marijuana card, so I'm good."

High heels click-clacked down the hallway at a rapid pace. Miss Claudia rushed into the waiting room, looking stunning with a royal blue dress and black leather jacket. She was a snazzy dresser and so beautiful. The boys looked her up and down and grinned like goofy kids who had a crush on their teacher.

Miss Claudia reached out her hand to Zack and Robbie, then gave them both a quick peck on their cheeks. They blushed. She had picked up Elizabeth from the airport first before her conference call.

"Ah, so good you all made it together. So nice to meet you both! Look at you boys, so handsome. I see Ty's features in you all. Oh my." She clutched her heart. "I really hope this works. Journey loves you all. I just have a feeling that you all coming will help her."

Robbie put on his formal voice for her, and Elizabeth held in her laughter. "Oh, not a problem, Miss Claudia. We absolutely love Journey as well. We're very grateful to you for bringing us together too."

"I'm so glad that I could." She waved her hand toward the hallway. "Follow me."

Standing over Journey's hospital bed was a surreal moment for them all. The mood was somber as they watched her —speechless. The loud machines beeped while the monitors had colorful displays showcasing her vitals. Seeing her lying there, bruised and bandaged, made it real.

Surprisingly, she didn't look as bad as Elizabeth had expected. She looked so peaceful. It was tough seeing someone who was so full of life and personality just lying there. It was as if she were in a coffin. The stillness was too much. Elizabeth was determined to bring Journey back. They had to find a way.

Miss Claudia left them alone, so that they could try to reach her. She assumed they would practice using their psychic energy, and that was exactly the plan the Fantastic Four had in mind. Elizabeth started to cry, but she tried to hold it together. The brothers both had teary eyes but remained calm.

Robbie touched her foot gently. "Damn, Journey. What happened, sis?" He folded his arms and shook his head. "She's gonna be pissed when she wakes up and sees what they did to her hair."

Elizabeth managed to smile and grabbed a tissue to blow her nose. "Hey, if the three of us created so much energy from just a hug, maybe we can try something with Journey."

"That actually makes sense." Zack agreed.

"Recharge her battery." Robbie smirked.

Elizabeth, her hands in prayer, took a few deep breaths. "Let's send her some healing light and love."

The trio held hands around the foot of her bed and began to meditate. For someone on the outside looking in, they resembled a small prayer vigil. However, these siblings were deep in trance, trying to connect with Journey's higher self.

Elizabeth said softly, "On the count of three."

"We're just gonna yell it in her mind?"

"Yes, Robbie," Elizabeth said.

Zack shook his head and said, "One, two, three."

In unison, they sent Journey a mind message.

"WAKE UP! WAKE UUUUUP! JOURNEY, WAKE UP! WE MISS YOU. WAKE UP!"

Robbie looked at his vibrating fingers. "My hands are like fire now."

Elizabeth put her finger to her lips. "Shhhhh. Look—her eyes."

Journey's eyes were closed, but they moved slowly from left to right, as if in a deep dream. The siblings sent their own personal telepathic messages one at a time, so as not to confuse her. Elizabeth moved up to the top of the bed to do Reiki on Journey's head where the surgery was. She then took crystals out of her pocket and placed one on Journey's third eye and one on her throat. Elizabeth's hands were pulsating and hot. She knew it was working.

Robbie whispered, "Yo, tell me if I'm wrong, but I'm getting she ain't do this shit to herself."

Elizabeth whispered, "You too?"

Zack mumbled, "Psychic warfare. Someone wants her out."

"But who?" Elizabeth asked.

Zack shrugged. "I don't know, man. But I feel it. I feel it strongly in my gut."

Elizabeth could tell he was afraid to share what he really thought.

He said, "I just know Journey needs to get it together when she wakes up."

"She needed us." Elizabeth moved her hand down from the crown chakra to the throat chakra to hopefully help her be able to speak again.

Robbie shook his head. "She did need us, but I hate to even say this, bruh. . . . This shit is straight karma. I feel Journey went overboard trying to get revenge on Ty. Now she got some bad juju on her. Maybe she messed around with the wrong people and some spirits attacked her or something." Robbie shimmied his shoulders as if something crawled up his back. "Y'all don't feel the energy in here? It feels off. Like a presence. Like it's not just us. Could it be some dark energy around her that pushed her?"

Zack kicked Robbie under the bed, alerting him. Miss Claudia walked back into the room slowly.

"Oh, hi there." Robbie smiled sheepishly.

"How's it going?" Miss Claudia looked at Elizabeth, who was putting crystals on Journey's heart and belly now.

Elizabeth felt confident in her work. "We saw her eyes move a little, like she knows we're here."

"I'm sure she does, my love. I'm just so glad you could all make it. It's too bad you can't all stay longer together.

Elizabeth turned to her brothers. "I think I'm going to stay. My school is virtual. I am going to meet with Ty when he comes back from his business trip."

Miss Claudia took off her jacket and hung it on the door. She sat down in the big reclining chair next to Journey. "That will be great for you to meet Ty."

"Word?" Robbie raised his brows. He put his arm around Elizabeth. "Yeah, we'll have to catch him next trip. I'm sure we'll be back."

Miss Claudia pointed to Zack. "Sweetheart, can you ask the nurse for some more chairs so we can sit and talk a bit more?"

"On it."

They spent the afternoon getting to know one another. Journey never showed any more signs of being alert. They knew she would come to eventually, but they just didn't know when.

Ty

Ty realized now how parents could have favorites. Growing up as an only child, he was lucky to be the only star in the spotlight. Now that Ty had met Elizabeth, he wished that he had met her first. He had no problem claiming her as kin. She was mature, intelligent, and extremely caring. Ty was in awe of her calm energy. She didn't give off the vibe that she was helping them for something in return. She didn't expect a handout like Journey did. There was no entitlement. Her heart was pure. Even after all that Journey did to them all, she still cared. Elizabeth felt sorry for Journey and wanted to help her heal. After her siblings went to see Journey in the hospital, she had come for a visit and even did a little bit of Reiki on Papa.

"Ty, do you mind me trying something? His throat is very blocked. I would be mad at myself if I left here and didn't help him."

Papa pulled his reclining chair back and was eager for her healing hands to work on him. Ty knew she had to be special. Papa didn't trust many people, especially after what had happened with Journey.

She held her hands over Papa's face and then his throat and heart for a few minutes, performing Reiki. Her eyes were closed, and she was making strange faces of concentration as if she were reading him.

He was so relaxed the entire time. He looked at Ty and said in his mind, "This one is good. She's more powerful than she even knows."

Elizabeth's forehead formed creases of concern. "Papa, what are you holding onto? It's so blocked." She turned to Ty. *"I see a lot of rage inside of him. A lot of pent-up energy. I feel like, like I'm going to explode. I forgot how to say that. Rage."*

Ty said, *"Furia. Or* estoy enfadado. *But he understands English. He just doesn't speak it as well anymore."*

Papa nodded. *"Si, anger. Rage."* He growled playfully, and they all laughed.

Ty was afraid that she would read exactly what he was angry about. Elizabeth continued as if she read his thoughts. *"It's not just about Journey. It's a lot of things. He's been holding on to resentment for many years. His wife? Where is she?"*

"My abuela. Mercedes was her name. She's been gone for a while now. Yes, maybe they had some unfinished business before she passed. They were together fifty-four years, so who knows what it could be?"

"Well, other than that, he feels pretty good. He's so strong mentally, just not able to voice it. I hope this helps a bit."

"We appreciate it. You didn't have to."

Papa tapped her hand on his chest. *"Tank you. Tank you."*

Ty started to go in his wallet. "How much do you charge for something like this?"

"Oh no, you're my family." She waved him off, laughing. She definitely was not Journey.

Elizabeth told Ty how the other two brothers were very gifted as well. He guessed their abilities could work in his favor. If they were all psychic, they would know he was innocent of any wrongdoing and that Journey was really the troublemaker. If they ever read his energy, they would know he did not do anything to hurt Journey. He just wanted her out of his house and truly out of his life for good. For some reason, Ty had this looming fear in the back of his mind that somehow people would blame him, since it had occurred at his house.

Ty was more worried they could fish around in Papa's mind to see what he saw or did as well. He wasn't sure just how powerful they were. He thought the more he spoke with Elizabeth, the more she'd open up. He felt a good connection with her. Ty could tell she wanted to open up more to him, but she was being careful. As for Papa, no one would ever suspect him, so Ty decided to not stress himself out. He would hate for people to even consider his sweet abuelo. He was too old and weak to be interrogated like a criminal. Yet, they still did have to question him. No one would believe that he pushed her, and what actually happened was even more unimaginable.

The police interviewed Papa the day of the accident. Before they took him into a separate room, they wanted to make sure he was able to handle the questioning.

"Is he able to speak?" the detective asked.

"Yes, but short sentences or one-word answers usually. He saw everything. He understands English but just doesn't speak it very well anymore." Ty tapped his forehead, referencing Papa's poor memory. "If you have a Spanish-speaking interpreter—"

"I'm actually bilingual. I can do it. I'm Detective Velez, Mr. Carter. Originally from Puerto Rico. Where's he from?"

He reached out his hand, and Ty shook it. "Okay, great. Cuba."

Ty looked vacantly into the living room. Detectives were taking photos like it was a crime scene. His stomach squirmed as he worried that people would think they had something to do with it. He just knew she had to be dead. No one believed she could survive that fall. Would he be to blame? He watched everyone moving in slow motion. The back of his head throbbed as he took it all in. Was this a dream? A nightmare?

"Why don't you have the medics take a look at that nasty gash?"

Ty held a cloth on his head.

"I'll only need a few minutes with your abuelo—alone." Detective Velez adjusted his horn-rimmed glasses and tucked in his shirt that was protruding from his beer belly. He was a short, stocky dude with a lot of attitude. He wanted to show he was in charge.

Papa mumbled to Detective Velez, "She jump. Diabla. Ella brinco!" He waved his hands toward the patio. His eyes held a steady stare, accompanied by a slight smirk. He actually looked pleased.

Ty's eyes opened wide at his grandfather as if to say, "Chill, Papa. You look crazy." Appearing happy was definitely not a good look. Ty was hoping he wouldn't say anything else, but he was sure if Papa said he made Journey jump, no one would believe him anyway. They would think he was just a delusional old man.

The EMT worker bandaging Ty's head wound said to him, "You're gonna need stitches. We gotta take you to emergency."

Another detective approached Ty. She was a very tough female who walked hard, yet had *a little switch in her step that softened up her appearance. Strong biceps, shapely body, smooth skin, and had her honey-colored locks in a bun. "I have a few questions for you, Mr. Carter. I'm Detective Dewitt. We'll meet you at the hospital once they patch up your head."*

They were in a private room at the hospital where Detective Dewitt's eyes examined Ty from head to toe with scrutiny. He wasn't sure if she was checking him out or already accusing him of murder. "So, tell me. How did this all start? I understand she is your daughter?"

"Yes, yes, well . . . We just recently met about a, about a month ago. I was her mother's sperm donor. We were just getting to know each other, and then she committed a few crimes that shocked us all. I just learned she stole money from my business partner and also drugged him."

"Drugged him with what?"

"That's just the thing. We aren't sure. We think it might be something from Colombia called Devil's Breath. It kinda turns you into a zombie."

"Devil's Breath? Never heard of it." She jotted down notes.

Ty held his head. "I'm sorry, I'm just a bit dizzy. This is just crazy."

"It's okay. We'll be quick, and then you can get back home. So, what happened?"

"We spoke on the phone, and I told her I was going to the police about what she did. Journey said she wanted to discuss it in person, yet kept denying it all. Next thing I know, she gets into an argument with my grandfather's nurse, Jocelyn. I asked her to leave. She wouldn't. The two get into a fight."

"Who hit who?"

"I . . . I don't remember. I think Journey punched her or something. I think it was after Jocelyn tried to lead her to the door. They ended up fighting for a quick minute, but I broke up the scuffle. Jocelyn ended up on the floor. She couldn't move. She hurt her back or something. Then Journey took an award off of my bookshelf and hit me over the head with it. I mean, really hard. I just remember waking up to people screaming, and then I heard she jumped. I guess I was unconscious for a while. I'm not sure how long, though." Ty's voice shook.

"So, you didn't hit her?"

"Oh, no, absolutely not. I just tried to escort her toward the door before all that occurred, and that's when Jocelyn and her got into it."

"Escorted her how? Did you have to grab or push her?"

"No, no, I just held her shoulders to get her to calm down." Ty's hands were trembling.

Detective Dewitt looked at them and looked him in the eyes as Ty wiped his brow of sweat. He didn't want to admit to her that he really damn near pushed her to the door. He knew that wouldn't work in his favor.

Panic filled his mind as he rambled to the detective. "It was so bizarre, since I didn't think she would want to kill herself. She seemed like she came to prove herself to us. She wanted to convince us of her lies. I don't know if she did it get back at us, but that would just be insane."

"Well, thankfully, she's not dead. She was rushed into surgery. Critical condition."

"Oh, well, thank God." Ty took an exaggerated sigh of relief. He saw how she studied his reaction as if she wanted to see if he was happy that she was alive or he was just faking it.

Ty realized he would still have to deal with Journey once she made it out of the hospital. "Look, Journey needs help. I mean serious mental help. It was really scary. I hate to admit it, but we were all afraid of her." Ty figured if he threw in the mental health comment it might lead them to really examine her mental state more. He was not going to jail for shit he did not do.

Detective Dewitt took a call from her partner Velez, who had just finished interviewing Jocelyn and Papa. "Oh, we're all done here. I'm going to drop him back."

She looked at Ty, "Need a lift?"

"Sure." He smiled at her kindness. He was skeptical too, since he figured she was fishing to get more information.

When they got back to his apartment building Detective Dewitt said, "Well, thanks for your time. I think we have everything that we need for now. We'll be in touch if you need to come down to the station for more questioning, and most likely you will. I'd like to interview your partner, the one you said she drugged?"

"Oh, no problem. I know he definitely wants to speak to you all." Ty pulled out his phone and shared the number with her to type into her phone.

"What's the name of your company?"

"C & C Investment Group. We run a real estate firm."

Her stern glare transformed into a glimmering smile. "Oh, you're the one building those luxury apartments in Midtown? I've seen the signs."

"Yes, that's us."

"I heard good things. Nice to see black-owned businesses doing that for a change."

Ty nodded modestly. He reached into his pocket and handed her a business card. Detective DeWitt looked at the card as if it were an invitation to other plans for contacting him. She bit her bottom lip and eyed him up and down.

"We'll definitely be in touch. Thank you. We'll get to the bottom of this, Mr. Carter."

"Oh, no problem at all. Thank you, Detective." Ty smiled, relieved it was over. He hoped her light flirting was a good sign.

"You take care of yourself. I hope that head heals up for you fast," Detective Dewitt said as she handed Ty her card. *"We'll be interviewing Journey after she gets out of surgery, probably tomorrow, if she's up for it."*

The lump in Ty's throat got larger and traveled down to his stomach. He felt like he was going to be sick. Detective DeWitt sashayed off with a little extra sway in her hips and looked back to see if he was watching. Ty just wanted the nightmare to be over and didn't need to add anymore notches to his belt.

The memory of being questioned was unnerving. He was shaken up after that phone call from Claudia. Just the thought of being interrogated again made him nervous and angry. But why would he be nervous? He honestly didn't do anything wrong. He was just going to let the cops find out the truth. They had enough proof to show she was off the hinges crazy anyway.

He was glad that it had already gotten out that Journey was the one who started the altercation.

The rumor mill was busy. Images of Journey fighting with them flashed through his mind. He pictured her diving off of his patio like it was a diving board. He still couldn't believe that had actually happened. Now she was awake. She was back. It was a lot to take in.

Ty went into the office and just took a deep breath. He felt like he needed to speak to someone who could calm his nerves. Then there she was, standing with her back to him, looking over a text message.

Natalia wore a cute beige pencil skirt that hugged her hips so nicely. Her shapely brown legs were sculpted like a dancer's. Her hair that was usually up in a conservative bun was flowing down to her shoulders with sleek Cleopatra bangs. It was her new look, and he really liked it.

"Natalia, Nataliaaaa!" He smiled brightly.

"Hey, babe." She covered her mouth. "I mean Ty."

"It's okay, baby. No one's around." He closed the office door and took off his hard hat.

She strolled over to him and embraced his broad back. "Noooo, leave it on. I always wanted to do it with the construction worker." She gazed into his eyes.

Ty grabbed her waist and caressed her soft bottom. He playfully put the hat back on.

She pulled back with a teasing smile, "Oh, wow. What's all this? You're in an extra loving mood today. In the office at that. You high?" She did a suspicious sniff of his face and hands for remnants of marijuana.

He chuckled. "No, I need to be, though. I just need a hug. I just heard Journey's awake."

"Huh? What? She's out of her coma? Really?" Her smile was bright, since parts of her still loved and missed the Journey who used to be her best friend.

"Yep. Claudia just called me. She's not speaking yet, but she's responding when you ask her questions."

"Wow, I'm glad she's alert at least. It's been so long. I thought she'd be gone for good. I'll reach out to Claudia today. Are you going to be okay?" Natalia placed her hand gently on his chest. "What are you feeling?"

His shoulders slumped. "I'm glad she's okay, but I'm also nervous about what's next. I'm just not ready to deal with all that shit again. I don't know exactly why, but I have a bad feeling about it all. I'm hoping that she tells the truth and doesn't create more drama than needed. We know that she's a good manipulator and has gifts to persuade people. It's not like I can tell people that she knows how to get into your mind and make you do things. They will lock me up and think I'm crazy."

"I know. It makes me wonder how many times during our friendship that she did it to me."

"Exactly. No one would believe me. Shit, I wouldn't believe me if I didn't see it with my own eyes. I knew she was psychic, but not to the point that she could paralyze someone temporarily. That's exactly what she did to Jocelyn after they got into it."

"I still can't believe it. That's so scary that she couldn't move." Natalia shook her head.

"I know she was very psychic, but not to the point of controlling somebody's body and paralyzing them. What she did to Jocelyn was really frightening. They were fighting, and before I knew it, I saw Jocelyn on the ground—frozen like a log. She was able to move the second Journey jumped, she told me." He chuckled. "God forgive me, but if I didn't know any better, I would actually believe that Jocelyn threw her out the window. She was kicking Journey's ass at first, until I broke it up."

"Lord. Yes, God, please forgive him." Natalie looked up to the ceiling.

"Well, I guess we just have to get ready for when she does get back to herself."

"I really hope almost dying changed her for the better. Maybe it will give her time to rethink her actions. Near death experiences like that usually do." Natalia grabbed her coat off of the back of her door.

"We can only hope. Where are you going?"

"This handsome fella was taking me to lunch."

"Oh, really now? Let me see if he's worthy."

Natalia came in close to Ty and removed his hard hat. She kissed him on the lips, and he embraced her for a moment. He removed her coat from her hands and held it open, so that she could slide into it. "Oh, he's very worthy. The ultimate gentleman." She giggled as they walked out of the office.

Chapter 3

Ty

A week after the jump

After a long day at the office, Marlon and Ty had a drink to catch up at their favorite bar and grill. It was a chilly Atlanta night in September, so they sat in huge lounge chairs facing the fireplace.

Marlon leaned in closer to talk over the loud, old-school hip hop music. "So, I finally had my interview with Detective Dewitt today." He gave Ty a knowing look with a head tilt.

"What?"

"She bad. Come on. You ain't see that shit, Ty? Ass was like pla-dooow!" They laughed. "I was like, what you need to know, Miss Detective? I'll tell you everything, baby. Shit. I confess. Lock me up, baby!" He shook his head, reminiscing on her voluptuous shape.

"You's a fool!" He laughed. "Yeah, I know. Nice looking lady. She was kinda flirting with me, but I'm good."

"Man, you crazy. That's worth smashing for sure. It's always good to have a cop in your back pocket."

"Yeah, not in your bed. I don't want no chick who might be power tripping and has a gun."

Marlon pointed at him and raised his glass. "Good point, good point."

Ty sat back and folded his arms. "So, how did it go? What happened?"

"Oh, you know me. I told her straight up. Journey Salazar is a certified crazy, manipulative bitch. I told her how she drugged me, stole money, and tried to blackmail me. I told her everything. I wanted it all on record if she lives through this." His hand went up to the heavens as if asking for forgiveness. "I ain't wishing for the girl to die, 'cause believe me, when she gets healed up, I'm pressing charges."

Ty rubbed the stitches in the back of his head where Journey had hit him. "I hear you. I just think we need to wait until she's fully alert and awake. She is getting enough payback right now, suffering in the hospital. Her mother told me she had another brain surgery yesterday. She's still in the ICU in a coma."

"Damn, she could be in a coma for a while." Marlon looked hopeful as he bit into his juicy cheeseburger.

"No, she's young and healthy. She should bounce back."

Marlon grabbed a napkin and wiped his hands. "Well, I got something to show you. Look at this shit." He fumbled for his phone in his pocket. Marlon passed his cell to Ty with the webpage pulled up to Atlanta Hood Scoop.

It featured an article from the *Atlanta Observer*.

Tragedy struck today at 2959 Peachtree Plaza in Midtown Atlanta. It was near fatal, and there are still some questions unanswered. The building is one of the newest developments by Tyler Carter of C & C Investment Group. A young woman caught everyone's attention as she dove off of his penthouse apartment patio in an attempted suicide. Foul play has not been ruled out as yet. The young woman is still unresponsive in a coma. Mysterious circumstances surround the Atlanta real estate mogul and his relationship to the young woman. Crowds gathered outside, appalled by what they witnessed. She leaped from the five-story building, but only made it down two floors and thankfully survived. She remains in critical condition at Emory Hospital.

A video clip from the article showcased a lady with a tight pink leopard bodysuit with overflowing cleavage, and pink satin cap on her head. She smacked her gum while speaking. "I was on my patio across the street, cleaning up, you know, just minding my business, when I saw this girl dive headfirst from the penthouse. She didn't have good aim—thank you, Jesus—'cause she ended up smack dab up on top of one of them AC units, then rolled on over to another balcony. I know that hurt. I still can't believe she survived. Lord!"

Ty mumbled, "Shit. That's all I need is more bad press." He passed the phone back to Marlon.

"Look at who wrote it." Marlon gave a knowing smirk.

"Oh, man, the second you said the *Observer*, I already knew Candace Overton was behind it. She just can't get over me not wanting a relationship with her toxic ass."

"She must have loved to see that you were involved."

"Exactly. Another excuse for her to sink her teeth into my business. We better tell our PR team to hurry up and draft a response, so that all employees are on the same page. I'm so glad they didn't mention Journey as my daughter."

"Well, you know she probably thought it was a girl you were smashing, but leave it up to her. She'll keep digging. Stalker ass."

"Yeah, she probably will. That's why we gotta work on damage control right now."

"I'm on it, Ty. Don't stress."

"But I'm concerned that they might think we have a motive," Ty said.

"No, no—with all the shit she did to us? I am sure we have more than enough proof."

"Yeah, all of the shit she did to us gives us more of a motive."

"Okay, okay." Marlon nodded his head. "I see where you're going with this. That chick with the pink leopard might be someone to have the cops talk to. Or she probably already did. So, I'm sure they can confirm that nobody pushed her." His eyes darted up as he scratched his bald head, remembering. "Yeah, but when they interviewed me, I was careful since they were trying to put words in my mouth. Like, 'So you were very angry with her since she robbed you and tried to blackmail you all? Did you want Ty to help you get back at her? Like I'm some fucking kid on *First 48*. Come on, man." He rolled his eyes and took a sip of his beer.

"Really, they were fishing like that?" Ty clenched his jaws.

Marlon nodded. "I'm glad I wasn't there, because if anyone had a motive, it definitely would be me. Come to think of it, I already spilled the beans that she was your daughter. Oh, my bad."

"It's okay. I had to tell them too. I just don't want it in the press."

"So, you gonna visit her in the hospital?"

"Yeah, at some point I will. I have to show my face so they don't look at me as a criminal." Ty wanted to tell Marlon so badly about what he knew, how Journey didn't jump of her own free will. But he decided to go against it, for now at least.

He leaned in closer to Marlon. "The part you're not getting is that we can be possible suspects. So, we can't show too much anger, not now."

"Suspects? Who told you that? Now, hold the fuck on, Ty. First off, I was in my bed, trying to sleep off that weird-ass Colombian drug that broad gave me. Second of all, we are the fucking victims here." He pointed to his chest. "We are! She stole from my wallet and our bank account like the little entitled bitch that she is. She drugged me. She motherfucking drugged me on some Jeffrey Dahmer shit. I was like a damn zombie. I still don't know what effect this will have on me long term! I am still waiting on blood tests to come back."

"Lower your voice, man." Ty waved his hands toward Marlon to calm him down. "The part you gotta understand is that we have no proof of—"

"Them damn videos are proof enough. You seen my eyes? My eyes were so glassy, I look like a fucking zombie. She took naked videos and photos. She gonna try to blackmail me or something. I know it. The bitch is treacherous. We can get proof of her cashing the check. I'm sure they got cameras there."

"Yeah, a check that you signed."

"Under duress!" He pulled back. "Nigga, whose side are you on? You need to grab your balls. I've known you over twenty years, and I ain't never seen you this soft."

"Come on. Don't be ridiculous. She knocked me out cold, and I had to get stitches. She could have killed me too. Whose side do you think, man? I have Jocelyn and Papa as eyewitnesses, but I'm sure they are still going to look at me as the main suspect. They could even say I swayed them to do what I want. Man, I'm just looking at it from all angles, that's all. What if she wakes up and she tells a lie and claims it was self-defense on why she had to hit me in the head?" Ty's eyes widened. "Or what if she doesn't wake up at all?"

"Nah, son. We ain't going down for this shit."

"Claudia is a lawyer with connections. She might try to sue me for emotional stress or some bullshit. Who knows?"

"Come on, man. You worrying for nothing. You taking shit too far. We got enough evidence. We good, man. Chill the fuck out. You beginning to worry me. We got eyewitnesses."

Chapter 4

Journey

Journey was overwhelmed by the commotion in her room. She felt all of these eyes staring at her with pity. There were nurses peeking in to see if she was really awake. They were checking to see if the rumors were true. Did "suicide girl" finally open her eyes? Journey was sick of feeling like a pathetic fish in a tank. Her head felt so jumbled. She felt trapped under the bright fluorescent lights. Journey also hated that no one could really understand her. It was like the words sat on the tip of her tongue, but she struggled to form anything sensible.

The only excitement she had was when Dominick watched the Oxygen channel with her. She loved true crime stories. As Journey dozed in and out, she heard Dr. Alexander scolding Dominick. "Why do you have on all that murder and gore? She's trying to heal. You are going to make her have nightmares watching all those *Snapped* and *Killer Couple* shows."

Journey opened her eyes and smiled.

"But, Doc, she likes it. Look——Journey don't you like it?"

She blinked twice to respond yes.

They both laughed.

"See!" He gestured toward Journey.

"Well, just try to change it up with some lighter things. Energy is everything. You of all people should know that, Mr. Shaman."

"Sure." He turned to Journey, shrugged, and smiled, while playfully rolling his eyes as she walked out.

Dominick was getting Journey's cues. She was really so grateful for his friendship. Sometimes he even stayed longer than his shift. He really cared for her, maybe more than his other patients. Journey wondered why Dr. Alexander called him a shaman. That was interesting. She couldn't wait until she could speak more.

The sunset painted the sky full of beautiful pinks and orange hues. Journey rolled over and saw Francesca sitting up, looking at her TV. Francesca's TV was not on. Journey couldn't remember her leaving, but also didn't remember her in the room most of the day.

"Hey there. Long day, huh?" She twirled an auburn lock of hair and smiled.

Journey tried to speak.

"Oh, come on. You can do it. I'm special like you. You don't have to talk. I get you. I can hear you without saying a word. Hellooooo. Have you not figured that out by now?"

"*Really? So, you can hear this?*" Journey sent the message to Francesca's mind.

"*Clear as day,*" Francesca answered without moving her mouth. "*Shoot, I think that's why they think your ass is crazy and tried to off yourself. I heard whispers of how you can do stuff to people. Are you, like, a low-key witch?*"

She turned her head and tried to sit up. "*Who did you hear saying that?*"

"*Careful, don't be jumping up. You're not healed yet. Well, if you really want to know, it was a few kids. They might have been college kids like your age. They were hovering over you, saying they knew you could hear them. There was a Latino chick with dark hair, baggy jogging suit, and these ugly-ass Converse, bright-as-fuck colors. She was cute. You almost looked alike. She was doing most of the talking, saying even if you were in a coma, you could hear them.*" Francesca mocked the girl with a higher voice. " '*It's just like an altered state of consciousness.' You know, a lot of that mumbo jumbo. Kinda a know it all. She was young, but spoke like a teacher. A nerd.*"

"*Be nice. That's my sister you're talking about.*"

Francesca sat up and smoothed out her hospital gown to keep it from riding up. "*Then there was a very slender, tall black boy. He was kind of cute and funny. Legs long like poles, chile. He*

*seemed to hang on every word of that girl. Then
there was a weird-looking white boy with bleach
blond locks. Them shits look like big-ass snakes
coming out of his head. You know them big, thick
dreadlocks? I almost thought he was an albino,
but his eyes looked hazel or light brown. He was
definitely a white boy, or mixed, I guess. He
talked really slow and low. He seemed to be the
type that just goes with the flow. I figured they
were your classmates."*

"Yep, we're all mixed with a little something.
That was the Fantastic Four. Elizabeth, Robbie,
and Zack."

"Well, there was only three of them."

"I know—I make it four. They are actually my
siblings. We call ourselves the Fantastic Four. It's
like our fun little gang."

*"What? Really? No waaaay! What kind of
Rainbow Coalition are you from?"*

Journey chuckled. "We're sperm donor babies.
We got the same dad, different moms. Our dad is
Cuban and Jamaican."

Francesca's eyes widened, and her mouth
dropped open in awe.

"I know, I know . . ."

*"Whaaaa, that's fucking wild, but cool too. But
now that I think about it, that girl did resemble
you like a lot. She had nice flowing hair with
glasses. She's like the nerdy, hipster version of
you. But then again, I don't really know how you*

look with hair or out of this ugly-ass blue-and-white gown they gave us." She tugged on the thin cotton gown and frowned at the flimsy material.

Journey sneered, *"I still can't believe they came."* The tightness in her chest lightened after hearing more details about her siblings. She really felt so much better knowing they weren't still mad at her. *"So, you saw them a lot?"*

"No, it was for one weekend, but the girl came back more. She was here much longer. She would come with your mom. She was always talking to you and working on you, doing some kind of healing stuff. Rahkeee? It looked like massage, but not really. She wasn't massaging you."

"You mean Reiki." Journey smirked. *"Yup, that was definitely Elizabeth. She's a Reiki healer and going to school to be a psychologist. My mom told me. She said she thinks that Reiki might have helped me wake up."*

"Yeah, I believe it. 'Cause you were out cold before." She fell back in her bed and played dead in her bed with her tongue hanging out to the side. They both laughed so hard.

"You're a spy and a comedian, aren't ya?"

"Well, I'm a prisoner here just like you. What else am I gonna do? I have to entertain myself somehow. It was pretty cool to watch. Your sister had a bunch of crystals on you, and it was really weird looking. I loved when she came, though. She had the room smelling so good with essential oils."

"I thought she hated me. Our last discussion was not a good one."

"Oh no, not the way she was acting. She really wants you to get better. She seemed almost obsessed with healing you. I was kind of jealous, and I wanted her to come over and work on me too." Francesca lay down and got under the covers.

Journey wondered where Francesca's cards and flowers were. Where were her family members or friends? She looked at her side of the room, which was barren. The sun shone brightly onto a windowsill that had only a box of tissues on it, while Journey's was full of cards, flowers, and balloons.

"So, what got you in here in the first place, Francesca? What do you want her to heal you for?"

"Oh, me? Vaping. I couldn't stop coughing. I had a high fever, and my chest hurt like hell. My heart was beating a million beats a minute, and I couldn't breathe. They thought I had some kind of virus or something. I was vomiting and had nonstop diarrhea. Spewing stuff out of me from both ends. Chile, I was a hot mess. It was a straight up nightmare. No one knew what was wrong with me at first. They diagnosed me with lung disease. I'm seventeen. Fucking lung disease? COPD it's called. And I still wanna smoke. I snuck out a few times to do it, but I ran out of my pods. I'm dying for a smoke now."

Journey gave her a scolding look.

"*I know it's no good for me. I started at thirteen. Me and my older brother used to sneak and do it, but now we just do it in the open. I know better now.*"

Journey said, "*Yeah, vaping is like a pack a cigarettes on steroids.*"

She sat up. "*I didn't even know that each pod is like twenty cigarettes. It's super addictive. They told us it was safer than cigarettes at first. Pure bullshit.*"

"*Well, I think it's best you stay away from that stuff, Francesca.*" Journey's eyes narrowed. "*Where have you been all day? I missed you.*"

"*They were testing me like a lab rat. Blood tests and more blood tests. I'm always waiting long. But, back to you. Don't try to change the subject.*"

They were startled by a knock on their door. A familiar face poked his head in. He was shadowed by an older woman, another familiar face. Yoga students. She knew him. Phil . . . Philip. Journey remembered her too. Helen. *Oh, shit. Heleeeen.* Her stomach churned. The memories of her bad deeds hit her like a baseball bat to the skull. She didn't want them to see her like this. She wondered who the hell had let them in there. Weren't they getting a divorce?

Francesca whispered in her mind, "*You know them? You want them here?*"

"*Yes, I know them. Both from yoga. But—this doesn't look good.*"

Phil smiled, and his handsome chiseled jaw brought back warm memories of their late-night chats and yoga sessions. He said softly to his wife, "Okay, are ya happy now, Helen? She is unable to do anything. This poor girl is fucking bedridden, and you just had to see for yourself. I told you before, I just came to visit her when she wasn't even awake. Nothing happened."

His tone softened, and he turned to Journey. "Hey, kiddo, it's good to see you awake." Phil turned his back to his wife. He mouthed toward Journey, "I'm sorry."

She was trying to remember everything. She knew he was her yoga student, but she felt something wrong, very wrong had also happened.

Phil said, "Can you understand me? The nurse said you can respond by blinking yes or no."

Journey blinked twice to let him know she understood him.

Helen's stringy, long jet black hair was thinning and pushed back into a tight ponytail. It was like a makeshift facelift to hide her wrinkles. Her dramatic eyebrows and heavy eyeliner made her look like she was in a horror movie. She actually scared Journey with her menacing eyes. They were full of anger and pain. Journey knew it was something that she had done. It made the memories flood back like a tsunami.

Helen whispered, "Nice to see you again, you little slut. And I thought you were my friend and my teacher. Nothing but a fucking con artist."

Phil winced in pain. "Easy, easy. Come on, Helen."

Journey felt a jolt go through her. Helen's anger was so intense she could feel her hate-filled stare vibrating through her entire body. Her throat tightened. She wanted to scream at her in retaliation, but nothing came out. Who the fuck did she think she was calling her a slut? Then Journey got a flashback of Helen's husband's warm hands caressing her ass and legs while she stretched him. She taught private lessons to Phil with a few added perks. He was a fine Italian man, very distinguished with his salt-and-pepper hair. He was older than her father, about thirty years her senior.

She never had sex with him, or at least she didn't remember going that far. Maybe foreplay, but no sex. She never even kissed him, but Journey was sure if she wanted to fuck him anytime, she could have. Journey and Phil had a simple agreement. She liked to call them "arrangements," and although they were not the norm, she felt they were pretty innocent. She was good at rationalizing her not-so-good deeds.

Phil paid her top dollar for their private "yoga" sessions. He left satisfied just from the way she talked softly to him in his ear. She was very seductive, making him feel wanted, making him feel like a man again. You see, Journey had a talent of bringing him to climax sometimes without even touching him, but by invading his mind with her telepathic skills. Journey would enhance the fantasy of what she wanted him to feel. Watching him beg her every time for a little bit more gave her a thrill too. Many times, his excitement released right on the yoga mat. It could happen while being put into the warrior one position, plank, crow, or even a headstand with Journey pressing her moist, soft skin against him, assisting him. Driving older men wild and teasing them with the promise of giving them more pleasure in the near future turned into a lucrative side business for her. The sheer sense of power was what she reveled in.

Helen was lucky Journey didn't have her strength back, or she surely would have slapped her clear out of the room.

Phil whispered, "Helen, *come on*. What's the matta wit' you? Have a heart. Stop it. You see where she is?" He ran his hands through his salt-and-pepper waves.

"Yes." She rolled her eyes at him.

"The girl's in bad shape. Are you happy now?"

"Yes. Yes, I am." She turned to Journey and whispered, "So, I guess you won't be giving out yoga hand jobs now. Heard you've been giving them to your married clients. Oh, not giving them, selling them, like a prostitute. Does your mother know you're a whore?" Then her unnaturally white teeth shone like sharp, bleached fangs. "I curse the day you were born. Homewrecker. Philip isn't going anywhere. You can't have him. Karma, bitch. Karmaaaaa." She almost sang it.

Francesca shouted in Journey's mind, *"What a bitch!"* She balled her fists.

Journey said, *"For real, and her breath is seriously kicking of cigarettes and coffee."* Journey really didn't remember everything that she had done with Phil, but she knew it went on for months.

"Damn, sugar, what you do to that man?"

"I guess you can call him a sugar daddy client, and let me tell you, he wasn't so hard to please. He definitely helped pay the bills."

Phil finally found his courage. "Okay, that's enough. She's unable to do anything. Ya gonna get us kicked outta here. I just came to visit her before, and she wasn't even awake yet."

"Yeah, but I'm sure you can't wait until she is up and running so you can suck her filthy pussy again. She's a manipulating swindler. Five hundred dollars a week for yoga? Or was it a thousand? Give me a fucking break. You're just throwing money away on a skanky suicidal whore." She blew out more rank air like a filthy muffler into Journey's face. "Yes, I know. I heard everything, Miss Journey. Phillip didn't cover his tracks enough. I doubt you'll have a job when you get outta here. Everyone knows. Cameras never lie."

Journey wanted her out! A tear trickled down her eye, but not because she was scared. She was furious that she couldn't do anything. This jealous wife was making Journey so nervous. She wasn't sure if Helen was going to hit her to try to pull her IV line apart. Where the fuck were the nurses? The doctors? Philip was not helping. He was being a full-blown pussy in Journey's eyes.

She looked at Francesca, who coaxed her on in her mind. *"Do something! Do something!"*

Anger stirred within her. Rage awakened her powers.

Journey yelled a telepathic message to Phil. *"Why would you bring her here? She swears we were having an affair. You need to go. Get the fuck out! You need to control your wife."*

Just like that, he said to her, "I'm so sorry, Journey. Let's go, Helen." He grabbed her arm and yanked it hard. He heard her. He definitely heard her.

Helen pulled away from him and whispered, "Karma, bitch."

Journey screamed into her mind, *"Don't hurt yourself on the way out. I'll show you what a bitch I am!"*

"Get out!" Journey was able to yell. The sound of her voice surprised them all, even Journey.

Helen and Phil jumped back. The door flew open, and Helen collided with an orderly bringing in some medical equipment on a tray. The cart crashed into her feet. Helen screamed at the young man, "Oh my God, what the fuck is wrong with you? You stepped on my foot! Jesus Christ, Philip. My toe, my toe!" She cried, and her arms went flying as she struggled to keep her balance. She ended up flat on her face.

Phil screamed, "Oh my God. Are you okay, hon?" He had a smirk on his face, trying to hold in a laugh as he pulled her off the ground.

The orderly's face was flushed crimson red. "So sorry, ma'am. I didn't see you standing so close to the door."

She was flustered and dramatically dusted off her cream khakis, looking for stains.

Journey whispered to herself, "Karma, bitch. Karma."

Francesca rolled on her side, facing her, and silently laughed. *"Good for her!"* she whispered. *"Did you do that? Holy shit."*

"Yep." She smiled.

"Shit, Journey. I'm finna to stay on your good side."

Journey was really baffled about how Helen came in ready to fight her while she lay in a hospital bed. Insane. From what she remembered from her conversations with Phil, Helen was always making excuses not to give him some sex. She guessed Helen had a low libido. His sacral chakra was always blocked, and Journey was just using yoga asanas to help him out. Helen was apparently happy after he started taking private lessons with her, since he seemed more attracted to her after he came home from being with Journey. She would thank her all the time for his "renewed energy." Phil told her she gave him a "strong erection" that made him feel young again. Journey would stretch him out, get his blood pumping, tease him a little, and send him home horny and ready to make wild, passionate love to his miserable wife.

Journey couldn't figure out why on Earth he would tell his wife unless she saw his CashApp payments. That was the only thing she could think of. Helen knew how much money he was paying her, so she must have been snooping. She also remembered the girls at yoga were gossiping about her and her "special clients," and it got back to Natalia. She remembered that it was the rumor that Helen saw his bank statements.

She thought, *If those girls at the studio were gossiping about me, it's all good. They couldn't just mind their fucking business. They were jealous I was getting paper. I will get back to myself and just take my business elsewhere. There are plenty of yoga studios in Atlanta.*

Journey thought the talk started because one of the managers kept asking her why she was at the studio so late at times. She just told them it was because Phil's schedule was pretty hectic running a law firm. She figured they thought it was a bit strange, since sometimes they would leave at 11 p.m.

They had cameras in the front. She hoped that was all Helen was referring to. What if there were hidden cameras? Shit. That would be bad, very bad.

Phil was paying her on average $2,000 a month for the private sessions, and Helen knew yoga didn't cost that much. It was just for the extra VIP services she added on to make him feel like a real man—obviously, a skill he said Helen was lacking.

She enjoyed Phil's company. He was an intelligent entertainment lawyer, super cool, and not bad looking for a man in his late 50s. Journey would miss his company and his money, because by the looks of it, when she got better, he might be banned for life from yoga.

Francesca interrupted her reminiscing. *"Girl, you fucked him, didn't you? I didn't know you liked them so old."*

"Nah, not at all. He was my private yoga student. He did pay me well, so she probably just saw the statements."

"Sucked his dick?"

"Nah. Well, I might have rubbed it by accident when adjusting his pose." She smiled.

"*Ohhh, you nasty. Sure, accident my ass. I knew it, I knew it!*" Francesca pointed. "*Hey, I am not mad. Get your money, girl. He was nice looking for an old dude. But he got poor taste. His wife was ugly as fuck. Her skin was so pale, she looked like an uncooked chicken.*"

They both laughed.

Journey got a text from him right after they left.

Journey, so sorry about Helen. She found out everything. She saw our CashApps, and she even tracked me to the hospital when I came to visit you last week. I hope to see you again, but it won't be anytime soon. Good luck with your healing, kiddo. I will make it up to you someday. Again, my apologies.

Just like she figured. She knew it. What a pussy! She didn't respond. Her mom had given Journey her phone back, since she was able to at least type. She had been using that or an iPad to communicate in the memo feature. It took her a little longer to type, since her full mobility was not there, but she was able to do it at a snail's pace. It was frustrating, but it was a start.

Going through her phone was overwhelming. Journey had so many texts wishing her well or trying to check up on her status. So many people showed they cared, from coworkers to clients and friends. She especially loved the text she received from the Fantastic Four. It was a photo from Elizabeth when they were all there with her. It filled her heart with so much gratitude. She was still loved even after all of the trouble she caused. Journey was so happy that they had all met, and sad that she didn't get to experience it.

Some of the texts had a hint of pity in them.

Lola: I hope you get help after your therapy. We don't want to lose you. Love you, girl.

Kennedy: Therapy worked for me. Try it, Journey. It can shift things. Sending you healing light. Namaste

Mickie: I used to work for 911. I can help you if you ever feel in crisis again. There is a better way. The world needs your beautiful soul. I'm here for you.

Journey wanted to throw her cell clear across the room. If she had the strength, she would have. *I didn't do this to myself. I am not suicidal. I am not fucking crazy.*

What baffled Journey the most was that she did not understand how her last memory was being in an apartment engulfed in flames. How could she have felt fire at her heels and have the intense desire to jump? It was terrifying, but somehow, she had been convinced at the time that jumping was safer than staying. Maybe she did have a hallucination. She figured she had to have seen something foreboding. It was almost like something or someone had taken over her mind.

Then it came to her. It had to be Ty. Who else knew how to do what they did? Who else had the power of telepathy, how to invade people's thoughts? He had twenty years ahead of Journey to learn and master his gifts. Even though he barely spoke about it, she felt he just played it down like he really didn't know how to use his abilities, but deep down, he was playing mind tricks on her.

After going through her phone and seeing all the text messages, her memory was improving. She wished she could forget some things that were coming back. Ty and Marlon were going to send her to jail for stealing money. Ty was furious about her seducing his partner Marlon's gullible ass, even though he gave her the damn check.

Before the accident, Journey had a strong drive for revenge. Her mouth watered for it, but somehow, it had faded. She didn't even care anymore. Getting her life back to normal was more important.

Her mother walked in. "Oh, boy, you are getting back to your old ways, I see." She pointed to the cell held in her limp hand and shook her head.

"Hey, Nini. Okaaaaay, so full disclosure," Mom whispered. "I deleted those disgusting photos and videos you had." She sat down next to her bedside.

Oh shit, oh shit, oh shit! Thickness formed in her throat as if it were stuffed with cotton.

She was so humiliated. She felt violated, and the shame of being seen engulfed her. She had a few with dick pics from Kendu, Philip, some clients, and definitely a damn near porno with Marlon. She had been saving those. What the fuck? Her mother actually got into her phone? Journey felt her mother needed to get a life and was so damn nosey. Her mother was probably trying to find out why she wanted to kill herself and went digging. Memories of her risk-taking behavior haunted her.

"Journey, I'm going to get you help for your mind after your body heals," she whispered. "Now I know your little secret on what you been doing to make so much extra money. Listen, I know you are free spirit, but what I saw in your phone was too much. I almost thought you were on a porn site. You have to have respect for yourself and your body, or no one else will respect you." Her voice choked up. "Where did I go wrong? A young lady should never, ever take nude photos. You never know where they will end up."

Not being able to speak back and at least share her side of the story was totally torture for Journey. But maybe it was a blessing, since what the fuck was she going to say? What could be her excuse? If her mother saw the videos with Marlon, Journey was actually sucking his dick in one of those videos. She was lying in the bed with him, topless, telling him to call her the master. Journey didn't even want to imagine what went through her mother's head when she viewed those videos and pictures.

"Why did you go through my phone, Mom?"
Journey screamed in her head. Her mother shimmied her shoulders as if a chill went through her.

Journey felt her body sink deeper into the mattress. If she could burrow a hole and disappear like
a beaver, she would. Journey let out a soft moan,
and her eyes widened.

"Why?" Her throat strained to say it.

"Oh my God, finally! You spoke! She finally
spoke," her mother yelled toward the door that
was cracked open. Her mother rang the nurse's
button, and she heard monitors attached to
Journey beeping wildly.

"Oh, no! I hope I didn't excite her too much!"
She caressed her head. "Nini, are you okay?"

She shook her head and moaned again. "Why,
whyyy?" It was the only word she could get out.
Her cell was protected by fingerprint and facial
recognition. How much her mother had to go
through to get into her phone was what made
her heart speed up and her body violently shake.
Journey wanted to jump up and scream.

The nurse came in and checked her vitals. She
turned off the machine making an incessant beeping sound. "She's fine. Her pressure was just a
little high. Maybe let her rest a little bit. Maybe too
much excitement for a day. I would take the phone
away from her."

"Noooooo," Journey mumbled. Their faces lit up
with smiles.

"Wow, I guess she really is getting back to normal. This is a really good sign." The nurse chuckled.

Her mother conceded, "Okay, I'll leave." She gently picked up Journey's phone and moved it to a shelf away from her. "Dominick is coming soon anyhow. His shift starts in thirty minutes." She bent down and whispered, "I also had to delete it before the cops saw it." Her mother raised her brows. "They may look at these things during an investigation. You know, Nini?"

Journey blinked twice. Her mom did have a point. She was probably right. Seeing all of her blackmail photos and videos of Marlon, Philip, Adrian, and other high-profile clients would not look good for her rep. The only downside was that Marlon had copies of what she texted him.

Stupid . . . stupid . . . stupid. Fucking stupid.

Dominick brightened her mood when he walked in with a big smile on his face.

"Good afternoon. Look what I got you." He talked softly and deliberate, as if each syllable needed to be deeply enunciated. It was like he wanted every word he said to be understood. With his deep baritone, he could be a radio announcer or even do commercial voiceovers. When he spoke, it reminded her of someone whose first language was not English, so they needed to be sure they said each word correctly. From time to time, she would hear his faint Spanish accent.

Dominick held up a Nike bag. He opened it and showed her the coolest high-top sneakers. They were brick red. Journey looked at her feet, confused. She shook her head no, slowly.

"Oh, you can't walk right now, but you will be able to soon. Don't you worry. These sneakers are more for right now. It will help you keep the shape of your feet. You see, if you are laying down too long with nothing on your feet, they will start to change shape. You are progressing fast, and we have to get you ready. I know you will be up and walking in no time." He leaned in and whispered, "I'm really not supposed to get you gifts, but it's okay. It's our little secret." Dominick winked.

She got a whiff of his cologne. He smelled so delicious. Was she developing a crush? She wasn't sure, but she definitely loved all the attention.

"Before we put on these fresh Air Nikes, I got a little foot massage for you. We need to keep that circulation flowing in these pretty little feet you have." Dominick put down his bag and pulled out a bottle of shea butter, then removed her socks.

Journey was surprised to see a fresh coat of ocean blue nail polish on her toes. She figured her mother must have done it. Dominick pulled out a tiny spray bottle from his bag and dramatically spritzed the air above Journey's bed and waved his hand.

"Smell that. Can you smell it?"

Journey moved her head gently from side to side, taking in the lavender aroma. She smiled at his childish excitement. She wondered if he was gay or just really loved his job. He had his hair gelled with little curls. His facial hair was trimmed neatly, and overall, he was a little eccentric in his style. Dominick was sexy in a bad boy kinda vibe that she was digging. Then he would switch into this very giddy, almost feminine nurturer. Journey enjoyed his company, but she was hoping that he wasn't gay, since all of his skills might come in handy someday. He wasn't her normal type, but he was handsome, and so compassionate. Journey wondered if he was the same outside of his work.

She thought, *Who wouldn't want a man that really knows how to take care of you?*

"Oh, wait. Before I start, lemme put on some spa music to make you feel at home." He reached for his cell. "Hold up! Is that another smirk? You are laughing at me. I see it. I love it. It's okay. Don't hate on this VIP treatment you are getting. How's this mix?" He showed his screen to Journey. "It's lo fi chill mix on Pandora."

Journey's brows rose up in delight.

"Ah ha! I knew my research would get me far. I saw your Tiktok and IG. Your mom gave them to me. I heard the kind of music you put on your videos. You got good taste."

Journey was impressed. He definitely must like his job since she knew right now, she looked like shit. Dry skin, chapped lips, and a pasty mouth was her current situation.

He must have the Captain Save-a-Ho complex, because he's going all out for little old me, Journey thought.

Maybe looking at her socials had inspired him to see what she really looked like when she got out of the damn bed.

As he glided on the lotion and kneaded it into her feet, she could feel his touch. His hands were warm and so caring. She loved watching his thunderbolt tattoo on his arm and hand as he massaged her. Maybe it represented his powerful energy. It was a relief to Journey that she had more sensation coming back to her.

He looked at her and smiled. Dominick seemed to really create a bond with his patients.

Chapter 5

Journey

"Sooo, let's get to the good stuff. I want to hear your voice soon. I mean, it's been a one-sided conversation for the last two months. I heard you spoke."

Journey snickered.

Dominick leaned in with a tilted head. "Oh, you think that's funny? Well, I hope you speak up soon. I won't pressure you. When you are ready. Would you like to watch *Snapped* after your massage?"

Journey nodded yes. He reached for the remote and changed the channel from the Food Network to her preferred show. Journey figured he must have really talked long with her mother, who told him everything about her. That could be good and very bad.

Dominick always wore bright green or aqua scrubs. He looked intimidating, with a lean physique and tatted arms, but his endearing smile and wide eyes gave him such a tender look. He had a splash of goofiness that made everyone like him. Journey wondered if he had a crush on her or the girl on her social media. He could just feel sorry the "suicide girl," because the way she looked and felt right now, it wasn't attraction.

Journey couldn't wait to really piece together what had happened, so that she could shout it out to the world. She might even buy a billboard and post it on Buford Highway.

I DID NOT TRY TO KILL MYSELF! I LOVE MY LIFE.

Yup, that's what the banner would say.

All the attention Dominick gave her made Journey wonder if her old flame, Kendu, even knew what had happened to her. Did he ever come to check on her? The last time she saw him, she busted him with her so-called friend Zuri. It was a friend who pretended to be a photography client of his, but she knew better. Having been betrayed, she didn't trust many people. She usually liked black men with deep chocolate skin like Kendu's, but there was something about Dominick that intrigued her.

He proceeded to rub the shea butter into her feet and shins. He caressed her so gently that it was almost sensual. She could feel the nerve endings on her legs and thighs tingle from his touch.

In between her legs felt a little spark as well. *At least that still works,* she thought. The fear of not having feeling below the waist was terrifying to her. She would rather be dead. Not being able to feel passion again, to connect with another; now, that would be the real reason she wouldn't want to live anymore.

Dominick looked at her with a deep gaze. "Is that okay? Not too hard, is it?"

As she shook her head to his question, she wanted to feel his touch more deeply, so said in his mind, "*Harder, harder!*" She wanted to see if her limbs were really alive.

She sighed. Journey could just fall in love with his voice alone. It was so soothing. He added more pressure. She was satisfied that he had heard her plea.

"You had a lot of bruising that healed quickly. You been through so much, Journey."

She took a deep breath. Her chest tightened with frustration. The sorrowful look he gave her was the motivation she needed to speak. "I didn't . . ."

Startled by the sound of her voice, he dropped her foot to the bed.

Her chest heaved as she tried to push down a cry, but she didn't succeed. She belted out, "I didn't do it. I didn't do it." Tears rolled down her cheeks. Ragged sobs erupted from her tight throat.

"Whoa, whoa, relax, mama. I'm so happy to hear your sweet voice!" He chuckled, but he also was concerned. He moved in closer to console her. "What didn't you do?"

"This! I didn't jump."

"Oh, shit. If you didn't, then—did someone push you?"

She shrugged her shoulders. "I don't know." Journey couldn't explain to Dominick what was really on her mind. What was she going to say to him? *My dad and I have magical powers. We're telépaths and he wanted to punish me for being a bad girl, so he threw me out the window with his mind?* Nope, that would never work. She would sound fucking insane. Well, it was not like she could get that many words out anyhow. She had so much to say, but it was so difficult to even form a full sentence. It was that "tip of the tongue" feeling, like when you want to remember the name of the actress in a movie, but you're at a loss for words even though you know who she is.

Journey was restless. She figured if she tried again and took her time, she could probably make some sense of it all for Dominick. She gave it a shot and looked directly into his eyes. Instead of speaking, she projected her thoughts to his mind. Much easier.

"Someone made me jump."

He jerked back. "They forced you? Did they have a gun?"

Journey shook her head and replied softly, "No."

"Take your time, Journey. I am actually supposed to call the detective on your case. They said we need to call them once you start talking. Are you ready to talk to them? I can call if you want."

"No, no." Journey started to realize she needed to plan out her next steps before jumping ahead. If she was going to be recorded, she wanted to make sure it was good and served a purpose for what she needed to do.

"Gosh, it's just so good to hear your voice. So good to have you back. Did anyone have insurance out on you?"

She shook her head no.

"Oh, you know how all these true crime shows are. Everyone killing off people for lousy insurance money or land."

"I know." Journey smiled. She was getting back into the groove of it. She felt a bit more like herself.

"You are doing so good. I'm so happy that your cognitive functions are coming back so strong. You'll be up and at 'em in no time once you start rehab."

He grabbed the remote. "Speaking of true crime." Dominick playfully raised his eyebrows up and down. He turned off the music from his phone as *Killer Couples* came on. Journey was ecstatic and wished she had a bowl of popcorn to go with it.

He sat in the lounge chair next to her bed to watch the TV with her. A dark shadow flashed behind him. Journey blinked, thinking her eyes were playing tricks on her. The figure glided behind him, then dashed behind the TV, then to the bathroom on the right. The figure didn't touch the ground. It floated.

Dominick followed her eyes and saw her point with a shaky finger. "What? What's wrong? There's nobody there?"

She was sure she had seen someone.

"The show just started and you're scared already?"

Then the shadow walked out of the bathroom slowly and took form right behind him. She couldn't believe her eyes. It was Janet! Janet's deep brown skin glowed. Her smile was oozing joy.

"Look at ya! Journey, Journey, Journey. Just look at ya!" Janet pointed at her and shook her head in disapproval.

Journey gulped and tried to play it off that her fears were ignited from the murderous show after all. It was obvious that Dominick was not experiencing what she was. She knew now it was nothing to fear. Janet was her friend—a dead friend, but a friend nonetheless.

She spoke to Janet telepathically, *"Am I asleep? Am I dreaming?"*

"No, ma'am!" It was Janet in full color, looking radiant, not at all dead.

"*You're here? I can't believe it. Your hair is so pretty.*"

"*I told you I had nice hair before I lived on the streets. You like my outfit?*" She did a slow spin, showing off her sky-blue T-shirt and fitted jeans.

"*Yes, you look so young. So amazing*"

"*Yeah, you get to pick the year you want to be on the other side.*"

Janet put her hand on the edge of the bed. "*So, look now, I ain't here just for fun. I told you not to abuse your gift. And what do you go on and do?*"

Journey gasped, and Dominick looked at her, confused, since there was nothing scary happening on TV. She pretended as if she had gotten a chill. He pulled the covers up on her a bit more.

Journey was in awe. Janet continued chastising her and laughing while she did it. "*Look at you in a hospital bed, damn near bald headed and looking crazy.*"

Journey tried not to smile. Now on the TV there was a gory scene of a man found bludgeoned to death by his ex-girlfriend.

Dominick was watching the show intently, and Janet pointed to him. "*You watch this one, ya hear? You go on ahead and get better, so you can fix the mess you made. Just know you are never alone.*" She stepped back into the bathroom but faded into the mirror without having to use the door. Journey didn't want Janet to leave. She had so many questions.

Journey was in shock and hoped she really wasn't going crazy. She was unsure if she had dozed off and was possibly dreaming. Either way, her heart fluttered in delight at seeing her. Janet was truly her first teacher to help her take her telepathic and psychic gifts to the next level. Journey was devastated that Janet had to leave the Earth so young at the age of 53. Cirrhosis of the liver was what took her. It finally took its toll after years of sobriety. Her body paid the price for decades of abuse. She was homeless for years, and everyone thought she was mentally disturbed because of her gift of talking to dead people.

When Journey had met her in the coffee shop, she thought she was off her rocker as well. She was talking to the air. Well, at least that's what it looked like, until Journey realized Janet could hear her thoughts and see spirits as well. They began speaking without moving their mouths. It was fascinating, and Journey took to Janet quickly, meeting with her regularly to practice her newfound talent of telepathy.

Journey found her determination to heal even faster now. Seeing Janet reminded her of her life's calling. She had a goal of creating a wellness center to help everyone, and it would have programs for the homeless as well. A Place for Janet was the name she had come up with as a dedication to her teacher. She was not going to let this roadblock in her health stop her. Journey had big plans for her wellness center to have yoga therapy, fitness programs, and much more.

Journey watched Dominick stare at the TV while now massaging her hands and forearms with so much care and love. She thought, *Yes, Dominick will help me. I can see him being on staff for my wellness center. Maybe I'll add a rehab room.*

Journey refused to let her setback stop her vision to build her wellness empire. She was getting fired up again. She knew that after all of the drama that had occurred between her and Ty, he probably would not want to help her at all, much less see her. However, she still felt he was her ace in the hole, and he might not have a choice but to help her. She still couldn't prove that he had made her jump, but she couldn't count him out either. Time would tell.

She should have asked Janet. Maybe her friend knew what had really happened to her.

Chapter 6

Journey

After hours of watching TV, Journey drifted into a deep sleep. When she awoke, the room was dark with a faint, flickering blue glow from the TV. She felt a presence as if she were being watched. Two silhouettes were at the edge of her bed. Chills galloped up and down her spine.

"Janet?"

The hairs on her forearms stood at full attention. Journey felt a gentle tap on her bed frame and then a tug of her big toe. *"Oh, relax, Journey. It's me, Francesca. I wanted you to meet my girl, Delilah, from room 561. We were waiting for the nurse on duty to fall asleep."*

Delilah waved and smiled, showing off her braces. *"Yeah, she is out there snoring and all."* She wore a high ponytail of golden brown locs. They were so shiny and beautiful. Delilah's gown had style. It was adorned with a big gold belt around it. It looked so strange to Journey, but she thought it was cute.

She pointed at her belt. "*New look?*"

Francesca said, "*Oh, her gown kept coming off, so she started using the belt. She's a little bit of a diva, chile.*"

Delilah said, "*Whatever. I'm a designer. You ain't know?*" She playfully tossed her locs. She had sass. "*I like to keep it sexy.*" She looked about 18 or so. Her skin was flawless as if she were dipped in deep, dark chocolate.

"*What are you in here for?*" Journey asked as if they were in prison doing hard time.

"*Oh, me? They think I have a tumor or something. They can't find out what's wrong with me. I'mma be geeked once they let me out, 'cause I gotta have my baby. I am sick of everyone here. They got me going stir crazy. I know you must be losing it. Can you move yo' legs yet?*"

"*I can feel them more now, but still not able to walk just yet.*"

She turned to Delilah. Journey tipped her head to the side. "*Wait a minute. Dial it back some. You have a baby?*"

"*Well, yeah, I ain't seen her yet, but they took her from me.*"

Francesca waved her hands in front of Delilah, cutting her off. *"All right, all right, let's not be a Debbie Downer. Your baby is fine. Your family got her. You came to meet Journey, not dump all your sad stories on her."*

"Yes, I had to see this miracle girl everyone keeps talking 'bout. Shit, if you can fall from a building and survive, maybe there is hope for me too." Delilah laughed.

The trio heard footsteps coming, and Francesca crawled into bed and shoved Delilah out. *"Go, girl. We gonna get in trouble."*

Dr. Alexander came in and saw Journey sitting up with the marathon of *Killer Couples* still on.

"Lord, I told Dominick this mess is gonna give you nightmares."

"No, it won't," she mumbled with a smile.

Dr. Alexander did a double take and stepped back. "Oh, my, this is awesome." She flipped the light on, and Journey squinted, trying to get adjusted to the brightness. "Ah, sorry. I know it's bright." She took out a flashlight pen and looked into Journey's eyes. "Do you know what year it is?"

Her voice cracked. "Yes. It is 2023."

"Do you know how old you are?"

Journey paused and searched the ceiling with her eyes for the answer. "Twenty-two, but no, twenty-three. I missed my birthday. It was, it was November second." She had a sinking feeling as if it had just hit her. She was in a damn coma during her birthday a month ago.

"How are you feeling?"

"So tired. Better, but tired."

"That's normal to feel that way."

She typed a few notes into Journey's charts on the computer. "Okay, get some rest." She turned off the TV. "I'll make sure the morning staff runs some more tests on you. You should be good to go to rehab soon. You are doing amazing. I've never seen such a fast recovery. You're truly a miracle." She brushed her shoulder softly.

Her sweet smell of perfume lingered. Dr. Alexander was Journey's favorite. She had such warm, feminine energy, and it really soothed Journey's anxiety from being there so long. She was caring like Dominick. Journey could tell they sincerely liked to help people. Journey laid down with a big smile on her face.

Janet's visit had sparked a memory. It wasn't the first time Journey had seen Janet since her accident. It happened when she was in a coma.

It was so cold. Journey felt her teeth chattering, then her body felt weightless. She was floating. Floating like a kite. It was similar to when she had out-of-body experiences. She felt at peace. Suddenly, she was standing in a doorway that was illuminated with a white light around its border. The light was so strong; it was seeping in from the bottom and the top of the door.

Journey had this urgency to see what was on the other side and pulled the door open. She felt a sudden rush pass through her from the back of her body to the front. Her foot was wedged in the door, but she didn't go in. The white light was so bright that it was almost blinding. Two long rows of people were inside, as if they were waiting for her. She couldn't make out their faces, but it just felt so good to see them. Journey felt their energy. She felt this immense feeling of love. Her body was buzzing from the vibration of everyone's auras being so strong. Her head was spinning. Their faces were fuzzy. It was as if she needed glasses to see them clearly. But she could hear them in her head. She could feel them. Her hands tingled, craving to embrace them all. She was home again.

Journey walked in slowly. The pulsating light was so amazing. She needed to get closer to it. She heard the people cheering, and some were pumping their fists as if she were a champion who arrived from winning the Olympics.

But a few in the front were yelling, "Go back! Nooo. Go back. You are not done."

It was then she noticed her great grandmother Mercedes, whom she had never met. Journey remembered her from photos that Ty had showed her. She was a beautiful, brown-skinned Cuban woman with short, curly hair and bright red lipstick. Absolutely stunning. She had the graceful presence of a 1950s movie star. Mercedes was adorned in a vibrant tunic of purple and gold with rhinestones around the V-neck collar with matching gold hoop earrings. Journey didn't understand how she looked exactly how she had in the photo, not a day over 30.

Mercedes' eyes were deep and peaceful. Her makeup, flawless. She spoke softly. "Journey, mi amor, why are you here? It's way too soon." She walked toward Journey, almost gliding. She grabbed her hand and pulled her gently back toward the doorway. Her eyes sparkled as if she had tiny flames hidden behind each pupil. Journey was in awe of what she was whispering.

Mercedes raised her voice. "It's way too soon, mi pequeña nieta! You have more work to do. He sent you here. Show him you can do better. Show him you can do better than me. You can heal. You don't have to do things my way. Learn your gifts."

Journey didn't know who him was. Was it God? Ty? She had no idea which "way" they went.

Janet came from right behind her in the crowd of unknown faces. "What you did was stupid.

Stupid as hell. I thought so much better of you. Don't you have any self-control? Now look at ya!"

"Okay, okay, stop yelling. I don't know what you're talking about, Janet."

"Oh, you have a selective memory. You're better than you think. You caused so much trouble that they wanted you gone. They wanted you gone!"

"I don't know what you're talking abo—"

"Oh, you will know very soon. Now, go and make it right." Janet's eyes were intense, and her lips flattened. Journey had never seen her get angry, so it frightened her.

The rows of people behind her joined together slowly and were moving at the dragging pace of zombies. They slowly turned around and walked in the opposite direction. The sky behind them turned from a light blue to vibrant hues of purple and pink. They all faded and transformed into beams of light. The clouds faded. Journey watched the sky change colors in awe. It was so serene.

"I said goooo! Don't just stand there with your mouth hanging open." Janet's eyes widened. She was in a panic. "Go before it's too late! GO!" Janet pushed her so hard.

She saw her own body on the patio. Her face was covered in blood from the gash on her head. Her legs were twisted in such an odd way, but she wasn't in any pain. She didn't even remembering jumping. It was as if her spirit was out of her body, viewing it all.

That last push made her fall back into her body. Journey winced. Her left eye was pounding. Her spine twisted, and the back of her head throbbed in excruciating pain. She gasped for air.

The sky opened up further and got brighter, almost blinding. The intense bright light beamed over her face now. Loud sounds invaded her ears. Sirens. Two faces stared down at her. A woman and a man were excited to see her open her eyes. She felt strapped into a bed. Her eyes were squinting from the strong glare. Journey had something over her nose and mouth. It was a mask. An oxygen mask. She wasn't in a bed; it was a gurney. Her eyes examined her surroundings. Gray cabinets were everywhere above her. She heard machines beeping above her. There were things hanging from shelves. Medical equipment. The reality hit her that she was actually inside of an ambulance. The sound invaded her eardrums. It made her head throb.

The paramedics shouted for joy, "She's back! She's back. She's breathing. She's okay. Stable." The female paramedic wiped her brow with the back of her forearm and sighed. "Close call, Kenny."

Her partner said, "This head injury looks pretty bad. Pretty girl. Jeez, she looks so young. Life must be hard on her to wanna take it."

"Yeah, young, pretty, and dumb for jumping out of a balcony." She put a brace on her neck.

Kenny shot a look of disapproval. "Shhh, Lena."

Lena sighed while making sure Journey was strapped in good on the backboard. "Oh, she's out of it. She can't hear me. She is so lucky to be alive. These broken bones are gonna be a bitch to heal. She better pray that she'll be able to walk from a fall like that." Lena shouted to the driver, "Get trauma on the phone. We gotta let them know to get ready for this one."

Ty

Claudia looked good for a woman in her late 50s or maybe early 60s. She had on some loose-fitting linen pants with a satin camisole that revealed her belly button just a little. Jazz music played in the background, and the candles were lit all around the dining room. She had a plan.

When Ty walked in, she embraced him with a long hug. Her fragrance was captivating, but Ty was on to her.

"Thanks so much for coming."

"Wow, this looks really nice." He got a bit nervous. It was a little too nice.

"Thank you, Ty. I don't get much company these days, so I might go a bit overboard. Don't mind me." She giggled like a girl with a teenage crush.

Claudia was headstrong and determined to always get her way, Ty had his reservations about her motive for their meeting. Claudia had invited him over for an early dinner, and he saw no harm in it. Dinner was also a good way to see where her head was. Ty figured she wanted to discuss Journey and her future since she was recovering.

"I ordered some rasta pasta from the Jamaican spot down the block. Journey once told me you like Jamaican food, since your dad was, well, Jamaican, right?"

"Right."

"I know you're busy, but I really wanted us to talk in person."

"It's no problem. It's good to see you again. So, how is she doing?

"Much better. She's speaking in short sentences and seems to be pretty alert under the circumstances. She's using her cell more too. Texting mainly, but she's acting more like herself. She is still sleeping a lot because of all of the medications she's on. She spoke with the detectives, but said she doesn't remember much. She just remembers coming to talk to you and then waking up in the hospital."

Ty felt instant relief, but also knew that was all bullshit. How did Journey forget all of the turmoil she caused? She just remembered coming to visit and then waking up? How convenient. *Sleeping Beauty, eh?*

"Yes, can you believe it?" She took a sip of her wine with her pinky out. "The doctor said it's common when you've been in a coma to be slightly forgetful or to have full blown amnesia. I'm glad she remembers who she is. Most of the times, it does come back slowly. I don't think you have anything to worry about; however, I'd like to be transparent. I'm still concerned."

Ty tilted his head, fishing for details. "Why?"

"Well, I'm praying when she comes out of the hospital, you and your company won't pursue any legal action." Claudia quickly put on her lawyer hat.

A lump formed in his throat, so he took a sip of his drink to swallow. "Well, I don't know what's going to happen, and I'd honestly rather not discuss it since Marlon was the most affected. He's really shaken up with what happened to him, and he actually is going to need therapy it seems."

Claudia dabbed her mouth with the napkin. "I saw the videos."

"What? She showed them to you?" He felt so embarrassed for Marlon.

"No, no. When she was in a coma, I went through her phone. I had to see what caused her to . . . to try and, you know . . . jump. What I saw was sick. It disgusted me." She shook her head and squinted from the memory. "It was a lot. Just too much. Did you see them?"

"Unfortunately, yes, some of it. It was hard to watch."

"I know. Tore me up inside to know, well, I, I just had no idea what she was doing. It was like porn. I'm getting her a psych evaluation because I did not raise her like that." Claudia cleared her throat as if to not put her foot in her mouth any further. "Her doctor said it's possible that by next week she can be released into a six-week rehab program. I'm just hoping we can really come to some agreement to keep this off of her record."

Claudia crossed her legs and attempted to fill up his glass with more wine. Ty held up his hand. He saw what she was doing. It was as if she were flirting with him and trying to get him drunk.

"Well, I hope the treatment will really help her, because she definitely does need a little bit more help. The way she deals with conflict is very combative."

"I am just hoping we are on the same page, Ty." She smiled slyly and tapped his hand. "We really should have a united front. She is our daughter."

"Claudia, I can't control what Marlon tells the cops about her."

"More wine?" She started to pour more into his glass before he could answer. "Can we call it a truce? I paid you back."

"Actually, she owes more than the five thousand that you paid. I found out it was also money in his money clip she emptied. About one thousand dollars."

Claudia leaned in more as she spoke, revealing her ample cleavage. Her nipples were piercing through her silky camisole.

"Oh, wow, but that's no problem. I'm sure we can work it all out." Her eyes were glassy, and she was being much more flirty. She was trying too hard.

"Look, Claudia, I think you're a very nice lady. This is not for me. I came to talk to you, that's it." He couldn't believe how much she was teasing him. He wondered if she had put something in his drink. He looked at it and stirred it around.

"Really, Ty? What are you looking for? Devil's Breath?" She laughed at her own sick joke.

"Well, just checking. It looked a bit weird." He laughed nervously.

"Do you really think I'd have to drug you? I thought I would be enough without that. I think I still got it for a woman of my age."

"Oh, you do, you do. Never said that you didn't." Ty winked to reassure her ego.

He fumbled for words and decided to send her the message telepathically. Maybe she would assume it was her own mind.

"Stop it! You're making a fool of yourself. Tell me what you have to tell me already."

"My, my, you're *so* intense. What a look you just shot at me." She stared at him. "Now I see where Journey gets it from."

"Claudia, I'm gonna head out. Thanks for dinner. Maybe you should get some rest and sleep that off. You're drunk."

"No, I'm not. I'm just a little tipsy." She laughed. "I always thought you were soooo attractive. I did good with my donor pick, didn't I? So, Ty, you never thought about it?" She traced his hand with her fingers.

"About what?" Ty pulled his hand away slowly.

"An older woman?"

"Oh, I've had a few in my day. I have nothing against it, Claudia. I'm just seeing someone right now."

"I see. So it's not me, it's you." She held up her wine glass and bit her bottom lip and leaned in again.

He laughed. "Exactly." Ty rose up from his chair. "Okay, I'm going to head out now. Thanks so much for dinner. You have a good night and keep me posted on when I can visit Journey."

He realized the wine got to her before he did. She didn't take his mental cues. He felt sorry for her. Claudia seemed lonely. She was also probably so stressed out waiting for Journey to heal. She needed a lover to release her tension, but he was not the one. He didn't want to complicate matters even further, so he made his grand exit.

Chapter 7

Journey

The trees outside her room showcased a colorful display of burnt orange, red, and browning leaves. It was a nice view and change of pace to get lost in. Journey was feeling confident that soon she would practice walking again and experience fresh air. She missed being in nature. The doctors and nurses said her next step would be the wheelchair, then a walker, then finally, walking. It was so painful to even sit up. A tear came down her eye at times, feeling so helpless when just two months ago she was able to do handstands and splits. Just the thought of knowing she was so close to being a vegetable or dying made her so grateful to be alive.

Journey couldn't wait to get back to herself. She was in and out of a lazy Sunday morning doze when she heard a knock on the door.

"Well, well, well! Someone is a celebrity! Special delivery for Journey Salazar," Dominick cheered.

Journey was sitting up and eating on her own. She still needed a little help, but she was much better now that she had gotten rid of that irritating catheter. This was her last week in the hospital, before she would go to Peachtree Long Term Care Facility.

"Wow! For meeeee?" Journey exuded so much joy, although she seemed paler than usual. Small bags under her eyes gave her a weary appearance, but overall, she was feeling much better. One of Journey's yoga clients who was a hairstylist had given her a nice pixie cut, so that her short hair had a little style to it. She had very short bangs and was now wearing diamond stud earrings and some lip gloss to feel cute again. Her crush on Dominick was growing, so she always made sure she looked presentable before he came in.

She wondered who the box of flowers was from and quickly ripped it open. To her dismay, they were long stem black roses.

"Black roses?" Her hands started shaking. This was a message, a threat even. "Who's dark idea of a prank was this?" When she read the card, it all came together.

> *I heard you're getting back to your old whorish ways. Get your own husband and stay away from mine.*
> *-Surprise! You know who.*

Journey mumbled out loud, "What a bitch. She is so lucky. She is soooooo lucky I am here."

"Whoa, whoa. What's that about?" Dominick sat by her bedside. "I didn't know you had enemies, mama? Not my sweet Journey. Is this something we need to worry about?"

"I doubt it. She is a crazy-ass yoga student of mine. Her husband used to get private lessons, and she swears that we were doing something. I'm so sick of her accusations."

"Wow, that's harassment, you know? Did you tell your mother about her?"

"Hell no. She's already a worrywart." She yawned and stretched her arms in the air, pretending it didn't bother her. "It's nothing. She's harmless. She is talking all that mess to someone who can't fight back. She wouldn't be so bold if I was back to my normal self, trust me. You know, she even came to the hospital a few weeks ago when I first came to? I couldn't speak yet. So, that shows just how much of a coward she is. She's just trying to scare me."

"What? Why didn't you tell someone?"

"I don't know why. I guess I was embarrassed to even share the story. She came with her husband, Phil. It was pathetic. She is that insecure that he had to bring his wife here to show her that I was still incapable of doing anything with him. She threatened me from the bed too."

"Nope. Unacceptable. I can't believe you didn't tell me."

"I didn't know you were my bodyguard now."

"This is harassment, and you should file something when you speak to the detectives. That's dangerous. What if she tries to get in here when no one is here? I don't mean to scare you, but it is possible. What's her name?"

"Helen. It's Helen Esposito."

"Okay, I'll make sure that the nurses know not to let her in. What does she look like?"

"You're going to laugh, but she kinda resembles Cruella De Vil. You know that evil villain from *101 Dalmatians*?"

His mouth opened partway in shock. "Oh, I know it well. That's hilarious!"

"Yeah, let's just say she has a strong face. Square jaw line and too much Botox, maybe. I don't know."

Dominick seemed to make a mental note as he said her name again in a softer manner, "Hel-en Es-pos-i-to," sounding out each syllable. "How long has this been going on?" Dominick looked at his phone and typed in her name in his notepad.

"What, her harassing me? It just started."

He lowered his chin, and his deep hazel eyes glared into Journey's. "No, I mean how long were you dealing with her husband?" He raised his eyebrows, wanting the details.

"Really?" It was evident by his confident tone that he knew there was more to the story. She wondered if he could read her mind too. She instantly forced an invisible field of protection around her. She felt seen. Was she that obvious?

"Journey, I think you should feel comfortable with telling me the truth by now. I'm practically family at this point. I'm like a big brother." He took her blood pressure and adjusted some machines on the side of her bed.

Journey snickered as she looked at his strong biceps, tattoos, and his sparking smile. She thought, *BILF —Brother I'd Like to Fuck*. She smiled to herself, hoping that wasn't a real acronym.

Journey tried to probe him to see if she could feel anything, but the only thing she felt was power and confidence. It was like he had his own force-field up and was not letting anyone penetrate it. He knew how to guard his energy. Journey was impressed. She knew there was something special about Dominick. He definitely was a lot more than a medical assistant. He had many gifts. She wasn't quite sure what they all were, but she felt he held onto many secrets, maybe just as much as she did.

Journey decided to confess. He knew how to break her, and she kinda liked it. "Ahhhh, those damn eyes of yours! You need to work for the police. I feel like I'm being interrogated."

He laughed and shrugged. "What? I'm just asking a simple question. Hey, it's no big deal. Shit happens. And you and I watch enough crime shows to know when someone is withholding the truth."

"Well, okaaaay. So, I flirted with him a little bit during our sessions, and he gave me big tips in return. I learned he wasn't getting much attention from his wife, so that's why he kept wanting sessions. I saw an opportunity. He's filthy rich with money to burn."

"Sounds like a business move to me. There's nothing wrong with that, mama. What does he do?"

"He's an entertainment lawyer. But that's all I did was flirt, no sex. He just likes me talking a little dirty to him. It was like acting really." She took a sip of water and couldn't understand how he had gotten her to open up so much. "It started off pretty innocent, but then the money started to come in. I mean a lot."

"Wow, impressive skills you must have."

She shrugged innocently. "He just kept rebooking. I think he got a bit obsessed with me. The irony is that Helen is the one that booked his first session with me. She felt he was so blocked and stressed and needed to release the tension from his work, so I helped." She giggled, remembering some moments with Phil and how much he adored her. He was definitely good for her ego. She turned into a self-proclaimed yogi dominatrix.

"Listen, I'm not mad at your hustle. As long as it was safe for you, and he wasn't a creep. You could be doing worse. I applaud your creativity." He adjusted her blanket over her since it was getting chilly in the room. "Sounds like innocent fun to me."

"Yeah, Phil was harmless. It wasn't really much." She snickered, recalling a memory. "If I could keep it one hundred with you, he would be so excited just to have me hold him in a position longer. It was kinda weird. He's an older guy, so I guess I was like an Afro-Latina fantasy for him." She covered her face in shame. "Oh God, that sounded so arrogant. I hope you aren't judging me." Journey felt so free, finally sharing this secret since no one else knew, not even her former best friend, Natalia. She felt so comfortable with him. He was not judgmental at all.

He gently touched her arm. "No, no not at all. I mean, I can understand that. You know, you being . . ." He cleared his throat. "Um, a fantasy and all."

"Dominick? Whaaaaa?" Journey laughed nervously.

"What?" He smiled shyly and reached for the remote. "So, what do you want to do with these flowers? Let me take a picture of them, so I have it as evidence in case she tries something else." He took a photo of the roses and the card with his cell. "Black roses. You gotta give it to her for being morbidly creative."

"Thank you. Please text me that picture and put those roses in the trash. She's so evil and insecure." She pulled the covers up some more.

"Done!" Dominick dumped the roses.

"Okay, what do you want to watch today? *48 Hours*, *Snapped*, or *Killer Couples*?" He rubbed his hands together like an evil villain.

She waved a scolding finger at him. "Oh, no, no, no. You're not going to just change the subject. Sooooo, am I a fantasy?" She smiled slyly with a tilted head. Journey blushed since her confidence was making a comeback.

"Come on, Journey," he whispered and leaned in close. "Are you trying to get me fired?" The warmth from his breath on her ear gave her goosebumps. They locked eyes.

"No, no. Not at all." She giggled. "I'm just amazed you would find me attractive, you know, looking like a bald-headed cripple and all."

His voice was deep and tender. He softly held her chin. "Oh, come on. You're beautiful on the inside and out. Don't ever say that about yourself." He removed his gentle grasp, catching himself. "And everything is not just about looks. I think you're basing things a lot on hair and makeup, but when someone really appreciates you for your soul, your feminine energy, your directness, and your sense of humor, then looks are just a bonus."

"Wow. I never thought you—"

"Please, just know I'm here for you as a friend, and I got your back always. Not just because it's my job. You should know by now, you are one of my favorite patients." He sighed as if it was something he'd been holding in for a while. "This might sound a little crazy, but I really feel we are connected. I care about you." His eyes darted around, seeming shy. He stared up at the lights, out the window at the rustling trees, and then back at Journey. "Not just from this plane or even this dimension. It's like we had shared a past life or something."

"You too? I believe in that too! I swear, it's so easy getting to know you. Maybe it's because you

took such good care of me in a coma. I already feel
like I know your soul. We must have been friends,
family or—"

"Lovers," the pair said in unison.

Nervous laughter filled the room. It was more
like relief that the feeling was mutual.

Journey said in his head, "*I LIKE YOU. I
REALLY LIKE YOU.*"

Her stomach trembled. She knew he felt the
chemistry too. That was a sign to tell her to keep
her big mouth shut. However, a part of her wasn't
afraid of his reaction, since she needed some
excitement. She wanted to feel love again. Being a
prisoner to the bed was not supposed to be a part
of her "Roaring 20s'" stories she told her kids one
day.

He furrowed his thick brows. "Why are you
looking at me like that?" Dominick slid off her
compression socks and pulled out some new fuzzy
purple ones her mother had brought. He adjusted
her positioning in the bed, so she wouldn't get bed
sores. Then he took some lotion from the counter
and began massaging her feet.

He said, "It's important to keep the circulation
flowing."

"It feels incredible. You know, when you touched
my face earlier, it just felt so familiar. It made me
remember something." She turned slowly to the
window, watching a bird float by. A large flock

followed behind it as the sun was beginning to set. Journey was afraid to look into his eyes.

"Remember what?" He was eager to find out. He sat up straighter, accentuating his broad shoulders.

"I'm embarrassed to say. I just remembered my dream, I guess. My memories are so jumbled. I had a dream that I was still in a coma, and you were trying to uh—let's just say, you were using some unorthodox ways to wake me up out of it."

He chuckled nervously as the blood rushed to his olive-toned face. "Unorthodox like what?"

"You had your hands . . ." Journey buried her face in her hands. "Ugh, I don't wanna say it. It's so crazy. You will laugh or run. I'm not—"

"Saaaay it." He chuckled. "See, now I'm curious. This is getting good." He whispered, "Say it. I won't tell anyone."

"It's soooo wrong." Journey laughed.

He leaned in. Their eyes held a long glance. "Continue." He waved his hands. "Had my hands where now?" Dominick snickered, trying to hold in his laughter.

Journey used her hand to seal her imaginary zipper on her lips.

"Is it that scandalous? Wow, I feel like I need to really make a cup of tea for *this tea*."

"Okay, Okay. You had them under my covers." She leaned into his ear. "On my nipples and—"

"Journey, *Journey*." He jerked back as if he was getting turned on from the vision and trying to remain professional. Dominick blushed from embarrassment, but Journey couldn't tell if it was more like fear.

She whispered, "Dominick, be honest. Have you ever touched me like that? I mean, I was out cold. You had free rein to do it. You coulda done whatever. And that dream felt more like a memory to me." She licked her lips, feeling her feminine power making his imagination go wild.

"Aye dios mio. Your dirty little mind is a bit out of control, mama. Well, yes, of course I touched you, but not like that. Never like that! I had to wipe you and bathe you. Clean your stools and change your catheter."

"Eww, yeah, I know. Don't remind me."

He shrugged. "So, um, touching you for work is not as sexy as you are making it sound."

Journey beamed him a message. *I know you're lying. Just tell me the truth. Not even once?*

She sensed his attraction for her and found it hard to believe that he had never copped a feel. Journey knew she would if she were in his shoes. Now that she was eating solid food again and gaining weight, she knew her body was going to be shapely again soon. After two months on a feeding tube, she had only lost fifteen pounds. She thought it was more since her legs looked so different, but the liquids they pumped into her had nutrients to give her the calories she needed. Journey knew all she needed was the gym to build back muscle and tone.

"Look, Journey, I tried to be delicate with you. I would never do that. We take an oath. I could lose my job. I need this job. So, I'm going to ask you to not play like that and to never share that dream. I mean never ever. Deal? People have accused others who work here for shit like that."

"Okay, okay. So why are you so defensive? Look, if it will make me relax and feel better, that's actually called healing." She laughed loudly. "I can't even lie. I probably would have enjoyed it. You are kinda seeeeexy. There, I said it."

His lips parted, and he was at a loss for words for a moment.

"Muy fresca! What's gotten into you today?" He reached for the TV remote and turned it up a bit more, while closing the door with his foot.

"Well, I'm just saying." She shrugged and whispered, "If you ever want to give me a special happy ending massage, I'm down. My sacral chakra needs some help. Maybe it will help my legs get some circulation down there." She raised her eyebrows and maintained a straight face for barely a second before a loud laugh escaped her.

"Okay, okay, chill out." He turned red again. He ran both of his hands through his hair, and his eyes scanned the door as if he were really contemplating her offer.

"I mean, you've helped me so much. I'm feeling like my old self again. Being in this bed so long, a girl's got needs."

"I'm flattered, but I gotta respect the code."

"What code?"

"Well, just a code of ethics. I . . . I couldn't go there, and besides, your mom, she wouldn't approve of . . . of us."

With a sly head tilt, she said, "Who said I was gonna tell? I'm not saying we gotta go together. It's just helping me out, and I can, you know, help you out. That's what friends do, no?"

"Nope, you're not taking me down this road with you. I don't know what kind of friends you have." He laughed.

"Okay, it's okay, but I feel a little sweaty. Don't you have to bathe me tomorrow?" She winked. Journey was having too much fun watching him squirm.

He swiped his hand slowly across his goatee, trying to hide his smirk. "See, you're bad, Journey. Nope. I think Evelyn comes in tomorrow to bathe you in the a.m. I have the night shift again."

"Okaaay, you can relax now. Was I making you uncomfortable?" She tapped his strong bicep. Journey felt her sex appeal oozing out of her, even if she couldn't get up and sit on his lap like she really wanted to. She was getting high off of seeing him fidgeting. "I'm just messing with you." She knew how to seduce with just her words and voice.

He chuckled. "You better be. You're not gonna get me in trouble. All jokes aside, I don't want to have to transfer to another patient if this sexual harassment continues."

He grinned to let her know he was teasing. "Let's do your exercises and please change the subject. It's getting a bit awkward in here."

Journey fell back on the bed, laughing. "Whoa! You scared me a minute there."

She got a peek at his scrubs, and they seemed tighter than usual. His arousal gave him away. Journey's confidence soared.

He started to do some exercises to improve mobility in her hands and wrists. He just grabbed her hand and held it. Journey put her fingers in between his as if they were holding hands. She felt a tingle from his energy. Such a strong heat vibrated from his hands. She knew he felt it too. A surge flowed through her body and sent blood rushing to places that had been stagnant for a while. Dominick smiled and shook his head at her teasing.

The room's door was ajar, so they could see the people passing by in the hallway. A nurse walked by and looked in. He quickly released Journey's grasp and went back to massaging her palms. They looked at each other. Journey loved how he made her feel so safe and cared for. She knew he was into her, and maybe when she started to walk again, he would take her more seriously.

After the nurse walked by, Francesca walked in the room right behind Dominick. It was so strange, since Journey hadn't seen her in a few days, so she had figured she was discharged or moved to another room when Journey was asleep. She just appeared out of nowhere. Francesca was smiling really hard, exposing her cute gap and almost every tooth in her mouth. She held her finger over her lips and shook her head no, as if she was going to surprise Dominick.

Journey didn't want to play along. For some reason, her gut urged her to tell him. She said in his mind. *"Don't be scared. Someone is behind you."*

He felt her. She didn't say a word. "Huh, did you say something?"

She mouthed the words, so he could read her lips. "Behind you."

Francesca shot her a scolding glare and snuck out. *"Oh, you ain't no fun, Journey!"*

Dominick quickly turned around, and there was no one in sight.

"What? Are you seeing things again?"

"No. Not at all. Someone was trying to sneak up on you. Don't you see her?" She pointed to Francesca, crouching down.

"I used to always see you looking into space when you just got out of a coma. I wondered if you were seeing angels or your spirit guides. It would be such an intense stare, like what you just did."

"No, not angels. You didn't see her? She ran out." Journey pointed at her. "It was Francesca. The girl that used to be on the other bed in here. I hadn't seen her in a while, and I figured she went home."

"Fran . . . who? What?" His face drained of color.

"You know, Francesca. I never got her last name."

His voice cracked. "What does she look like? Short, long red—"

"Long red hair. I guess it was like strawberry blonde, now that I think of it. A lot of freckles. Gap in her teeth? Lots of personality. Her family was from Mississippi by way of Chicago."

His stare was blank as if his soul had left his body.

Journey sat up. "What? What's wrong?"

Dominick's energy ignited. "Wow!" He stood up and paced. His voice was slow and steady. "How could you know all of those details? When exactly were you talking with her? Did you know her before?"

"Helloooo? Francesca was my roommate. She was the first person to see me wake up. I think it was her that got me out of my coma. She was pretty talkative, mainly when everyone was gone."

His jaws clenched with tension. "Journey, that's impossible." His eyes widened with fear.

"What do you mean impossible? You're acting weird. What . . . what's up?" She felt his energy. He was terrified. Journey took a deep breath and tried to invade his thoughts again, but she only heard muffled words. She needed more practice in that area. It was only easier for her when the other person was a willing participant. She slowly moved the covers down and pushed the button so she could sit up further. "She was right there most of the time, sleeping." Journey pointed to the other bed. "I thought she would at least say goodbye when she left. What's wrong, Dominick?"

"What's wrong? I don't know how to tell you this, but Francesca died a month before you got here. A month at least."

She shook her head. "That's imposs—What? But she was right here in 3D. She wasn't a vision or a dream. Not funny. Stop playing!"

He said flatly and rubbed Journey's arm, "I'm telling you, she passed away in her sleep. I went to her memorial service. But the strange thing is that everything you said was one hundred percent accurate. Her lungs collapsed, and I was here when she coded."

Silence swallowed the room as they stared at each other. The only thing that filled up the space was the constant beeping of the monitoring machines. The hairs on her arms stood up as she recalled how it was odd that she never really saw him or any of the doctors interacting with Francesca. It started to make sense to her. She was usually never around when other people came, and it seemed she was pretending to be asleep or hide. So, no one really ever acknowledged her in the room.

"That's wild. So she was a fucking ghost? That's beyond crazy! I was having full blown conversations with this chick." Journey realized she had the same gift as Janet, so it was not as crazy as it sounded.

Dominick sat back down, taking it all in. "I believe her spirit is not at rest. She probably thinks she is still alive. That's the only explanation I can think of. She struggled a lot in her life and had a lot of guilt around getting sick, so maybe her spirit is fighting the reality of that. I am going to have to do some prayers to help cross her soul over."

"You know how to do that?"

"Yes, it's a long story, but I come from a long line of healers. From the Incas in Peru to Mayans in Mexico. They are in my bloodline and passed on a lot of knowledge. My grandmothers on both sides were shamans. They taught me a lot. I have to do a short ritual with candles to pray for her and send her spirit to the higher plane. It's as if opening a portal."

"Wow, you know how to do that? That's impressive, Dominick."

He nodded and smiled. It was then that Journey remembered Dr. Alexander called him Mr. Shaman as a joke. Maybe there was some truth to that after all.

"Oh shit, then what about Delilah? She was a pretty black girl who was hanging out with Francesca. She had a tumor, or they thought she had a tumor. Something like that. She had a gold belt on her hospital gown. I thought that was hilarious. She must have been a ghost too. Did she have a baby?"

"Well, we learned she was pregnant when she passed. She had a little boyfriend that knocked her up. The baby was too young, so they couldn't save it when she passed."

"Ah, that's so sad."

He leaned in closer. "Oh my God! I can't get—" He realized he was shouting and lowered his voice, covering his mouth. "This is incredible. You met Delilah too? She was a sweetheart. She died over a year ago, maybe even more. I've got to tell Doc *now*." He backed away from Journey, in awe of what he was hearing. He started texting Dr. Alexander.

"Oh God, noooo. Don't tell. Are you sure? The doctors are going to think I'm a freak. Put me in a mental ward or something."

"No, not Dr. Alexander. She is into all things metaphysical. We've seen strange things happen many times that can't be explained by science, but not everyone gets it. She will."

"Really? So, you aren't afraid of me?"

"No, no absolutely not. You're gifted. You're a medium." He seemed to be crafting a message via text. "So, let me get this straight. She was just talking to you close up in 3D, like you could touch her?"

Journey nodded yes.

"How many times do you think you saw her?"

"Holy shit. I don't know, maybe seven or eight times. So, I've been hanging out with ghosts all the time? This is crazy, Dominick." She rubbed the goose pimples forming on her arms.

"Have you ever had that happen before the coma? You know, seeing spirits?"

"No, but I'm psychic. I can feel things about people. I can see things in my dreams. I am freaking out, Dominick. This is a *lot*." She looked at her hands that were shaking. Fear sat in her stomach like an unwanted guest.

"No, don't freak out." He rubbed her shoulder. "I can't believe you were speaking to them. You are beyond talented."

"Well, it was mainly telepathic. I just thought she was psychic like me too."

"Sometimes after brain traumas people do experience increased psychic phenomenon. I'm going to have Mackenzie, I'm mean um, Dr. Alexander talk to you. She had an experience to share with you, so you know you're not alone."

"I really like her too. She's my favorite doctor. I peeped her crystals. I figured she was one of us."

"Oh, yeah. She's a high-level thinker. Spiritual and in tune with holistic medicine as well, not just traditional medicine."

Journey got a tad jealous of how he had a twinkle in his eye when he spoke of the doctor with such reverence. She wondered if he had a crush on her. Dr. Alexander was so tall and gorgeous and brought elegance and grace to a lab coat.

"I would love to speak to her about it. I also think I died and came back in the ambulance. I'm remembering some wild shit. I don't know if I'm bugging out or not. But after all this ghost stuff, I probably didn't imagine it all."

"What? They didn't tell you?"

"No, tell me what?"

"You did die for at least a couple of minutes. I heard you coded on the way here in the ambulance, and they brought you back. It's very possible you traveled to a higher realm and came back even stronger. That is very common with near-death experiences."

"So, you really believe in all this stuff? You don't think it's woo-woo?"

"No, not at all. I just told you I grew up with healers. We are all born with gifts. Modern society tries to dumb us down, so we don't believe we are magic. Mexican and Peruvian ancestors I have were my coaches. My family extends back to their very first indigenous cultures. So, a lot of things the modern world might deem as 'out there,' spooky, or witchcraft was just a way of life. Our people connected to the Earth and the stars."

"That's so true."

"There are always certain rituals they performed. It's just our way to honor Pacha Mama—the Earth.

"Remember, my family is from Colombia. However, they are very Catholic, so—"

"Oh, you don't have to tell me. I have some religious folks in my family as well who are afraid of their own roots."

"I have read a lot about honoring the Earth from my spiritual and yoga books. You know it all stems from the motherlands, right? Africa?"

"Of course. You are being connected with source. It's so fascinating."

"I was once very gifted as a child, but I didn't want the weight of it all. My family would force me to do readings for people as young as six years old. As I grew older, I was afraid to see things others couldn't. Only in the last five years have I been getting back to re-learning. My spiritual awakening, if you will. You know? Embracing who I am. I've been through a lot of deep transformations in my life. Facing the dark shadows of your soul is not always easy, but we have to deal with the process and stare fear dead in the eyes."

"Shit, I know what you mean. My shadow lurks behind me and makes me really look at my past mistakes under a damn microscope."

"Deep. Well, you are such a wonderful soul, Dominick. I really appreciate all that you do and helping me understand what's really happening and not making me feel like a freak of nature."

"Oh, never that. And this job is not always easy, but you make me love my job. Most of my patients make me suffer. Thanks to your mom and amazing doctors, you're on the road to recovery. Having magical powers can't hurt either."

She waved her hands in the air. "Yeah, and now this. I find out I'm a full-blown medium. Having parties in my room with ghosts. You can't make this shit up."

"Did those ladies mention anything else to you . . . Francesca and Delilah?" He looked so curious, almost nervous.

"About what, you?"

"Oh no, just in general."

"If I see them again, I'll tell them you said what up." They laughed.

"Oh, no, don't do that. They don't know me like that. They were both very sick when I took care of them, and they were not alert. I don't really want them talking to me. I will try to cross them over later in a meditation."

"Cross them over? I'm impressed that you can do that. That's so cool. You say it like it's something everyone does." She laughed.

"Thank you. I don't tell everyone, you know. I trust you."

"I know. They might put you in the padded room next to me." She laughed.

Journey remembered Janet saying, "Watch that one." When she looked at Dominick, she wondered why. Was that a warning, or was she predicting their flirtatious connection? She figured Janet probably noticed she was catching feelings for him.

Dominick paused and tilted his head, looking at her. "I forgot to tell you how beautiful you look today. Your smile always makes me smile."

Journey smoothed out her short haircut. "Why, thank you, kind sir." She batted her eyelashes and giggled. "My mom brought me these diamond studs. I barely ever wore them. I love them now. Makes me feel feminine again."

"I see you have on lip gloss too." He pointed at her playfully and clapped. "You're looking like a celebrity from the hospital bed. You need to do an IG live." They laughed.

"Well, my mom is bringing a friend to visit me. She will want to make sure I'm looking present-able." She rolled her eyes.

"This is true. Miss Claudia is a little bit of a diva."

"You think? I see she did my mani-pedi as well. I'm surprised she didn't do my brows and lashes too."

"Glad she didn't. You are a natural beauty. No makeup needed."

"Dominick. I think I wanna keep you as my med-ical assistant."

"Well, just say the word. That can be arranged. It might already be in the works. I may know a little magic myself." He winked.

Chapter 8

Journey

Dominick took away Journey's tray of food. "I do have some news to share. It's not definite yet, but I heard some news on your treatment plan. Word on the street is that you'll be released soon."

"Wow, really? That is awesome news," she shrieked with excitement.

There was a tap at the door.

"Knock, knock." It was Dr. Alexander, doing her rounds. "Well, well, well. Will you look at the little conversationalist." Dr. Alexander reviewed Journey's chart on the computer. She smiled brightly.

Journey loved her energy. It was as if she exuded love and kindness. She could see a faint green and yellow glow around Dr. Alexander.

"If that's not a speedy recovery, I don't know what is. Only a week since you have been out of a coma, and you're speaking with ease. Just incredible."

"She's ready to break out of here." Dominick pointed to the door and laughed. He was her biggest cheerleader.

"Well, we just came to give you the good news. All of your tests came back really good, so we'll be releasing you within a week and transfer you to Peachtree Long Term Rehabilitation Facility."

Dominick interrupted them. "Soooo, did you see my text?"

Dr. Alexander reached into her lab coat for her cell. "Oh no, sorry. I've been running all morning. I missed it. What happened?"

He was so excited and tapped Journey's leg. "Go ahead. Tell her who you met."

Journey felt all eyes on her. "Oh God, really? Just put me on the spot why don't you?"

"Who did you meet? One of my favorite celebrities or something?" She looked at Dominick, excited.

"Noooo . . ."

"Who then?" She smiled.

Dominick said in a whisper, "Francesca and Delilah. Delilah Santos was a year ago."

The mood shifted as soon as Dr. Amadi walked in and nodded hello. He was passing by and seemed to want to hear the scoop. He motioned for Dr. Alexander to move out of the way so he could view Journey's chart on the computer.

She stepped back and looked up, as if searching for the memory of the patient. "Wow, she knew them? Wait, Francesca, the redhead teenaged girl?

But wasn't that like a month ago or so? I vaguely remember Delilah."

Dominick nodded slowly with widened eyes that darted to Dr. Amani, realizing he wouldn't get it. His back was turned to them as he typed away in the database.

She urged him on, waving her hands. "What? In a dream or in a vision? I'm not getting you. Make it make sense."

Dr. Amani snorted. "Yes, exactly how did you see her?"

Journey sighed. "I saw her a lot. I know it sounds crazy, but I thought . . . I thought she was my roommate."

"Really? How can that be so?" Dr. Amani chuckled. "Roommates with what, a ghost?" He turned to Dr. Alexander. "Oh, no, no, no. We will have to book the psychologist, Dr. Brinson, for an evaluation." He caught himself and tried to lighten his tone as he turned toward Journey. "It's just to be sure you are okay. She can help diagnose the situation better."

Dr. Alexander and Dominick gave each other a disappointed frown.

She felt she didn't need to be diagnosed. She wasn't crazy. "But I've had full-blown conversations." Journey looked to Dominick for validation. "You see. I told you they wouldn't believe me."

Dr. Alexander chimed in. "Oh, we believe you, honey. I really think it's quite common and nothing to be alarmed about. She will get a psych evaluation at the clinic as well." She cut her eyes at Dr. Amadi.

Dr. Alexander leaned in close and talked softer. "Listen, some things like this happen during a traumatic experience."

Dr. Amadi shook his head. "Yes, they are very rare. Just make sure she gets that booked. So glad to see you doing better, Journey." He adjusted his glasses that seemed too big for his head. "Lunch?" he said to Dr. Alexander.

She was hesitant, as if she really didn't want to go, but had to kiss ass to stay in his good graces. "Yes, I'll be there shortly, Dr. Amadi."

"Can I get a moment with you all first?" He waved them into the hallway. "Good day, Miss Journey. Please be sure to tell them when you see or hear anything again."

"Okay." Journey took a deep breath. Her throat tightened. She was already regretting telling them anything at all.

Dr. Amadi marched off with short, deliberate steps, and Dominick and Dr. Alexander followed.

They were in the large hallway right outside Journey's door, but it was sealed shut. She couldn't hear what they were saying. She closed her eyes and took a few deep breaths and just wished she could be there. She wanted to hear what they were saying about her. On her seventh deep breath, she felt a whoosh feeling go through her as if a spirit flew into her body.

In reality, it was her body that flew through the wall and hit the ceiling with a light tap. Journey was suspended in midair! She felt as if a parachute were holding her afloat. Her body tingled. It was such an exhilarating feeling. She bobbed and weaved in the air. She felt her head bump into something and looked behind her. It was the bright fluorescent lights on the ceiling.

Holy shit, she thought. *I'm doing it again.* She wanted to laugh but was afraid they might hear her somehow.

She was above all three of them, but she came down slowly to stand behind Dr. Alexander. No one saw her. Journey's heart pumped so fast she could hear it in her head. It was such a relaxing feeling. She tried to control it. Part of her was afraid she would touch them or they would see her, but she had to remember she was invisible to them.

Dr. Amadi folded his arms. "She must get a full psychological evaluation before she leaves."

"Yes, Doc, but it's not as outrageous as you think. You know people can see things after a coma or some type of traumatic episo—"

"Let me explain something to you." He adjusted his stance. His tone was very reprimanding. He pointed his finger toward Journey's room. "This child was all over the local news. Her mother is a very well-known attorney. Connected with all of the judges. Wins ninety-five percent of her cases. I did my research. I got the medical director down my back. We can't afford any more malpractice suits. We need to pull out all the stops to make sure we do everything right down to all of the evals and medication given. We don't need her to go to home with another suicide attempt."

"Oh, don't go putting that into the Universe." She shook her head and looked at Dominick.

"Pha! Universe? You young folks and all of your woo-woo nonsense." He laughed.

Dr. Alexander's lips tightened as if she were holding back from cussing him out. "With all due respect, Dr. Amadi, it's no longer considered woo-woo, as you put it. There have been thousands, no millions of near-death experience cases that have been documented and studied. Patients are having profound experiences they report when they are close to death or after an incident. They're most common in patients who survive severe head trauma or cardiac arrest. It's not woo-woo."

"I've been practicing medicine before you were born, so I'm well aware of the delusions people have when surviving shock. When you can show me the true scientific data, we'll talk. For now, let's handle it the right way to just make sure we do our due diligence. Put a new referral in for the psychologist, Dr. Brinson, to evaluate her. We need to do that immediately. See you at lunch."

"Sure, will do." Her eyes followed him as he took his hurried pace to the cafeteria.

Dominick looked at Dr. Alexander and mouthed, "What an asshole."

They both chuckled. Journey, still invisible to them, moved to the right behind Dr. Alexander, and Dominick's eyes followed.

She asked, "What? Why are you looking at me like—"

"Oh, nothing. My eyes are playing tricks on me. I just need some sleep." He blinked hard and wiped his eyes. He saw Journey; she was sure of it.

"Yes, you work so hard. Get some rest." She squeezed his shoulder, and he blushed.

Journey noticed his aura expand with pinks and greens, the colors for the heart chakra. He definitely had a thing for her. Journey knew it. She didn't mind, really, since she felt Dominick was not on Dr. Alexander's level, so she doubted they ever had anything going on.

Journey tried to get back the way she came, but her body felt frozen. It felt like an invisible layer was in between her and the wall. She willed herself to float back up, and then suddenly, she dropped back into the bed.

Whoosh!

Whoa. What a rush, she thought. Journey opened her eyes and clutched onto the handles of the bed. She couldn't believe all of the gifts she had were coming back even stronger than they were before.

Dr. Alexander sat down next to her. Her soft perfume was so soothing. Journey listened intently. "Boy, you fell asleep fast. Sorry for disturbing you," Dr. Alexander said softly.

"Oh, no, it's fine."

Dominick released a sigh, and he and Dr. Alexander exchanged glances.

Journey's chin pointed toward the door. "Dr. Amadi thinks I'm crazy, right? A psychologist?"

"Girl, don't mind him. And after what you've been through, it's standard to get evaluated. We just want to make sure you are okay. And let me tell you, eight years ago, I wouldn't have believed anything you just told me either. I went through my own traumatic experience." She motioned for Dominick to close the door. "My ex-husband nearly killed me. I woke up in the hospital a whole 'nother person, you hear me? I was speaking with an accent."

"What? What accent? You sound like you're from here."

"Exactly. Now, hold on to your pearls, honey. Would you believe that I'm British? Born and raised."

"What? No way!"

Dominick nodded his head. "No, she's telling the truth. There are actually documentaries on her. She's an anomaly."

"My old accent comes back and forth with certain words. Certain memories trigger it, like TV shows or food from home, but my original British tongue is gone."

"That's crazy. What caused it?"

"It's really still not a hundred percent understood. It's a very rare condition. Sort of a phenomenon. Less than two hundred people in the world have ever had it. It's called Foreign Language Syndrome. So, don't worry about the therapist. We know you're not crazy. Dr. Amadi is just an alarmist, and he doesn't really get into the metaphysical world. I studied both. Trust me, people thought I was crazy or was acting out in need of attention. It was very stressful and hurtful for no one to believe me for months."

"I can't even imagine."

"The mind is complex, and we still don't understand all the levels of consciousness. Just look at what you can do as a gift." She turned to Dominick, who was typing up notes in her file. "I'm sure Mister Shaman can give you some pointers on how to maneuver through it." She said to him, "See, I knew there was a reason I assigned you to her." She rose up and tapped the bed. "We'll catch up soon. Make sure if you see or hear anything to write it down so that you'll remember."

"Okay, I will."

"I have a lunch meeting with the boss, but this is fascinating, Miss Journey. Just fascinating!" Her eyes were bright with joy.

Journey felt like a celebrity and was so relieved she wasn't losing it. Her psychic abilities were expanding. Communicating with the other side was wilder than any of her other gifts. She hoped she could handle it or learn how to control it more. She was getting just as good as Janet.

Dominick said in a very serious voice after clearing his throat, "Can I be your manager? You might be the next medium with a reality show."

Journey smiled. "No way. I don't want that attention. But now, I'm a little nervous."

"Don't be. They weren't trying to hurt you, right? They were just comforting you when you needed a friend. They didn't scare you, did they?"

"No, no . . . not at all."

"Well, maybe Francesca gave you the push you needed to wake up. I'm so glad that you did."

"Me too." Journey rubbed his forearm and then pulled it back, realizing she was being too flirty.

They smiled at each other, knowing their bond was deepening.

Ty

Ty felt at peace. His eyes observed the unique shapes that the puffy clouds made in the sky. Silence lingered. It forced him to take it all in. The fishing boat was still. The birds said hello with pleasant chirping as they flew to their destinations. The brilliant blue sky shone through the tree limbs. The sun was beaming so brightly on Papa's smiling face. He was grateful he had on his favorite Mickey Mouse shades for protection. The sunglasses made his eight-year-old self feel like he had a little style and he was a grown-up.

Papa and Mama had come to visit the family for a week from Miami. Mama went shopping with his mother, while Papa always made sure they had their one-on-one quality time together. Papa loved to spend quiet time alone with his grandson. They went fishing, and even though they rarely caught anything over one pound, his stories were always entertaining to keep little Tyler captivated.

This dream made Ty remember when his grandfather's English was much better, before the dementia took over. It seemed since then he'd reverted to being in Cuba.

"You know we are special, ah?"

Tyler held his fishing rod still, waiting patiently for something to tug at it. "I knoooow. You say it a lot, Papa," he whined.

"Yes. Do you know why?"

"Not really." He shrugged.

"Our family has special gifts. You especially, mi nieto," He tugged on the rim of his Atlanta Falcons baseball cap.

"Really? Like what do you mean, Papa? Superhero gifts like Superman?" He laughed.

"Let's play a game, and I'll show you. Ah, let me see. He took a deep breath and looked to the trees that swayed gently in the breeze. "What color is that bird right there?" He pointed to a bird.

"Oh come on! That's too easy! It's red, of course. Rojo for you." He smiled, since Papa also encouraged him to speak Spanish when possible, so he didn't forget it.

"No, no, look again. Close your eyes and tell me what color you see. See the bird's true essence. Every living creature has one. Close your eyes and tell me."

"Close my eyes? So, how am I supposed to see?"

Papa's clean-shaven face was as smooth and youthful as a 40-something-year-old man. He only had a few streaks of gray at this time. Papa tilted his head down with a demanding glare. "Tylercitooooo."

"This is a weird game. Okay, okay."

"Use your imagination, but tell me the first thing that you see when you close your eyes. The first thing, okay?"

Ty followed instructions, and when he closed his eyes this time, he looked at the bird through his mind's eye. The bird was illuminated with streaks of colors, like a glow. It was the coolest thing Ty had ever seen. "I see colors! I see them. White, green, and purple. Is that it?"

"Ah, that's it. That's it." He clapped and almost dropped the fishing rod.

What Ty didn't realize then was those colors he saw as a child were really the bird's aura.

"Really? I don't get it. I didn't just imagine it? Mommy says I have a good imagination. I see stuff all the time, but she says—"

"Your mommy used to see things too. She was just afraid of it. You shouldn't be. You will understand it in time. You will go through a few changes in the next few years. I want you to embrace it, and even though you are going to feel different from your friends, realize it's nothing to be ashamed of."

Ty wished he remembered that chat during his teenage years when his abilities heightened during puberty. He didn't have anyone around to show him the way during that time.

Suddenly, they were transported into his current living room, and they were back in the present time. Papa was speaking clearly and standing up by himself. Ty knew he had to be dreaming. Or was he?

Papa pointed his finger at Ty, who was sitting on the couch. His eyes held so much wisdom and concern. He knew something was coming but wasn't sure what.

"Be prepared. It's time to embrace your magic. I regret not teaching you the way when you were younger, because I was afraid of the harm it could do. I want you to listen to me carefully because the time is now. We need you to protect the family. Protect our legacy. You need to get to know the others. The others will help you protect the future of our bloodline. The Garcia family. Don't forget who you are, and we must teach the others. Our blood line needs strength."

"Protect the legacy. Si, Papa. Si, Papa, I will. I will not forget." Tears ran down his face as he received the message from his grandfather, even though it was not very clear what it meant. He knew it was an important message to cherish. He felt so emotional.

***

Ty mumbled, "Protect the legacy. Papa, don't go. Don't . . ."

A soft hand stroked the back of his head, and a sultry voice said in his ear, "Tyler, Ty, are you okay? You were dreaming."

Ty rolled to his side to find Jocelyn naked next to him. Her hair was wild with big, fluffy curls. She sat up on her side, and her hard, cocoa brown nipples greeted him in the morning light.

His voice was still groggy. "Oh, wow. That was a dream? It felt so real. So real." He sat up slowly. I need . . . I need to write it down." He grabbed the small notepad by his nightstand and jotted down what he could remember:

PAPA, FISHING LAKE
8 YEARS OLD
PROTECT THE LEGACY
THE OTHERS NEED TO ALL MEET

Jocelyn watched him in awe and smiled. "I never remember my dreams. It must have been good. You were mumbling a lot, like you were having a full-blown conversation with someone."

"Yes, I was with Papa, but we were much younger. Then it was in the present time. It was so real." He looked at the sunlight shining through the curtains. "What time is it?"

"It's 7:15 a.m."

"Whaaat? What, what are you doing here?" He suddenly regretted saying it like that.

She sat up straight, and her breasts bounced with her. "Well, I'm so sorry. You made love to me all night, until I had almost had a damn seizure. I couldn't quite gather my things to make it to my room. And you didn't want me to go. You begged me with your tongue. At least that is what it seemed like. Maybe it was the wine. We had a lot."

He laughed nervously and patted her thigh. "I'm so sorry. I didn't mean for it to come out like that. I just don't want Papa to see you coming out of my room. You know he is nosey."

"Ay, please, Ty. Let's be real. He knows already. He's no fool."

"Well, I'd rather we try to be discreet and just respectful. It's just in his condition, who knows when he could say the wrong thing in front of company?"

Jocelyn sighed dramatically. "I think he'd be happy to see us together. And what company?"

He got up, and she watched his muscular naked body walk to the bathroom. Ty started to wash his face. She admired his broad back and firm backside.

He caught her checking him out in the mirror. "Well, you do know I'm dating someone I—"

She rolled her eyes and changed her voice to a snooty proper accent. "Yes, I know. Miss Natalia, the secretary."

"She's not a secretary. She's a property manager."

He came back toward her and sat down on the bed. He was looking at her curves, her hard nipples, and her soft lips. Ty looked at the clock to see if there was time.

Jocelyn's voice cracked. "I'm just going to be honest with you. I'm tired of just being a secret side piece of ass. It was fun at first, but it's getting hard for me to pretend I don't have feelings for you."

Ty lay back on his pillow and pulled her in close. His morning hardness swelled for Jocelyn's body once again. He wanted her to focus on the task at hand and skip the melodrama talk.

She lightly tapped his dick, and it rose up to the call of duty. "Ya see, ya see . . . oh, that's all you want from me. I bring a lot more to the table then sex." She jumped up and walked slowly so he could see every inch of her curves and ass jiggle. She went to the bathroom to wash her face and swished some mouthwash in her mouth.

Ty ached to mount her voluptuous body. If it's true what they say about men thinking with their penis, this was definitely one of those times. Her complaining just sounded like mumbles as if Charlie Brown's teacher was talking. He ignored her.

"Jocelyn, baby, come here." He pulled her back to bed. He eyed the extra condoms on the nightstand. "Come heeeere, come here. Stop acting like that. You know I care about you." His hands caressed her hair and her butt as he pulled her in closer. He buried his head in her neck to inhale her natural scent.

"I'm tired of hiding. I just want one man who wants one woman. You know, in my other job at the clinic, I see so many STDs. It's scary. Atlanta has some of the highest rates. Everyone out here is doing everyone else, and I—"

"Chill, chill. Look, I explained to you when this all started how I'm not ready to settle down again. I'm still healing from my divorce, and I don't want to commit just yet to anybody. I enjoy your company. I love making love to you." He put his hand in between her legs and felt how warm she was. She flinched. "But I also appreciate how you take care of me and Papa. I don't want to lose you, so please don't minimize our connection. I know it's not just sex, and I know you know that." He bumped his forehead gently into hers.

Jocelyn seemed to hold back tears as she spoke. "It's just after all we've been through with Journey, and then you're going to be with that puta's best friend. She's a spy. I don't trust her."

"They are not friends anymore. We're just dating. I'm not with anyone." He looked up at the ceiling, trying to find the right words. "Look, we promised when this started . . ." With clenched jaws, he said,

"We promised we wouldn't talk about my personal life, and I wouldn't want to talk about yours."

"Well, you are a part of my personal life." She reached down to Ty's erection.

He thought, *That's it, focus. Give me what I need. That's it, baby girl.*

Her voice softened as she tried to change the subject. "It's so beautiful. So long and thick." She started to stroke it. She knew he wasn't listening to her plea.

His lips parted with pleasure as he fell back onto the pillows. He liked this conversation a lot better.

She said, "I love it. I hate that I love it *so* much. Is this what you want, Ty, huh?" She wrapped both hands around his hardness, making slow and steady movements. She weaved her fingers together like a basket and moved them up and down. He throbbed in her hands. She kissed him gently on his stomach and his belly button. He tried to remain focused on her succulent lips, her plump breasts, and thick thighs. His hands glided across her soft skin. Ty's body tingled, aching for her once more. He loved how sensual, yet aggressive she was. She knew what she was doing.

She whispered in his ear, "I love you, Ty." She bent down and took him in her mouth.

He sat up on his elbows to watch her skillful display of fellatio. She gently pushed him back down and climbed on top of him, kissing his chest and stomach while he moaned in pleasure.

"I just want to feel . . . oh, I just want you to feel me. Feel how good it could beeee . . . "

Ty was taken aback as she slid him inside her hot wetness. He clutched her butt cheeks and moaned while she squeezed him tightly inside of her. His mind clicked, and he realized that there was no condom on. It was feeling so good, but then his stomach churned. Danger was near. He had to stop. He had to stop.

He eased her off of him slowly. She pushed her body back down and screamed in pleasure. "Papi, no . . . keep on . . . keep on . . ." She continued to grip him in as if she wanted him to melt into her.

He noticed the condoms on the dresser again. Ty knew it was torture to have to stop when he was just about to cum. "What, what are you doing? Come on, let me get a condom." His arm reached for the nightstand as he pushed her off slowly.

"Fuuuuck, Ty. It was feeling soooo good. I'm sorry. I don't know what came over me. I just wanted to feel you. Didn't you love it, Papi?" Jocelyn collapsed on his chest, smiling. "I want you to come inside me."

Ty's eyes narrowed. She had just finished complaining about diseases, and now this? He took a deep breath, trying to control his anger, and then he heard her voice in his head.

"I'm ovulating right now. I want to have your baby. I want to be Mrs. Carter. I don't want you to be with anyone else. I know you love me. Why

are you fighting it? We are perfect for each other. I need you."

The thoughts were foggy and jumbled, but she sounded obsessed. She really was in love with him. His rock-hard erection went flat like a deflated balloon. His temper flared.

Ty grabbed her shoulders and looked into her eyes. "Jocelyn, are you trying to get pregnant? Is that what your plan is?"

Her bottom lip trembled. With a downward gaze, she said, "What? No, I just wanted to feel you inside me. You just feel so good. I'm sorry."

"I've never violated you like that. I can't believe you just did that shit." He got up and grabbed his basketball shorts from off the ground and put them on. "Now, if the shoe was on the other foot, you would have called that rape, right?"

"Aye, please don't be dramatic. It's not like you didn't want it. Your dick was throbbing for it again."

"Yes, I wanted it on my terms, not yours. You ask permission for that. You don't do that. Only woman I am doing that with is my wife. I don't fuck around like that, Jocelyn."

"Neither do I. You can relax. I've been tested. I'm clean."

"Are you on any birth control? We never even discussed that before."

"No, but I'm not going to get pregnant right now. We're good. I do it naturally. I have an app I use that tracks my period."

"Oh, and when you're ovulating?" He sneered and shook his head.

Jocelyn knew he felt something and started to look for her panties on the ground.

"Nah, we gotta stop. We have to stop. I'm not where you are with the whole 'in love' thing. I don't want to lead you on, Jocelyn. I mean, I care about you, but this it too much."

She began to backpedal. "No, you're not leading me on. I'm not asking for it to happen overnight. I just thought I should tell you how I feel. I don't want to stop."

"We'll have to talk about this later. Look at the time. I have a nine a.m. phone call."

She took the cue. "Okay, I'm going to go make breakfast." She slowly started to gather her clothes and get dressed in the bathroom.

He heard her sniffling. He felt sorry for her, but he was still furious with her little tactic. Getting a glimpse into her mind made him even more nervous.

It was time to really connect with Papa and see if he could share more about the legacy. He knew that dream meant something, and he wanted to find out if Papa had actually come to him with a message while he slept. He needed to find out everything, and he needed to find out today.

Chapter 9

Ty

Ty thought, *What an awkward way to start the morning*. He was disturbed by how Jocelyn was trying to trap him. In the past, he would have thought it was his paranoia and that maybe he was just imagining her voice in his head. However, after the incident with Journey jumping and Papa speaking to Ty telepathically, he couldn't ignore it anymore. He also knew Journey used her telepathy to get what she wanted as well. He wasn't even sure if he could call it a gift anymore since it was so dangerous when abused. He knew it from his own experiences.

After a cold shower, he went to his office to hop on a call with a potential client. His coffee and breakfast were already there waiting for him. Jocelyn poked her head into his office sheepishly. "If you need me to warm it up for you, let me know."

Ty took a sip. "No, no, it's fine. Thanks." He got on his computer, getting ready for a video call.

"I'm sorry about what I did earlier. I don't know what got into me. It's just—"

"Please, let's just forget about it. I have to hop on a call." He dismissed her with a wave. She nodded politely and closed the door.

It was going to be hard to stay away from Jocelyn since he couldn't lie, he did have feelings for her. But he figured it was for the best. It was getting too messy. He did eventually want to settle down again, but he wasn't sure about her being *the one*, especially if she was already planning a pregnancy. He didn't like that sneaky side of her. What else would she be planning?

Natalia was more aligned with him and much more of a go-getter. They had a lot more in common as well. He couldn't play both of them for much longer without feeling guilty.

After his meeting, he heard salsa playing in the living room. Papa and Jocelyn were singing "No Le Pique a la Negra" by Joe Arroyo. It was a fiery-paced salsa song.

"Oh my God, come, Ty. You gotta come look at this! Ven aqui!"

Ty did a light jog to the living room and was amazed to see his abuelo standing up and swaying to the music with no cane. He was actually keeping up to the beat and clapping loudly. His smile was wider than Ty had seen in a while. It was a miracle. Papa looked like he was amazed by his dancing too. Ty almost asked to turn the music down like he normally would. However, he refrained from doing it, since Papa probably needed it louder, and it was definitely cause for a celebration.

Ty quickly wiped a tear that escaped his eye. He was overjoyed. Even though Papa was standing near his La-Z-Boy, he came in closer just in case his legs gave out. Jocelyn danced in front of him as a safety net as well.

"Would you look at that. This is amazing." Ty shook his head in disbelief.

Papa shuffled his feet and moved his hips. He wasn't exactly on beat, but that was all right with Ty. He was showing off, soaking up all the attention. Papa gently grabbed Jocelyn's waist. She danced salsa with him with her arms around his neck. It brought so much joy to Ty's heart.

Papa looked back at him and pointed to Jocelyn's back and said, "Mi novia!" They all laughed. He was such a jokester. Ty was grateful that he still had his sense of humor.

"Watch it! Jocelyn is your nurse, and that's it. Behave, Papa."

"It's okay. At least someone wants to be my boyfriend." She kissed Papa on the cheek while they danced.

Papa gave him a knowing look. He sent a message to his mind. *"Jealous? You are a fool. She is perfect for you. Don't lose her. We need her."*

Ty was shaken by the mental intrusion. Chills ran down his back as he realized the message was very real. His smile transformed into a frown because he still couldn't believe what he was hearing. First Jocelyn, now this.

"If you are really talking to me, nod your head yes."

Papa kissed Jocelyn's hand to thank her for the dance. He turned to Ty and nodded with a slight grin.

"Whew, Mr. Garcia put the moves on me." She fanned herself. "Look at him sweating. Let me get a towel for him." She walked out of the room.

Ty whispered, "Did you come to me this morning in a dream?" He forgot to continue conversing via telepathy.

"Si, si!" Papa nodded his head.

"You can do that?" He scratched his head.

"No, we can." Papa pointed to Ty's chest and then his. Telepathy was much easier for Papa, so Ty went back to communicating that way.

Jocelyn came back with a small washcloth and dabbed the perspiration off the top of his forehead. Her cleavage was very close to his face, and he was enjoying being pampered. Papa looked at Ty with a sly smile.

Ty started laughing and said, "Jocelyn, you're gonna give him a heart attack with that cleavage in his face."

She looked down at her posture and stood up straighter, realizing her butt was poking out.

"Aye, please." She rolled her eyes at Ty.

She was so sexy, and she didn't even have to try. It came so naturally to her.

He took a sip of his coffee. "So, what's on the agenda for today?"

"I was going to do some physical therapy with him, but the dance workout was enough for now. I'm going to run to the supermarket. I'm making shrimp and broccoli for lunch."

"That sounds really good." He looked down at his emails coming in through his phone. "Well, I'll be home for most of the day. If you wanna take a long lunch, feel free."

She pouted. "I was going to eat with you and Mr. Garcia, but if you insist, I might stop at Home Goods for some things."

"Some things?" He raised his eyebrows.

"Yes, more candles," she confessed.

"Sure, we have like one million already, but do what makes you happy." He thought about how she burned candles for him when she ran a bubble bath, or when they made love. She put them around the room. She was definitely a romantic.

He examined her body in her sky blue scrubs as she packed up her purse and fixed her hair in the hallway mirror. Ty realized he couldn't be mad at her for long.

"Do you want anything?" She grabbed her keys off the hook.

"No, not now. Maybe later." He bit his bottom lip and shot her a telling glance.

Jocelyn giggled and sashayed out the door. She seemed relieved by him flirting with her. That was his way of forgiving her and squashing their fight.

"Hey, it's a chilly morning, you know? Where's your coat?"

She returned, and her eyes were soft. Jocelyn wore a gentle smile. "I didn't know you still cared."

"Just wrap up and drive safely."

Ty picked up Papa's crocheted blanket that his mother had made for him and put it across his legs. He couldn't wait to finish talking to Papa. He picked up his cup of coffee and took a sip.

Papa smoothed out his blanket and hummed the salsa song playing in the background.

"The weather was glorious, wasn't it?"

Ty looked confused, and then remembered his dream of fishing with Papa.

"Yes, the water was beautiful too. It felt real. So, that was really you?" He was fascinated by how detailed the dream was. *"Did you have the same dream?"*

"It was not a dream, Tylercito. I have been trying to get through to you for years. I had not used our family's special gift for a while, because it caused nothing but torment, greed, and abuse of power. I fell for so many of the same temptations. It nearly destroyed me. When I was in Cuba, many of my dark deeds had a hit put out on me and the family. The gambling world in Cuba was dangerous, and I was working with the Mob."

"I heard rumors about it. That's pretty dangerous, Papa."

"Yes, and selfish. Very selfish. My punishment now is growing old in this body. I am able to reflect on everything I did. I see it all clearly now more than ever. I feel as if I am being punished for living the way I did for so many years. I took advantage of a lot of people. I think the spell is starting to break. I danced today. I danced."

"I know! That was amazing."

"I don't want you to be afraid of your gift, but I also do not want you to abuse it. You see, Journey has a rare talent, some things she has not even discovered yet. I know her well, because I used to be like her when I was young. She possesses a great desire for control, the urge to have money and power. But in her mind, she's convinced that she will use it to do good, when all the while she steps on people who get in her way.

"God forgive me, but I wanted her gone for good. I know her too well. I had this urge to be accepted. I was so obsessed with manipulating others that it could have gotten me and the whole family killed. And you would never have been born if we didn't escape."

"Wow." Ty's mouth opened in shock, taking it all in. *"So, what did the dream mean?"*

"I needed to bring you back in time. I needed to remind you of some things you can do. We need Elizabeth. Next to Journey, she is one of the strongest. She's also the one who is the glue. She is the balance who can bring them all together. She possesses strong powers to heal and to see ahead, a prophet. When she came to visit us for that short time, she helped me get better. She put her hands on me. Her touch is divine, full of light. It opened me up to believe I could live again. Did you know she also brought Journey back from her coma? She is just getting started with what she can do. I want to train you, her, and others so that they can prepare."

"You really think that is why you're walking and talking more?"

"I don't think. I know. She cleared my energy. I need her around to help me get better, so I can be a better help to you all. I know I can't truly be younger, but I can at least get better with walking and talking."

Ty put his hand on his shoulder. *"Papa, she's in college and lives all the way in California".*

"Oh, never mind that. Elizabeth will find a way. I've been visiting her in her dreams too. She is starting to understand we have a bigger mission. We have to protect the legacy of our family. Our bloodline."

"Really, how come you never shared this with me before? What are we protecting? What are we preparing for?"

Papa patted Ty's thigh. *"Oh, you will see, Tylercito. You will see. I have told you many times when you were a child, but you have forgotten and were just too young to understand. Also, your mother was a big threat to everything that I was trying to teach you. She had many powerful gifts as well, but she was afraid of them. She would block you from understanding what was happening with you. She thought if she did, it would just go away. Your mother knew a lot about what you could do, and I think you may have even frightened her."*

"Really? How?"

"As a child, you would predict when people were sick, who would be at the door before they opened it, and the one that really shook her was you knew who was going to die. You could even see what organ was going to fail. You were very specific at times, even if you didn't know how to say the word."

"*Wow, you know, I kinda remember that. I remember dreaming things and telling her about them.*"

"*Yes, you would have very prophetic dreams up until about seven or eight years old. She would tell you they were nightmares, so that you would forget them. Millie didn't want you to grow up feeling like an outcast like she was.*"

"*I thought she had a good childhood.*"

"*She did, mi nieto, she did. But she also had some lonely times too. Her gifts were special. So special to the point of moving things with her mind. They call that telekinesis. You see, she had a vicious temper as a teen and almost killed her first boyfriend back in Miami.*"

"*What? How?*"

"*He cheated on her with one of her girlfriends, and she attacked him with a machete.*"

"*Oh my God, that sounds about right. Mom was always grabbing a knife on Dad.*"

They chuckled.

"*I'm surprised she never used it on him for real as abusive as he was.*"

"*You see, that's the thing. She wasn't holding the machete. It was on the shelf way above his head. They were in the shed in our backyard. That was where they would sit and talk to get privacy, but she used that as a place to start an argument with him. She accused him of cheating, and the machete fell straight down on his hand. He almost lost a finger. She didn't remember what happened, but I heard the screams. There's no way she could've reached that machete since it was up on the shelf. I had to rush him to the hospital. The cut was so brutal.*

"He told everyone in town she was a bruja. The boy spread the word that she just raised her hands toward the shelf and screamed, and the machete came flying down like a bird aiming for his hand. Most people ignored him and took the story for a big lie, then many others were believers."

Ty's mouth dropped in shock. *"She never told me that story."*

"Your mother was so afraid she would hurt someone again. She never wanted to talk about it."

"So the kid never reported it to the authorities?"

"Oh, definitely not. I told him to keep his mouth shut after I heard the rumors he was spreading about Millie. I told him we would kill him if he didn't keep his mouth shut."

"No, Papa, I can't believe you did that. Wasn't he just a teen?"

"Well, I didn't say it out loud. I visited him one night and gave him the fright of his life in a dream." He tapped his temple. Papa laughed out loud. *"But the message was clear. I put the fear of*

God in him. I was really surprised your mother didn't kill Carl sooner with her temper."

A lump slid down his throat and thumped in his chest. He couldn't believe what he just heard. *"What! Why would you say that? She didn't kill Dad. That would be like suicide too, since they both died in the same car accident."*

Ty sat on the couch next to Papa in his chair.

"I speak to her all the time. You know we can do that too? Her last moments alive in that car, she said she just wanted him to die. Her anger let the car spin out of control. She moved things with her mind and with your fear, along with her anger."

"No, no, no. I thought it was me all these years. I thought maybe I killed them in that accident." Ty's voice cracked. "She had bruises on her. He was constantly beating her. She had bruises all over her." He started to cry as if reliving it all over again. "He was yelling and being so aggressive, driving so fast. It was terrifying."

"I know, Tylercito, I know. You told me." He patted Ty's back.

"Yeah, but I didn't tell you I wished him dead. I wished it on him, and then the car went out of control. I thought I did it all these years."

"Your mother is so sorry. She didn't want you to carry that burden for so many years."

Ty sobbed in his hands. He was so happy Jocelyn had left. He wouldn't want her to see him like this.

"I can't believe all these years I thought it was my fault."

Papa stroked the back of his head.

"Can you talk to her, please, and tell her I love her, and I miss her."

"You can tell her yourself soon one day. Now that you are finally opening your mind and letting me get through, there's so much I need to teach you and the others. We must get them back. We need them all. I'm not getting any younger. We need the others, especially Elizabeth."

"I only know four of them. There are more children out there, but I don't know them. The last I knew, it was seven of them in total. I am not allowed to reach out to them, but maybe Elizabeth can. I don't even know how old the others are. They could be babies for all we know."

"We need to find them to show them the right way, so they don't go to the dark side of the gift. When they go that route, it's not easy to come back. Journey is dark pretending to be light. I don't think she will come back. She may show improvement with enough support. I tried get rid of her before she destroyed everything you built, but she is a fighter. She will be back to her old ways soon, so we must get the others to help us. We can't do it alone. There are others out there that might be even more destructive than her."

"Okay, Papa, I will. I will work on it. I will reach out to Elizabeth today."

Papa seemed tired, and he lay back in his La-Z-Boy chair. Ty had so many emotions stirring within him. He still didn't really know what Papa saw that was making him worried, and honestly, a part of him was afraid to find out.

Chapter 10

Ty

The morning sun illuminated the room's panoramic view of downtown Atlanta. The C&C conference room was full of chatter. The weekly team luncheon was a success. Ty and Marlon smiled at each other, pleased about what was next for the company they had built together.

Marlon fist bumped Ty. "We're doing it, brother."

"Yes, sir. That we are." Ty nodded in agreement.

The staff was engaged in side conversations, catching up with fellow co-workers. They were excited about what was to come with the upcoming event at Sweetwater Luxury Condos. They were even going to have live performances with artists such as Yahzarah, Ludacris, Zane Taylor, and Common, just to name a few. It was going to be a classy affair. They were making it a huge deal to get the community excited about their new development.

Ty cleared his throat and clapped once. "Can I get everyone's attention, please? Attention? Please make sure all your tasks get done by Wednesday. Tanya, can you make sure the artists' travel is finalized?"

"Got it, Mr. Carter." Tanya got up from her seat and collected her iPad.

"Justin, please make sure all of the vendors contracts are ready and payments are in so we can start promotions."

"All right, chief." Justin gave a salute. He adjusted his glasses nervously.

Ty looked at Marlon and then the team. "I think you are all doing a great job. Let's make this an amazing event for the community."

Marlon chimed in, "Yes, we are killing it. So proud of everybody. Meeting adjourned."

The crowd still lingered. "We need the room for a moment. Marlon, Natalia, please stay."

Natalia was chatting with Justin and about to walk out the door. She turned back. "Sure, what's up?"

"I want to talk to you about the spa lounge idea that you brought up before."

"Really?" She was pleased to give more creative input.

"Yes, I really like it, and I think we should do it. It'll be a good way to incorporate the local spas and salons that don't offer the services that we have."

Marlon said, "Yeah, I really like that idea too. It'll help develop new partnerships for us. Maybe we'll be able to get our residents special offers."

Natalia's eyes lit up. "Oooh, I love it. We can make it very peaceful and have a little serenity section by the waterfalls. The vendors can set up their booths there. It's going to be so relaxing."

"Lord, yes, I need a massage too. Make sure they all look good, though." He pointed at Natalia with a scolding finger.

"Really, Marlon? What makes you think they're all going to be women? We want men massage therapists too."

Ty pushed his seat back slightly. "Oh, really now?"

Marlon raised his brows. "You see, you done put your foot in your mouth."

They all laughed.

Ty rubbed his hands together and smiled. "Well, I was thinking to add something else to the mix. What do you think about Reiki? I want to bring Elizabeth to work on people. She's really good."

Marlon put both hands on the conference table. "Hold up, hold up. Elizabeth, your nerdy sperm donor kid? Nah, man, that's all right."

"You always gotta give me a hard time, man." Ty sighed. "Come on, don't call her that. She's a good kid. Incredibly intelligent too."

Natalia started to write notes. "I actually love the idea. She is so sweet and very talented. I enjoyed getting to know her."

Marlon shook his leg as if trying to contain himself. "Yeah, so sweet, huh? So was Journey. So sweet until she almost killed us and herself. I don't know about them psychopath genes you got, my nigga." He laughed at his own joke.

Ty grinned but held in his laughter. Marlon was so rude sometimes, but he was used to it.

"Well, we know Journey is troubled, that's evident. However, I don't think Elizabeth and her are cut from the same cloth. Did you ever think that maybe some of Journey's traits could be from her mother's side?"

"Ah, you may be on to something." Natalia tapped her pen to her temple.

"And for the record, Elizabeth also knows that Journey is a bit off. That is why she came to town to help her. She's very aware of everything, and the main reason I want to bring her back is twofold. Ever since she did a little bit of Reiki on Papa, he's improved tremendously. He's been able to walk more, dance more, and he's even talking more clearly."

"Get out. Papa hitting the dance floor?" Marlon laughed.

"Well, the living room dance floor with Jocelyn."

"Hmmm . . . that damn Jocelyn. Whooo!"

Ty cut his eyes at Marlon, and Natalia caught their exchange.

She added, "I'm bugging that he's talking so good now. That's crazy!"

Ty continued, "And Papa even said it's because of Elizabeth. He's expressing himself so much better now, and even in English." Ty couldn't tell them that a lot of the messages were through telepathy, but either way, it was the truth. Papa seemed like he was not too far off from being a mute, and now he was making so much progress. "So, I guess my psychopath genes have some good qualities to them. They got a little magic in them." Ty sprinkled imaginary fairy dust on Marlon's face.

Everyone laughed.

"Claudia said that Elizabeth worked on Journey, so that might be one of the reasons why she got better so fast."

Marlon sat up straighter. "Oh! So that's who we have to blame for waking up Sleeping Beauty?"

Natalia yelled, "Marlon! Be nice. How can you be so cruel?"

"No, no, I'm not. Me, cruel? I don't know about this, y'all. You gonna bring her up in the mix and then what? You don't know. She might put her magic hands on you to manipulate you."

"Don't be ridiculous. She's a true healer and doesn't have her hand out for anything. I think she will be great for the event."

"Yeah, Marlon. Ty's right. I wouldn't mind trying it out too. I heard Reiki works wonders for stress. It's pretty popular in spas too. It balances your energy and releases tension." Natalia arched her neck and rubbed her lower back. "My back has been killing me lately too."

Marlon jerked his head back, and he gave Ty an accusing glare. "Hmmm, I wonder why?"

"All right come on, Marlon. Knock it off. We're still in the office."

"I'm just saying." He shrugged.

Natalia rolled her eyes but couldn't hold back a smirk.

Ty clapped his hands together and folded his laptop closed. "All right, so we agree on the spa lounge. Natalia, I want you to work on setting up the lounge, since this is your baby. Get one of the interns to help you. Try to find about two to three other spa services we can feature in there."

"I'll do my part and reach out to Elizabeth and get my assistant to book her flight and hotel."

Marlon crossed his arms. "I see you gonna do what you want, because I still don't agree with Elizabeth coming, but whatever. Just know you've been warned."

Ty playfully slapped Marlon's back. "I think you need to be first on the Reiki table. Maybe she can work on you to help clear out some of them mean-ass chakras."

"Hell nah. I'm not letting none of your kids ever touch me again." He laughed. "Fuck out of here."

Natalia hesitated before asking, "Ty, are you . . . Are you thinking of visiting Journey? I have a feeling Claudia is hoping you do. I think you should. I can go with you, but that might not go over too well."

Marlon faked a cough. "You think? Shit, y'all are the reason she went psycho on all of us. Shiiiiit, she might turn that place upside down. Blow the whole hospital up."

"Marlon, chill." He put his hand on Marlon's shoulder. "I think I should. I have to show concern. Show that there's no bitterness, just to make the peace. Claudia keeps mentioning for me to go."

Marlon sucked his teeth and folded his arms.

Ty continued, "It might be good for everybody. Believe me, I'm still pissed, but we can handle everything, all the legal shit, once she's out of the hospital."

"Man, you're crazy. Ain't no way I can see her without sending her straight back into a coma. She didn't show any concern when she busted your head open, did she? She's the fucking devil. Diabla! Your grandpa knew what was up when he called her that."

"At the end of the day, it would look better not to be enemies for Ty. Your situation is totally different, so I can understand that." Natalia turned to Ty. "It can be a quick drop off of flowers. Just show your face and go."

"I'll talk to Claudia and see when it will be a good time." Ty really was nervous and still very angry, but he knew it would be the right thing to do. He turned to Marlon. "Like I told you before, she didn't say anything bad to the cops. She claims she doesn't remember much."

"What? She just blacked out and went crazy on everyone? Bullshit. I got the photos and texts to send her to remind her evil ass of everything she fucking did. She's a calculated bitch. She's just playing amnesia for pity. Just be on guard when you go there. I'm just saying." He rose from his seat.

"I hear you."

Ty gave him a fist tap as they walked out. "Trust me. It's all gonna work out. You'll see."

Ty

Ty was actually excited to bring Elizabeth back, since they did have a nice connection. She was not as outgoing as Journey. She was more reserved and respectful. She treated him as an elder and not a peer. Journey never saw the distinction. He could tell she was raised more old-fashioned than Journey. She actually made him not regret being a donor.

He gave her a call, and she answered right away.

"Good afternoon! What a nice surprise. How are you, Ty? Is everything okay?"

"Everything is great."

"I heard Journey is talking again. Claudia called me. Have you spoken to her yet?"

"No, not yet. I'm planning on visiting her soon."

"Yeah, I'm going to reach out soon myself. I hope you're up for it. I know it won't be easy after all that she did. Just know she's not well. She really suffers internally."

"Yes, I know. We'll see. Listen, I am calling for an opportunity. We're having a grand opening for one of my newest buildings. For part of the day's events, we're going to host a spa lounge, and I thought it would be great for you to come and do some Reiki. I don't know how much time you can take without being drained, but I figured it would be cool if you could do little samples on people for a few minutes. I can pay you for your time, and I'll make sure you get breaks in between."

"What? That's amazing! I would love to do that. I've done Reiki where I did ten-minute demos of it, and people still got huge results."

"Well, I know you're in school, so not sure if you can come."

"Oh, it's okay, really. I work remotely, so it just depends on what time it is and what day."

"We're hosting it in three weeks."

"Oh, that's even better. I'm on winter break that week. Let me just ask my parents for permission, and I'll get back to you, like today. I can't wait to come back to Atlanta. How is Papa doing?"

"Funny you asked. He's one of the main reasons I wanted you back as well. He's actually dancing salsa, singing, and talking more. He thanks you, because he feels it was your hands that healed him. He hasn't been able to stand or dance without his cane in years. I am just amazed. He definitely wants more Reiki."

"Don't you worry. I will take care of him. That is such a great news! I'm so happy you are all open to Reiki. It's still new to a lot of people. It's not always an easy sell."

"Oh, trust me, he's your number one fan now."

"Thank you. That is so sweet. And you wanna know something so crazy? I've had dreams with Papa and you for the last couple of weeks, so I think it was a sign, and then now you call me. How auspicious."

"Really?" Ty was curious about what messages she picked up since he knew Papa loved to bounce around in people's heads when they were sleeping.

"Yes, they were kind of cool dreams. Just us riding around in a Mercedes Benz van. There was a whole bunch of us, and we were all family. I also saw us in a classroom. Papa was much younger and teaching us something. It was all of my siblings, you, and a few others that I didn't know."

Silence. Ty took a gulp. Chills ran down his forearms, and it made the hair stand up. "Wow, you are really talented, Elizabeth."

"Why? Does that dream mean anything to you?"

"Well, yes, it means a lot. Since Papa has been talking more, he's saying that there's more that he wants to teach us all about our family gifts. It's no coincidence that we all have a little bit of something. so that's probably why you saw the dream of him in the classroom. It'll all make sense when you get here, so let me know what your mom and pops say, and then I will book everything. I can speak to them as well if you'd like."

"Oh, no, it should be cool. So good to hear from you, and I'm so glad that I'll be visiting again. I'm really grateful."

"No worries at all."

Chapter 11

Jocelyn

Jocelyn admired her hair in the mirror. She had just used so many bobby pins to hold her full hair up in a huge bun. She got dolled up with matte red lipstick, eyeliner, and mascara. She adorned silver hoop earrings that nearly touched her shoulders. Jocelyn turned around and checked out her body. "Yes, that's right. I still got it." She did a little shimmy in the mirror in her red halter top and tight, dark jeans. Her silver bracelets sang a tune when she moved. She felt very hip and stylish. It was a nice change from wearing scrubs all day. She couldn't wait for Ty to see her outfit. She got a kick out his adoring eyes on her body. He liked her hair up, so she knew that would get his attention.

Jocelyn cracked the door slowly to do one last check. Mr. Garcia was snoring lightly, and she nodded in satisfaction. She made him some warm milk before he went to bed. That always did the trick. He was conked out by 7 p.m. Mr. Garcia did not miss out on sleep.

"Good, sound asleep." He worked hard today and was improving in so many ways. When Jocelyn turned around, she met Ty walking down the hallway. He was in a rush.

"Hey there. You look really nice. I like those earrings." He waved his hands in the shape of her curves. "I mean, I like the whole outfit. Red really looks good on you."

He was half dressed. She looked him up and down. "Thank you. Are you going out? A date?"

"Ah, yeah. A concert. Maxwell is in town."

Her eyes looked at his open shirt, revealing his smooth abs. He was buttoning it up as he talked. She was annoyed he didn't think to ask her.

"But seriously, I like that look on you."

"Well, you only see me in scrubs." She whispered, "Or with nothing at all. I do clean up well."

He pulled her gently toward him. He spoke in her ear. His deep voice made her quiver. "Oh, come on. Don't act like that." He got closer to her and pushed her back against the wall. Jocelyn could feel his arousal growing. "Damn, mami, these jeans. You're turning me on."

She knew he wanted to take her right there, but he couldn't.

"Careful." She pushed him gently in the chest away from her. "You don't want to smell like my perfume, Ty. Your girlfriend may get jealous."

"There you go with that. She's not my girl. We're just dating." He loosened his grasp and slid his hand down her backside.

She nodded and smiled. "Okay, well. I'm leaving in a few, so if you need anything else from me, you can just text me."

His eyes lowered from rejection. "Hey, hey . . . so where are you going? You got a date?"

She shrugged and paused. "Something like that. Going to dinner," Jocelyn said with a sly smirk. He came up close to her again. It was just a sin for somebody to be that damn fine, she thought. Jocelyn had the urge to tell him how good he looked. How she wished he would stay home with her and make love, lay with her, and play in her hair like he did many nights. She wanted to tell him how sad she was since she didn't get invited instead of Natalia. He could have invited her, but she'd rather suffer in silence.

"All right, well, you have fun."

"Oh, I will. Good night, Mr. Carter." She only called him that when Mr. Garcia was around or when she wanted to remind him of the place he put her in. Just her worker and sex buddy.

"I'm sure you're gonna hear it a lot tonight, but I want to tell you, you do look very beautiful. A ten!" He kissed his fingers like an Italian who had just made a succulent dish.

His cell rang, and he put his hand up to excuse himself. It was Natalia.

"Hey, lady. Yes, reservations are for seven thirty. Okay. You close? Oh, cool! I'll be ready soon. Just come up."

Jocelyn walked out the door and looked at her reflection in the elevator mirror. Truth be told, she really didn't have a date after all. She just wanted to show Ty that she did have a social life. She actually planned on going home to watch the rest of the *Handmaid's Tale* on Hulu.

As Jocelyn made it to the parking area, she heard the sound of high heels plummeting down on the concrete path toward the entrance. The woman's form came into view. She realized it was Natalia. A sinking feeling made her stomach growl.

"Hey there, Jocelyn. How are you?" Natalia was clueless.

"I'm good!" She exaggerated her pitch as a voice that was truly happy to see her and not pissed that Natalia would be making love to her man tonight.

"You look pretty, Jocelyn. Going out? Got a date?"

"Yes, and you look nice too. Ty says you're going to a concert. I'm just going to have some fun." She purposely didn't answer her in detail, hoping maybe she'd report back to Ty.

"Yep, the concert should be nice. I'm excited. Maxwell is amazing. This is my fourth time seeing him on stage."

Jocelyn clicked her car alarm. She was even more visibly annoyed with hearing about the date that she should be on.

"Well, I'm glad you can make him happy. We're all in a nice big family now. Huh?"

"What's that supposed to mean?" Natalia's head did a slight tilt. She wasn't used to slick comments from her.

"You know the C&C family?" Jocelyn tried to clean up her low-blow comment. "We all work for him. We're friends with him, and we're like sisters now." She smiled flatly. She really wanted to say they were "dick sisters," since they were sharing the same man.

"Oh, okay. Now I got it."

Natalia seemed to sense the sarcasm in Jocelyn's tone, but played it off.

"Have a nice night and a lot of fun." Jocelyn waved as she hopped in her car, stewing. There was so much that Jocelyn wanted to say, but she knew if she caused any more trouble, she might get fired. Jocelyn couldn't understand why he was so into that girl. She was cute, but she wasn't better looking than her. She just didn't trust Natalia 100%. Who was to say Journey and Natalia wouldn't become friends again and she would go back reporting things to her loco ass? She knew in time, Natalia would be jealous of her connection with Ty and Mr. Garcia. She didn't have anything against Natalia, since she was always nice and respectful. The girl just had poor choices in friends, even though she was supposedly enemies with that little demon, Journey.

To this day, Jocelyn wondered what kind of witchcraft Journey had used to control her body. She was paralyzed on the floor when Journey told her not to move during that big fight. She heard it in her head. Journey's mouth didn't move, but her voice was loud and clear. As much as she tried to fight the command, her body definitely could not move until Journey jumped. She never wanted to be near that witch again. It was a terrifying moment in her life.

The irony was now Journey was the one who couldn't move. She was like a cripple who couldn't walk. *That's what she gets.*

Jocelyn also felt like she was the side chick. She felt like a used piece of gum on the bottom of his shoe. Even though Ty paid her well and treated her like family, he just wanted to use her for a sex toy. She clenched her jaws as she drove home thinking about it. He really was protecting himself more now, too, since the condom incident. Her hands gripped the wheel tightly, and she turned her music all the way up.

Jocelyn realized it would be a fantasy to tame him as a perfect husband or the perfect mate, because she knew he had a serious issue with commitment. He was terrified of it. She knew after his ex-wife Ava cheated on him, he had no plans to marry anytime soon. Men always want you to forgive them if they cheat, but when it's done to them, their big fat egos can't handle it. She heard him talk about them being polyamorus, and that still didn't last. Made no sense to her if they signed up for an open relationship. Jocelyn wondered if she had Ty's child, could that change the way he felt? She hoped that if she did, he could experience being a father from the beginning and not feel like just a sperm donor.

Jocelyn had seen a few women come and go before they started to become intimate. They seemed very beautiful, but they always wanted something from him, and Ty would break things off before they got too serious. She figured back then that he might have been sort of a player, but she noticed that once they started their sneaky relationship, he really stayed home a lot more and kept to himself. He didn't seem to be going out on dates at all.

But there was something about this one. This girl Natalia definitely had him infatuated with her. She did have an advantage. Natalia understood his industry of real estate and seemed to have a lot of passion and drive. Natalia always wanted to talk about real estate, and that seemed to just bore Jocelyn when she overheard them speaking. He liked hard workers like himself, so she was sure that turned him on. Plus she was younger, so she was probably also a yes-man like the rest of the people that worked for him. Jocelyn didn't fall into that category. She didn't hold back and prided herself on telling him how she felt about anything she didn't like. She didn't kiss his ass.

She was probably going to have to quit soon, if he didn't see with his own eyes that she was the best choice. She might not know much about business, but she knew a lot about loving him and loving his family, minus that puta, Journey, of course. Jocelyn felt she would be the perfect wife. He could bring her to the company Christmas party and parade her around at those fancy real estate award galas he went to. They could go on exotic vacations together.

After all, she was more connected to his culture. She was Caribbean. That baby would be much mucha bonita, with Jamaican, Cuban, and Dominican roots. That would be an international baby. If she waited too long, she would waste her life and her precious time when she could still have kids. Jocelyn knew it probably wasn't going to happen, but she hoped and prayed Natalia would mess up soon so she could step right in.

She hoped that one day soon, Ty would take her out on dates and finally court her outside of the bedroom. She knew she was a catch, and she deserved it. He never really got to know her. Jocelyn felt like the more they got to know each other, he would really fall in love. She hoped to talk with him more on a deeper level, so that he would see she was more than just a sexy Latina nurse.

The good thing was that Mr. Garcia was on her side 100%. He was more powerful than he led on. She watched him sometimes and saw if he no longer stared into space, he was in deep thought. His cognitive function faculties seemed to be almost back in order. She'd only seen him as the old feeble man who could barely move or talk. She knew it had something to do with his great-granddaughter, Elizabeth. The two of them combined could heal him.

She would continue to give him physical therapy and dance with him. Papa was her cheerleader, and she would love to have him as a father-in-law.

Chapter 12

Ty

Ty still got chills when he knew she was coming. It was a good feeling. His body just reacted to her when he saw her. It was deeper than a sexual connection. He knew that Natalia understood him. He had to admit it to himself. He was falling for her.

Natalia walked in as he held the door, watching her every move. Her small, dainty steps were urgent. Even with the fear of being late, she floated down the hallway and was so radiant. Her coat was in her arms, and she wore a cream off-the-shoulder wrap dress. It accentuated all of her firm curves and brought out her cocoa brown skin even more.

She paused as in deep thought. Her lips pressed together. She shook her head as if deciding the right words to say. In that instant, he knew. It was Jocelyn. They probably just saw each other.

"Hey, sweetheart, what's with the face?"

"Oh, nothing. Just had a weird conversation with your . . . your grandpa's nurse or physical therapist? That's what she does, right?"

Oh boy, here we go, he thought.

She paced up and down the foyer slowly. "So, I just have to ask you this, Ty, and please be serious. I won't be mad if you did, but have two you to ever . . ." She pointed to the bedroom with her chin.

"Come on, no. No! She works for me, and that's all. She not my type," he lied. Ty put on his coat, trying to be busy. He wanted to change the subject so badly. "You look really nice." He gently took her coat from her hands and held it out for her to put it on. "Let's get out of here before we're late for the dinner reservation."

She ignored him. "I mean, she's a very attractive girl. I wouldn't be surprised if you did. I know how you have a strong appetite. If I were a man, I'd hit it."

"Oh God. Please stop. Really, you'd hit?" He snickered, trying to play it cool. They got in the elevator, and Ty needed to know. "What happened? What did you guys talk about?" He realized if he said, "What did she tell you?" he would sound guilty as hell. He was already having a hard time denying it without looking guilty.

As they walked to his car, she said, "Oh, it wasn't what she said. It was how she said it." She smoothed out her dress and put her seat belt on.

"Really, what . . . what did she say?" Ty was terrified to even hear the answer. First, Jocelyn hopped on him, raw doggin' it with that damn tempting body trying to rape him. And now she was shit talking to Natalia, filling her head with only God knows what. He would have to have a little chat with her tomorrow.

"Sorry, I could be reading into it too much." Natalia sighed. "She just seemed a little sarcastic. Had a little bit of a mean girl vibe. She said something to the effect of 'I'm glad that you can make him happy and that we're family now.'"

"Yeah, I doubt she said it like thaaaat. She's not worried about me. She has her own life. Didn't you see her all dressed up? She was going out on a date or something. Jocelyn is like family."

"Well, you know what really stuck out in my head is I remember Journey once mentioning it to me that you were doing your nurse. I've never seen anything strange since I've been here, but . . ."

"Exactly! Exactly. And you know Journey is not a reliable source." Sweat started to form on his top lip. He really wanted to end this conversation. "She has a wild imagination, and we all know how she feels about us together, so she would have told you anything to keep you away from me."

Natalia shrugged, not really convinced, but she left it alone. Ty was relieved, since he didn't want his night to go downhill in a jealous fight.

***

After the Maxwell concert, they came home exhausted, but feeling really good. The songs played at the concert definitely put them in a romantic mood. Even though the night got off to a rocky start with Jocelyn throwing shade his way, he really enjoyed how Natalia was acting more like his woman. She was holding his hand, fixing his shirt collar, finishing his sentences, just doing the cute, corny stuff that made him feel like she cared about him. Ty felt like he was part of a couple again, and he realized how much he really missed being with someone.

Maybe he was in denial that he would never get married again, because she could be the next Mrs. Carter, the last one. It was the one-woman-until-the-end-of-time issue that he had had to deal with. He wasn't sure if he could handle that type of commitment.

They pulled up to the driveway, and Ty rubbed his hand on her thigh.

"Ty, thank you. I had such a good time. I don't know the last time I went to a concert. I haven't enjoyed myself like that in a while."

"You want to come up and enjoy yourself some more?" He pecked her on the lips. "Spend the night with me."

"Isn't your Papa there? I don't want him thinking I'm some type of trollop. It's after eleven p.m."

He reached in and gave her an open-mouth kiss. "It's okay. You're my little trollop."

She giggled. "Stop it."

"Come on up. We're grown. He's sleeps like a log, and he's down the hall. He won't hear me beating that back out."

They both laughed.

"Oh, you mean *you* screaming?" she asked.

"Meeee? I'm quiet."

"Yeah, yeah, whatever, Mr. Moaner."

Ty

Ty and Natalia lay in the sheets still moist in sweat from their lovemaking. The candlelight flickered, giving the room a yellow glow and the sweet scent of vanilla and citrus. Their chests were heaving up and down slowly as they caught their breath from their passionate lovemaking.

Ty bit his bottom lip, and the guilt consumed him. He was staring at the ceiling to avoid eye contact. His chest felt so tight. He was beginning to hear things more, and now he remembered why he had blocked out his so-called gift for so many years. It was a blessing and a curse, because he didn't want to know so much sometimes.

He could feel Natalia's anger vibrating throughout his own body as if she were a volcano about to explode.

Did this nigga just call me Jocelyn? Are you fucking crazy? Fucking Jocelyn? I knew it. I knew it! I knew he was fucking her. He just made me dry all the way up. She couldn't hold back her disgust and just rolled her eyes at him. She pulled the sheets over her naked body.

"Look, it was a mistake. I don't know what happened," he said softly to her.

When he'd had Natalia's hips in the air and her face buried in the pillows, he kept picturing himself plunging into Jocelyn's plump ass. Natalia had a nice body, but there was something about Jocelyn that turned him on even more. He reminisced on how good it felt when she did ride him raw. The tenderness, that moistness, and the comforting heat of her pussy made him go against all his beliefs. He wanted them both. Natalia was driving her hips back at him so fast. He was loving every minute of it. All of the nerves in his body were turned on. He needed her to slow down before he ejaculated too soon. She was moving her body so sensually. He could not hold it any longer.

The big mistake happened when he said, "Jocelyn, slow down, mami. Ohhh, damn. Natalia, slow down." A golf ball–sized lump slid into his throat and sat on his chest.

Did I just say that shit out loud?

Her deep arch in her back sloped into a hump. "What did you just call me?" She panted.

"Nothing. Stay right there." He felt so good picturing both of them in the bed with him.

A few minutes went by without them speaking. The tension was building in the room, and he didn't know how to fix it.

Finally, Natalia broke the silence. "Look, no one is pressuring you to do anything. I would just appreciate you being honest with me. The last thing I wanna be is a third wheel or the dummy that's in the middle of some crazy love triangle. I don't wanna invest too much into this. If it's not going anywhere, I'm not trying to waste my time, Ty."

"Now, hold on, hold on. How are you going to make all these assumptions over a name? I'm sorry, but you know I could've called you my property manager Gisel or Marlon. It's a name I use on a regular basis. And we were just talking about her before the concert. Sometimes you slip up and call somebody the name of the pet that's in the house. It could have been anyone. I'm so sorry it happened, but it didn't mean anything. I promise you. We have nothing but a professional relationship. She's more like family at this point." Ty hoped he was convincing.

"Hmmm, that's a good one. I might even had believed you, if this wasn't poking me in my back." She held up a bobby pin.

"What is that?" He held her hand to see. It was pretty dark.

"A bobby pin. Not mine either. Now I am even more disgusted. At least change the sheets before you fuck me."

"Wrong again. She makes the bed, you know? It probably just fell out of her hair. You just keep looking for something, huh. What's really going on?" Ty got defensive, but he knew she was right. A part of him felt maybe Jocelyn had even planted that shit there on purpose. His stomach turned as he could feel Natalia's anger begin to boil.

"Nothing is going on. I saw what I needed to see. We're good." She got up to go to the bathroom, and her voice trailed softly. She didn't even want to look at him. "Since you don't want to talk about it and tell the truth, let's leave it alone."

Oh, shit. Oh, shit. She knows. I'm going to keep denying it, but I think she knows.

Chapter 13

Journey

Physical therapy had proven successful for Journey. She only had a few weeks left and was already home with Dominick as her medical assistant. It started off challenging, but with consistent therapy and her determination, she finally started walking again with help. It was a slow process and frustrating for her, since she hated feeling like a burden to others. Only a small part of her would admit that she liked the special attention from Dominick. He was definitely her hype man, who would celebrate even the smallest wins. She also thought he was trying to help her get back to her original weight. He was the master at getting her ice cream or sneaking in a slice of pizza. She couldn't wait to do yoga again and lift weights to build back up her muscle tone.

Being trapped in a hospital bed for almost three months definitely made her weaker, but she was determined to start teaching again very soon. One of the yoga studios that she used to sub in said she could teach a few days a week and sit in a chair, so there would be no pressure on her body.

Journey's mother and Dominick went with her to the psychologist, who had an office in the Peachtree Long Term Rehab Center's building, where she went for her weekly therapy and exam. Now, she was already walking with a cane. However, this appointment was a long walk to the next building, so Dominick pushed her in a wheelchair.

"Are you nervous?" Journey's mom asked.

"No. I mean, I know what I saw, and if they want to label me as crazy, then so be it."

Dominick interrupted. "You know you're not. Don't think that at all. We believe you. You are just a seer. You are extremely gifted. There is no way you could have made it up."

Claudia put her finger to her lips nervously. "But maybe she shouldn't share so much." She stroked Journey's hair gently. "I don't want them putting a label on you."

Dominick reassured them. "I doubt they will. Dr. Brinson is a psychologist who, from what I have heard, is very progressive and open-minded. We're here now."

Journey knew the doctors wanted to do a mental health check to see if she was a danger to herself or if she was just off her rocker. The suicide attempt was really the only part of her story she couldn't figure out or explain without sounding like she had a loose screw. She knew that she hadn't jumped at her own will. She knew that deep in her soul.

She hadn't seen Francesca or Delilah since she transferred to the new facility. However, she saw Janet from time to time in her dreams, or even just heard her voice with a message. That was the only thing she never shared with anyone. She didn't feel like sharing any of her messages. They were private and mainly just Janet scolding her for taking advantage of people. They didn't need to hear that.

Dominick wheeled her in and returned to the waiting room with her mother. Journey just wanted to be in and out. She didn't want to make small talk. Journey plastered on her best smile. "Hi, Dr. Brinson."

She was a tall, mocha brown woman with a regal presence. Dr. Brinson had honey-colored locks, high up in a bun, and large wooden hoop earrings. Her outfit was a bright green flowing dress underneath her white lab coat. If she took off her lab coat, she could easily fit into a poetry lounge or art gallery circles. Her vibe was very down to earth.

"Hi there, Journey. Nice to meet you finally. You have a very interesting backstory. I've heard lots about you."

"Do you think so? Do you not get a lot of coma patients?"

"No, no, I wasn't even referring to that. I love that you're a yoga teacher. Yoga is one of my favorite stress management tools I tell my clients to use. I just love that you're already ahead of the game."

"Well, yes, I can do as much as my wheelchair allows."

"The doctors tell me you're healing pretty good, so you should be up and at 'em in no time."

"I'm walking slow with a walker and a cane. I really needed the wheelchair since your office was kind of a hike."

"Yes, we are on the other side of the building."

"I pray that I will be walking without help in the next month or so. I hate that damn cane."

"I'm sure you will."

"I do like being wheeled around, though, I can't lie." She smiled.

"I'm sure it's probably a load off those legs." She flipped through her big yellow legal pad and got her pen ready. "So, Journey, I also hear that you're an interior design major. That's an awesome way to relieve stress as well, being creative. Art therapy is so popular."

"Let me guess. My mother told you that? Because I technically dropped out of college. I'm not seeing the benefits right now, but I can do a lot of other things with my business."

"Oh, I get it. College is not for everybody, and you have to do what works for you."

"Exactly. *See* . . . you get it. Why don't you talk to my mother?" She chuckled.

"Well, my job is to talk to you today. We can get mom in another session, if needed." She leaned back in her chair and starting writing notes on a pad.

"Lord, she probably needs it. She's been so stressed from all of this."

"How have you been doing overall? I know being confined to a hospital bed for so long can take its toll on someone."

"Tell me about it. I was losing it in there. I'm a pretty active person, so it has been torture. I'm grateful to have a support team behind me."

"That's so important to have people around you that care. So, tell me what you've been seeing?"

She took a deep breath. "Sure. I just wanna preface this with an official statement on the record that I am officially one hundred percent sane." Journey pointed to her chest adamantly.

Dr. Brinson wrote some notes and kept a straight face while she nodded. "That's fine. Tell me what you saw and we can work through it."

"Well, I saw two girls in my hospital room, one in particular who I actually thought was my roommate for a while."

"Two girls? So, do they have names that you recall?"

"Yes, Francesca and Delilah. Francesca was the one in my room most of the time, and Delilah was a friend of hers that she brought in. Both of them were a little younger than me, about seventeen to twenty. And they still had on hospital gowns, so I just thought they were in there like me."

"What happened when you saw them?"

"They just talked to me similar to how you and I are speaking. I wouldn't even know that they were freaking dead unless someone had told me. I always thought ghosts were supposed to be translucent or something, but it didn't feel like that at all, which is why I wasn't even scared."

"Oh, so these were actually real people?"

"Yes! Actually people. Not in my imagination, They are definitely real, or they were, at least. I know it just sounds so crazy, but I am not that. I promise you, even my medical assistant and my doctor confirmed that they were actual patients. You can ask him. Dominick is the one that wheeled me in."

"Oh, no need for that. I believe you."

"I mean, how else could l know their names and even why they were in the hospital? They told me specific details." Journey wagged her finger defensibly. "There's no way I could make it all up."

"It's okay. It's okay. Just relax. Has this ever happened to you before your accident? Seeing or hearing things?"

"No, not really. I do see and hear some things because I am pretty intuitive. I'm very good at just reading people's energy, getting psychic messages, but I never saw dead people." Journey left out that she was also telepathic and could read minds sometimes, but she didn't want to be stuck there and be dissected like a lab rat. So, she kept those secrets to herself.

"Does anyone in your family have the same gift?"

Journey sighed with relief. "Oh, I didn't think you'd call it a gift."

"Well, yes, of course it is. Many people have a stronger insight than others."

"Yes, some of my siblings and my father have it. As far as I know."

"How often are you having these visions?"

"I haven't seen them in while, since I left the hospital, but I was seeing Francesca almost every day that I can remember. I really felt her spirit helped wake me up out of my coma."

"Speaking of that, your mother told me that you had amnesia at first. Do you remember what happened that day? Can you take me back to the day of the incident that put you in the hospital?"

"Damn, I had a feeling we were gonna have to talk about this." Journey rolled her neck out, stretching it as if getting ready for a workout. "Ty, that's my father, we had a misunderstanding. He was accusing me of stealing from his company, but his partner, Marlon, actually gave me a donation." She was denying it so much that she was actually starting to believe her own lie.

"Really. A donation for what?"

"A new business I'm starting. It's going be a wellness facility. I would even want therapists like yourself there. It's still in the early stages of development, but I was raising money. The main issue really is that Marlon is his business partner, and he had an intimate relationship with me."

Dr. Brinson held a poker face while she took notes. "Oh, I see. How do you feel about that?"

"Look, I knew he was much older than me. So, I was fine. I don't like young boys. They can't keep up." She tilted her head to side as if recalling a memory. "But Ty, he wasn't happy at all. I really needed to talk to him in person to share my side of the story. But when I got there, there was nothing but yelling. The nurse that works there put her hands on me."

"Nurse?"

"Well, she is for my great grandfather, his caretaker."

"Oh."

"I can't lie. I kind of lost it when she grabbed me. She tried to kick me out. She really acted as if it was her house when she is just the fucking maid-nurse or whatever. I really think I blacked out then." She took a deep breath. "This is confidential, right?"

Dr. Brinson put her pen to the corner of her mouth and nodded. "Completely confidential. So what happened after that?" She actually looked as if she needed some popcorn, since the story seemed very juicy.

"Well, I remember her putting her hands on me, and we started fighting. I knocked her down. From what I heard, Ty claims I hit him too or took something to hit him. I don't even remember that. He's freaking huge. I don't even know how I could take him. I am not a fighter, but if somebody touches me, I do get violent. I might be a yogi, but

I still have hands." Journey got very anxious as if she were reliving the moment. She put her hand over her heart. "My heart. It feels as if it's knocking on my chest."

"Take a deep breath. Just take your time." Dr. Brinson's voice was soothing and got softer. "Close your eyes and see yourself there. You are in a safe space here. We just want to find out what happened. Breathe in through your nose and out the mouth." She did a few deep breaths to show Journey the way. "That's it. Just relax. Let's try to remember what happened, bit by bit."

Journey followed her lead and breathed deeply. Her body relaxed and sank deeper into the wheel-chair. She closed her eyes. "I remember there was something on the stove when I got there. I heard it bubbling, and it smelled good. Then after the argument and fighting with them, I just remember smelling smoke. I thought the food caught on fire. The flames were crackling. It was quiet. No one was yelling or fighting anymore. Just the sound of something burning. My body started to get hot and drip sweat. I could smell the walls burning. I remember seeing the entire room behind me on fire. The flames danced around the curtains and enveloped me. There was nowhere to go but . . . but out. I couldn't see anybody else. The smoke filled the room. I just had this urge to escape." Her hands began to tremble as she relieved the fear that took over her that day.

"So, you saw the fire?"

Journey kept her eyes closed. Her voice was almost a whisper, as if embarrassed to share her vision that apparently never happened. "I didn't just see it. I felt it. I smelled it. The heat was so intense, then I kept hearing in my head, 'Fire! Jump! Jump!' I thought maybe the firemen were there to catch us. I don't know what I thought." Journey's voice cracked. "I was so afraid when I saw the flames closing in on me. It happened so fast." She started crying. "I even remember feeling soot in my nose. It was stinging. Like I couldn't breathe. I remember now. How could I just have just imagined all of that?"

"When you heard someone say *fire* and *jump*, who was saying that? Your father?"

"No, no. It was a man's voice, but it was older and raspy like." She gasped, and her eyes opened in sheer shock. "Oh my God. Oh my God! It was Papaaaaa. It was Papa's voice!"

"Was he there?"

"Yes, but I didn't hear him say it out loud. I heard him in my head."

"You mean like telepathy?"

"Exactly. Wow, Doc, you really get this stuff.".

Dr. Brinson smiled and kept scribbling notes.

"Maybe I am really crazy." Journey shrugged, feeling defeated. "I can't imagine him saying that to me when he can barely talk or walk. Why would he say that to me?"

"Do you think maybe during all of the turmoil, maybe it was a defense mechanism you created? It was your way out?"

"No, no, no! I would never jump! If I'm going to escape, I'm gonna head to the front door. That's not fucking normal. Pardon my French."

She waved her hand. "Oh, it's fine. Why did you think Papa would say that?"

"Maybe he has the same power I have and my dad has. It makes sense. We definitely all have some kind of gift. I don't know him enough and never asked Ty if Papa was psychic too."

Dr. Brinson tried to play along, but Journey could tell she wasn't really believing that as a possibility.

"So, why would Papa want you to jump? I didn't hear you mention him in the argument."

"I know it. I think it sounds insane. I don't know. I just have a feeling I didn't imagine that."

Dr. Brinson took down more notes. "You're not insane. Be careful. Words have power. This was just your experience and what you remember. Do you think maybe you and your Papa have any bad blood between each other? Did you get along?"

"I never thought we had any issues. I was always nice to him, but all I can remember now are his gray eyes just staring at me with hatred. It never happened in real life, but that's what I see in my mind now when I think of him. Like he can't stand me. I don't know. It was just soooo freaking real.

Can I be making this all up in my mind? Can people really hallucinate like that? Like that detailed?"

"Yes, it's very possible that you saw everything as you described. It sounds like a hallucination."

"This is so scary, Doc. I just . . . I don't remember everything. I just know I jumped and woke up two months later in pain. I woke up with no hair, with bruises, and scars. I am still traumatized." Her chest started to heave as she tried to suppress her frustration. Tears trickled down her cheeks as she spoke. "I missed two months of my life. I missed my twenty-third birthday. I am missing out on my life right now." She slapped her legs. "Look at me. I can't do hardly anything for myself. I'm grateful to be walking again, but I want to be able to do it on my own."

Dr. Brinson kept writing fast. "And you will. You got a second chance, Journey. You survived, and you are healing. It's a process. You are bouncing back, and we'll figure it out. It's okay if you don't remember everything now. It takes time after experiencing something as traumatic as that."

Journey's voice was shaking. "I really thought someone pushed me, but everyone is saying the witnesses saw me jump. It's so scary to me. It was on the news. So embarrassing. I am just so mad because people really believe I wanted to kill myself. How could that happen?"

"You've never had suicide attempts before, correct?"

"No, never! Absolutely not. So, what can you do to help me?"

"Well, one step at a time. We're going to run a few diagnostic tests to see what's going on and get the big picture on how I can help."

"The more I think about it, he was never really that friendly to me. But I just figured he was senile. I don't want this to happen again." Journey began panicking. "What if it happens again? I think I need some kind of drug or something. What if I black out in traffic? Or what if I try to jump again? Now everyone thinks I want to kill myself, and I don't. I promise you, I never ever had the urge to take my life."

"Well, that's good, but there are ways to help. I don't think you need meds just yet. We can start a holistic treatment plan with plant-based medicine to help you with anxiety and stress."

"Oh, wow. Plant based?" Journey put her fingers to her lips and took a puff of an imaginary blunt.

Dr. Brinson laughed. "Yes, in moderation, and possibly CBD. I might get you a prescription to micro-dose psychedelic mushrooms as well."

"Mushrooms? You are cool as hell. You can do that? Get out of here. I'm already hallucinating. You want me to see more? I have a brother in Colorado who is always doing that, but he seems high all the time. I don't want to be a zombie now."

They both laughed.

"No, no, that won't be you. Micro-dosing is in very small amounts. It's very gentle. From what you're telling me, you might be borderline schizophrenic based on hallucinations. I'll write up a prescription. However, you have homework."

"Whatever you tell me to do to make this go away, I will do."

"I want you to journal every day on how you feel, and if you see anything unusual again like your friends in the hospital, write it down, everything that you remember. Let's meet in two weeks, so we can see how it's going."

Journey soon realized that if they diagnosed her with anything, maybe it could work in her favor. Maybe Ty and Marlon would be more understanding and forgive her if they realized she had a mental issue. She really did want to understand what happened in her mind to make her want to jump. Could someone have control over her mind? She couldn't understand who or how. Journey wondered if a spirit maybe possessed her at that moment. She had to figure out what had happened, or she really was going to go crazy.

Chapter 14

Journey

Dominick helped Journey get back into her bed, and he sat in the reclining chair.

"Can we go hang out in your room downstairs?" she asked. "I really need a change of scenery. I need to walk around the house more."

"Are you sure you can handle the stairs?"

"Dominick, I need to practice. I don't wanna be stuck with this cane forever."

"Okay, I will help you."

She walked slowly down the stairs and held on to the banister tightly. He was in front of her, going slowly to break her fall if she slipped.

When they got to his bedroom, she said, "See, I told you I could do it."

"Okay, I was wrong. I thought it was too soon. Just promise me you won't do it without me."

"Oh, you don't have to worry about that. I had enough falls to last a lifetime. I want to get better. I don't ever want to see a hospital bed again."

They laughed.

"I hear you. I hear you."

"It looks good down here." She walked around slowly with her cane, observing the changes. "You've made it your own. It smells good too." She looked around at the floor pillows near a table with candles and some photos.

"That's incense. I meditate a lot. I made little prayer altar to set my intentions every morning."

He also had about twenty books on spirituality, anatomy, and holistic health on his dresser.

"I need to get back into all of this myself. I read and meditate, just not every day like I used to."

"So, how was your session? I see you were pretty quiet with your mom around, like you didn't want to share."

"Oh, I just didn't want to worry her since she gets frazzled. It wasn't bad at all. Definitely not what I expected. Dr. Brinson was pretty cool, and let's just say non-judgmental. She didn't even blink when I mentioned seeing ghosts. She didn't think I was crazy."

"There is no doubt that you are a psychic-medium, because you knew way too much about Francesca and Delilah. Also, you have to realize a lot of doctors aren't as old school anymore. Many of them get it and understand there is a metaphysical answer to some things, not always medical."

Journey put her hand up. "Hold on. Since I'm not a hundred percent out of the water. She said it's possible I could be borderline schizophrenic."

"No, no, I doubt it."

"Well, it's not related to seeing spirits, but because of the jump and everything I saw. It was so real. I forgot most of it until today. She was amazing. She helped bring me back to the memory. It wasn't really hypnosis, but she knew how to relax me so much that I could sort out the jumbled-up memories. Clearly, I was hallucinating, since no one said there was a fire. But you could not tell me I didn't experience all of the fear around being stuck in a burning building. It was terrifying seeing it all over again. She asked me so many questions to help me remember, and the one thing I forgot was the voice that made me jump."

Dominick leaned in. "The voice?"

"Yes, the voice. It was Papa, my great grandfather. He was there when it happened."

"Really?" He tilted his head. "Wait, hold up. This is new. He told you to jump?"

"That's just it. He said it in my head. I remember it so clearly. Like, why would he want me to jump? I know I had to be losing it."

"Do you get along with him? Come on. You're not really believing he made you—"

"Look, anything is possible. With my family's gifts, anything is possible. I really don't understand it, since he's not really all there. He looks out of it most of the time, dementia."

"Here's the thing, though, Journey. Even though his mental faculties might not be like you and I, maybe he has a gift too. It could be he just wanted you to leave the house or stop fighting."

"I never heard Ty say he had the same gifts as us, but that makes sense if he does. Maybe he just wanted to stop the drama. Maybe he didn't really know how to tell me how to leave."

"It's a stretch, but you never know. He could have wanted you to leave."

"Yeah, but to *jump*? That shit was loud and clear. I don't know. That just sounds crazy as fuck. I'm sure there is a better explanation. My brain hurts trying to figure this mess out."

"Things might come back more. You just went through so much only three months ago, Journey. Don't stress yourself."

"Speaking of stress, I almost forgot that the best thing that came out of the session aside from remembering those details is she will give me a prescription for medical marijuana and mush-rooms."

His eyebrows raised, and he smiled. "Really now? I forgot she did that."

"Yeah, but it's just going to be micro-dosing, nothing crazy. I don't know much about 'shrooms, but the weed I'm happy about. She mentioned CBD, but I want the real shit." She snickered.

He whispered and looked toward the door's window. "Weeeell, since you're going to be doing that, I can get you the real good stuff. 'Shrooms. I can get it. I know a guy."

Journey put on a bad British accent. "Do you now? I would like to partake in those festivities."

He mimicked her accent. "Say no more, madam."

They both chuckled.

"I always wanted to try it, but I was always scared I might do something crazy with people I was around, so I never went through with it." She tapped his arm and smiled mischievously. "But this is the perfect time, since my mom is leaving for her conference."

"Sure, let's do it!"

"You just got to watch me to make sure I don't do nothing crazy."

"Oh, no, it just makes you feel really nice. You know that from being in the military, I had my own traumas to heal, and 'shrooms really helped me get through it."

"Really?"

"Yeah, it's very healing. You feel like everything is peaceful in the world. You may see colors, you may see a lot of bright lights. It's just a good Zen feeling. It's cosmic medicine. Connects you to the stars."

"Word. Okaaaay, say no more. I need it. I'm down. Take me to another dimension please. I can't wait."

"You just have to keep it to yourself because these are technically from the streets. Your mother would kill me."

"Hell no, I'm not telling her shit. It would be our little secret."

Ty

Ty walked slowly into their home, and Claudia greeted him with a warm hug.

"Well, what a nice surprise."

Ty forced a smile and waved at Journey. He couldn't believe how different she looked with her hair so short. Her face was slightly slimmer, but she didn't look sickly like he thought she would. She had on light makeup and earrings. She was actually very lively and pleasant. Maybe being bedridden had humbled her.

"I can't believe my eyes," Journey said, putting down her cell phone. "Ty!"

"Hi, Journey. Nice to see you."

She beckoned him closer, and when he got to the bed, she held his hand. "Come, sit, please. Wow, I'm still in shock."

Ty's stomach teased him, yanking and churning. He released her hand. His nerves were so bad. He wasn't sure how he could face her without wanting to strangle her, but he knew he had to put on a happy face. After all the pain she had caused, he couldn't believe that he was genuinely happy to see her. He was happy that she was alive. Maybe everything happened for her to repent and take a look at all the evil she'd done.

She must have felt his compassion for her, since all of sudden, she was overwhelmed with sorrow and cried. Ty patted her arm gently, and Claudia rushed to grab some tissue from the dresser.

"What's wrong?" Ty asked.

"I didn't think I would see you again. I didn't think you'd come. I don't want you to hate me."

Ty just shook his head and patted her arm. He didn't respond, and his silence was deafening. Claudia passed her the tissue box and stood over her on the opposite side of the bed, stroking her short waves.

Journey blew her nose. "I'm so sorry for what I did, for anything that I did. I don't remember everything either, but my mom told me some of it, and therapy is helping."

"Yes, her doctors say it's probably from shock. Happens a lot from trauma."

Ty thought, *Yeah, the trauma she caused does have a lingering effect on people.* He tried to keep a clear head and listen to her. He was happy she was in therapy because she truly needed it.

Journey continued to sniffle and pat her eyes. "I don't remember everything, but I do know I did not want to jump, not on my own free will."

Ty wondered if she knew. Did she know what gave her the urge to almost end her life? He protected himself in case she was trying to read him. He took a deep breath and pretended he was deep inside of a steel room. That was a trick he had learned to protect his energy. It was his imaginary fortress.

He took a chance and asked her, "What made you want to jump if you didn't want to? That was a very bold move. Terrified us all. You gave your mother a huge scare."

"I'm still unsure. I actually remember after seeing my psychologist that I heard a voice telling me to jump. I remembered the fire I was trying to escape, but I know now there was no fire."

Ty shook his head. "No, not at all."

Claudia jumped in. "It's a part of your illness. They said she could have been hallucinating." She looked at Journey. "Remember, Nini? Don't be ashamed. Ty is your father and needs to know." She opened her eyes wide to remind Journey not to take the blame.

Journey ignored her mother. "Well, I heard Papa telling me to jump. Isn't that crazy?" Her voice got softer. "I know it sounds crazy since he barely talks, but I heard him in my head." She tapped her temple.

Ty swallowed. He clenched his teeth, and his head felt a little woozy from concentrating so hard on protecting his energy. Her eyes squinted, and if she was trying to get a reaction out him, he was not going to give in. He felt Journey peeking into the corners of his mind.

"Well, I can assure you, Papa did not tell you anything. He was in too much shock with everything that happened. Let's not talk about that day anymore. I know it's not a good memory. How are you feeling?"

"Much better. I'm able to feel my legs and walk now. Slowly. I mean, I look like a ninety-year-old and shit, but I'm walking again. That was my biggest scare. I thought I would never be able to do yoga again, never be able to walk again. I'm just so sorry how things got out of hand."

She looked at her mother as if trying to give her a message. Claudia wasn't getting the hint. "Mom, do you mind giving us some privacy for a few minutes?"

Claudia seemed surprised by the request. She pursed her lips together as if offended. She fluffed up her hair in the mirror. "Oh, wow. That's fine. I'll let you both get reacquainted. I have a few phone calls to make anyway to the office. Just call me when you're done." She bent down to give Ty a hug and kiss on the cheek. "Thanks for coming."

"No worries."

She put her hand on top of his shoulder. "No, really, she needed to see you." She took an exaggerated whiff of the air. "Mmmm, you smell amazing by the way."

Ty blushed.

"Eeew! Ma, stop. He's too young for you."

"Oh, hush. He smells good. There is nothing wrong with giving someone a compliment. Right, Ty?" He nodded his head in agreement. She waved goodbye and rushed out the door, blushing.

Ty cleared his throat. "I'm glad you're getting help from a therapist. The important thing now is to work on healing and take it easy."

"I know. I just want to know . . ." She swallowed. "Does Marlon hate me?"

He took a deep breath and bit his bottom lip. "Well, I can't say you're one of his favorite people right now. He's still pretty angry. What you did to him, to us,"—Ty shook his head— "Journey, was unacceptable. It was dangerous."

"I know, I know. Please, I'm paying for it now. Believe me. It was stupid. I was childish about how I handled everything. Like everything. I'm so sorry for everything that I did, I really am, but I didn't deserve to be pushed." She choked on her tears. "I didn't deserve that. I could have died. I could have been brain dead. I—"

Ty jerked back and shook his head in disbelief. He couldn't believe she was even going there. "Now, Journey, didn't you just tell me you jumped? Eyewitnesses saw you jump. It was even on the news." He got a bit defensive. His tone was stern and deep. "No one pushed you."

"I am gonna just say it, because all this time, I thought maybe you had something to do with it." She softened her voice as if she felt someone would walk in on them. "You know as well as I do, we don't need to touch people to make things happen. I found out I could just think things sometimes, and it will work. It was like magic. I felt so power-ful. I think my anger brings it on. I was able to do little things before, like make someone trip or spill their drink, but I've gotten stronger. I noticed the angrier I am, the more I can—"

"What are you talking about, Journey?"

"Like when we were fighting. When you tried to throw me out, when you put your hands on me to shove me out the door. It . . . it just got me so angry. I didn't want Jocelyn to hit me anymore. She pulled my hair and kept hitting me. So, I told her to lay there and stay there, and she couldn't move. But I said it in my mind. Do you remem-ber that? She was yelling that she couldn't move her legs?" She had a slight smile as if enjoying the memory of toying with Jocelyn.

"Yes, I remember that." He leaned in and raised an eyebrow. "But I thought you didn't remember details."

"I don't. I just remember certain things that stuck out to me."

Ty wasn't buying the amnesia façade.

"I say that to say that maybe you just wished something about me, and it forced me to do it." She paused, waiting for a reaction, but Ty just listened. "Maybe you didn't mean it, but it happened. Like, you've been doing this way longer than me."

"Journey, if you remember so much now, you should remember you spit in my face and knocked me out cold on the floor, splitting my skull so that I needed stitches." His heart was beating faster, remembering that traumatic day. "You attacked me, and I wasn't able to wish anything, even if I wanted to."

"I'm sorry, Ty." She covered her mouth. "I don't know what happened. It's like I blacked out. At first, I thought it was you, but after I saw my therapist, she helped me really think through the process and help me relive the whole memory. It was terrifying. Now I can't shake that voice. The voice that told me to jump. It was Papa."

Ty froze and tried to crack a smile, but he was trembling inside. He quickly forced a chuckle. "Oh, please, Journey. No, it definitely was not him. He was a witness to everything, but he has no way of telling you that. You've seen him. How he speaks."

He thought, *Fuck, she knows. She knows!*

"Well, that was my experience. I just know there's no way I could have jumped on my own. I never wanted to commit suicide. I never had the urge to hurt myself ever! I wasn't drunk, I wasn't on any drugs. I mean, come on. Why would I even do that? It just doesn't make any sense."

"I'm so sorry you can't remember that detail, but so many witnesses saw you climbing out on the balcony. It had to be a hallucination."

Journey sent him a telepathic message.

"I know you're lying. You know something. I feel it. Just tell me the truth!" She screamed louder in his mind. *"Just tell me the truth, Ty! I won't be mad."*

Ty backed away slowly, trying to act casual.

She screamed again. *"Why aren't you telling me the truth?"*

The scream made him hold his head for a second. It felt so intense, like he had headphones up to the highest capacity.

He said into her mind, *"Get out of my head a little, girl. Get out."*

Journey's eyes narrowed. Ty was trying to remain brave, but he could see she was holding her own. She definitely was more powerful than before.

"Your mother said it herself. Hallucinations, right? What did the therapist actually diagnose you with?"

"I don't know if she's even right, but they said it's borderline schizophrenic, possibly, but that doesn't mean there wasn't some psychic interference to make me do something. I had to think about it but, I noticed that Papa never really liked me."

"What do you mean? He barely even speaks to anyone."

"No, I remember how he would look at me. Something about him, Ty."

Ty's headache was intense. He grabbed his head with two hands and bent down a bit. He was trying to control his imaginary force field, but he kept hearing this immense buzzing in his ears. He felt so dizzy. He had to make his energy field stronger to protect his mind.

"Oh, no. Ty, you're bleeding!" Journey pointed to his nose and handed him a tissue.

He quickly touched his mustache and felt blood. He went to the bathroom and realized he had dripped blood onto the collar of his shirt. "Damn," Ty mumbled in the mirror. He was actually embarrassed. He wiped it off and splashed water on his face. He realized he was clenching his jaws so tightly, fighting to keep her out, that it made his head hurt even more. He wasn't good at keeping up the poker face. It was getting hard to put up this front, as if they were best buds now. His frustration was building, and it was really difficult being around her when he felt she was probing him all the time. He wanted to yell at her and just admit it.

Yes, it was Papa! Yes, you are so right! He hates you for what you did. He wanted you dead.

Ty kept remembering his grandfather talking in his mind the night she jumped. It was the same thing he was rambling after he woke up from being unconscious that day. Before the paramedics arrived, Papa was screaming that she was the devil in Spanish. "Diablaaaa!" The last thing Ty needed right now was more problems with Journey. He didn't want her stressing him out. He loved how healthy Papa was becoming, and he didn't want to drain his energy with more of this drama.

The bathroom door squeaked open slowly.

"Hey, are you okay?"

"No, I'm not feeling well. I think I'm going to leave now. Hope you feel better, Journey. We'll be in touch." Ty rushed out to escape her intrusive energy. She was too much. Way too much. He was furious because he knew exactly what she was doing. No one had the right to tamper with his mind. No one. He knew he was a hypocrite too, since he also did the same things at times.

As he walked out, Dominick was walking in. He saw Ty holding his nose with a bloody tissue. "What's wrong, man? Are you okay?"

"Just a little nosebleed. I'm good."

"You should have a seat and—" Then he heard Journey crying, and he ran to her aid instead.

Dominick came to the side of her bed and bent down. "Hey, hey, Journey, what's wrong? Why are you crying?"

"No one is listening to me. No one believes me. I'm not crazy. That was Ty, you know?"

He ran back outside. Ty was already close to the door. "Hey there, you're Journey's father, right?

Ty nodded, observing Dominick's green scrubs.

"Oh, I'm Dominick. I'm her caretaker."

Ty put away the tissue and attempted to seem normal, even though he was shaken up. "Oh, yes, I heard some great things about you from her mother. Nice to meet you."

"You got a little something there." Dominick pointed to his nose.

Ty rubbed under his nose, and he realized he was still dripping blood. "Oh, geez, yeah. Thanks, man." Ty grabbed another tissue from his pocket to wipe it away.

Dominick seemed concerned, but Ty speculated that he also had an agenda. "Why don't you have a seat right here? Lean forward. Keep that light pressure on it. I'll be right back."

He got some paper towels from the kitchen. "Just give it ten minutes. It should stop soon."

Ty took a deep breath like he was a child put on punishment. "I just want to get home. I'll be fine, really."

"Ten minutes. Just give it ten minutes. It's actually good I have a moment to chat with you without Journey. I have to ask you. Do you know what happened? She keeps thinking somebody pushed her."

"No, no such thing happened. We were just discussing it. You do know that she suffers from some sort of mental illness. Her mother already told me."

"Well, that's what the doctors say, but there's a spiritual aspect to it I think as well. I'm sure you know your daughter is very gifted."

Ty shrugged. He was not ready to get into a metaphysical discussion with this guy. He took the paper towel off and realized the bleeding had stopped. Ty scrubbed his head with his palm. "Look, man, it's obvious that you're very caring and you want what's best for her, but do yourself a favor and don't get sucked into her life. Just stick to your job, or it might get messy." Ty could tell that the young man was crushing on Journey.

"You see, it's a part of my job to see what's in the best interest of my patients."

"Well, just make sure she gets the best mental health care she can. That's my main concern." Ty rose up from his seat. "All right, you have a good night. I have to get outta here."

He was sure that Dominick was trying to be some kind of knight in shining armor. He had probably already slept with her, being that she seemed to be so promiscuous.

As he stepped outside the door, he felt sharp jolts go through him about Dominick. Visions of him flashed before his eyes. He saw Dominick screaming on his knees, like he was trapped somewhere. It was very bizarre. He saw him in small room, screaming for help. He felt that that young man was in trouble, but he couldn't figure out if that was a symbolic message to him being trapped, or something even worse to come. He was probably going to be added to the list of victims that Journey terrorized. Poor guy had no idea what he had signed up for. Claudia said she was having him move in and take care of Journey full-time after she was done with rehab. Ty had no doubt that Journey had manipulated her mom into making that happen.

Chapter 15

Journey

After Ty left Journey's room, she was so emotionally distraught. She needed to understand what had just happened. She couldn't get into Ty's mind like she wanted to. He was too powerful. She felt him blocking her. It was like an intense headache. He could not deny his fear. It was obvious. He couldn't wait to get away from her. His nose kept bleeding, which was confirmation he was straining to keep her out. Ty knew more about what had happened to her that day, and she wanted to find out the details. When he left so suddenly, she just couldn't hold back the feeling of rejection and betrayal.

Dominick rushed back into the room. "Wow, I just met your father."

Journey said, "He finally came for a very short visit and well, it didn't end well. I think he's hiding something. I kept questioning him. He knows something, man."

"I just had to sit with him for a minute to get his nose to stop bleeding."

"Really? It was still bleeding?"

"Yeah, does that happen often?"

"Well, it's something that happens to us when we're using our powers—I mean our intuition. I really think he was blocking me. He knows I can read him."

"That's wild. Are you serious?"

"Yes, I needed answers. I kept asking him, Why did I jump? Did Papa had anything to do with it? That was when he got really defensive. Then the nose bleeding started, and he just left in a hurry, saying he didn't feel well."

"Wow, that's pretty suspicious."

"Yes, and to add to the drama now, my mom just texted me that I need to put something in writing for Marlon. Something that shows remorse and also to let him know that I've been diagnosed with mental illness. She got into lawyer mode and is convinced that he's not gonna come after me if I can show proof that I have a mental condition."

"You do know there's nothing wrong with you, right?"

"I *know,* but I have to play the part." She slammed her phone down, annoyed by the multiple texts coming in from her mom. The doctor had explained that she could be borderline schizophrenic, but she knew she was not. She knew what the hell she saw. Just then, her phone rang.

"It's her," she said to Dominick.

He said softly, "I'll be right back. I'm gonna talk to Doctor Alexander." He closed the door.

Claudia sounded concerned. "Journey, are you okay? Did you see Ty?"

"Yes, yes. I'm not ignoring you. I saw *all* of your messages, Mom, all seventy-two of them." She snickered.

"Oh, stop. It was like six or seven of them. You're so dramatic, Nini."

"I'm sorry. I was just talking to Dominick about Ty's visit."

"How was that?"

"It was nice. He came in cool, calm, and collected. It was fine. Quick but fine. He had to leave in a rush. He had a nosebleed."

"Oh, no. Like you have sometimes? I wonder if that is hereditary or something?"

"Maybe." Journey played coy and didn't want to give her mother another thing more to worry about.

"Okay, well, just handle the Marlon thing today. I just have a feeling he's going to come after you. Tell him you're very sorry. Be extremely sweet. I know you hate this, but you have to do it. You know you were in the wrong. What you did was uncalled for. You could go to jail. This is not a game."

Journey let out an exaggerated sigh.

"It's really important, because I really think he's going to press charges soon."

"Fine. I'll do it, Mom." She was sick to her stomach to know she had to grovel. Journey thought it would be just a waste of time, but she agreed it would show some good faith. She would pretend not to remember much about the incident, even though watching the videos brought it all back. She knew her mother was right. She had to cover her ass. She did want to protect her reputation, but if she had to pull the mental illness card, then so be it. She sent Marlon a text.

Journey: Hi, Marlon. Why haven't you visited me yet? I would love to talk to you to clear the air on everything that happened. I'm really, really sorry.

Marlon: Who is this?

Journey: It's Journey. Ty just came by, and I was hoping you were going to be with him.

There was no reply for a few minutes. Then her phone rang. His voice was deep, raspy, and filled with contempt.

Marlon screamed, "Don't you ever, and I mean *ever*, fuckin' call me or come near me evaaaa again in life. On God, it might be your last motherfuckin' day, little girl."

Journey was shaken by his rage. Her voice cracked. "Marlon, I just wanted to apologize. I really—"

"Fuck your apologies. Stay the fuck away from me, Journey. I mean it! You better be lucky I didn't come to visit you. What you did could have killed me. You could have destroyed me. You are going to jail for this shit. Trust." He hung up on her.

Journey's hands shook as she texted back frantically. She mumbled in disbelief, "Jail? Jail?" He was serious.

She texted him again.

Journey: I had a breakdown of sorts. I have mental illness that I can't control, so I'm very sorry for whatever I did. I don't even remember most of it. They diagnosed me with schizophrenia. You can ask Ty. He knows.

Marlon: There's not a damn thing wrong with you. I'm already onto your manipulative ways. Fuck you, you crazy, manipulative witch. What you are is a pathological liar and a sociopath.

His words slapped her hard in the face. The sting almost made her tear up. She was filled with anger and regret for doing what she did. She never wanted anyone to hate her.

Dominick came back into the room and noticed her typing away with tears in her eyes.

"Hey, are you all right?"

"Yeah, gimme a minute." She continued texting.

Journey: You know what, Marlon? FUCK YOU. I was trying to make up, and you won't even hear me out. Your heart is so damn cold. But that's all

good. People like you will always get what they
deserve.

    Marlon: I sure hope so. I want you under the jail
before you do that shit to someone else. THAT'S
WHAT I DESERVE. JUSTICE. From theft, drugging me, and kidnapping. You are so lucky I don't
have proof of that Colombia powder you blew in
my face.

    Journey threw the phone on the foot of the bed.

    "Sometimes I . . . I really wish I never woke up!"

    "Journey, don't talk like that. What happened?
Who were you texting?" He came to her side and
hugged her as she cried.

    "Marlon, Ty's partner. He was just so nasty to
me. He just cursed me out even though I said I was
sorry. I told him about my . . . my diagnosis."

    "And he still cursed at you. What the hell?"

    "I know." Journey sniffled and wiped a tear.

    Marlon's evil words stung. She was still shaking.
Granted, she knew she was no angel and probably
deserved it for being so vindictive. She had wanted
to get Ty back for lying to her about Natalia. She
did use Marlon. She could understand why he was
so mad at her, but he didn't have to be so nasty
about it, especially since she apologized. They had
a little bit of fun, and she realized she probably
didn't even need to use Devil's Breath to loosen
him up, because she knew that he wanted to sleep
with her.

She got up and grabbed her phone from where she had thrown it and sent another text.

Journey: Last thing. I deleted the videos, but they could be in the clouds. Just floating through the clouds.

Marlon: What does that mean?

Journey: Nothing. You have a good night, Marlon. I thought we could have an adult conversation, but you've proven me wrong. You will never hear from me again.

Marlon: Good. Do not text or call me anymore. This is harassment. LOSE MY NUMBER.

Journey then sent emojis of the clouds. She smiled and turned off her cell.

Ty

Marlon stormed into Ty's home office. Jocelyn let him in on her way out the door. Marlon slammed the office door behind him. With protruding eyes, he yelled, "Ayo, Ty, tell me you are losing it or something. Please tell me you didn't go visit that crazy daughter of yours."

"Well, good evening to you too." Ty stopped typing and closed his laptop. "Marlon, lower your voice and chill out. Have a seat." He waved his hand toward the leather chairs in front of his desk. "Yes, I did. It's just—"

"You done unleashed the madness! Once again, she's back. You've awakened the dragon. She's gonna get hurt if she keeps on fuckin' contacting me."

"Slow down. Slow down. What happened, man?"

He tapped his foot nervously. "I should block her, but I'm gonna need all the text messages as evidence when I file an order of protection. I'm doing it first thing in the morning."

Ty slammed his hand on the desk. "Focus. Tell. Me. What. Happened."

"So, she texts me out the blue like we are cool and shit." He shook his head side to side like a girl with an attitude. "Talking about why didn't I visit her? Is she fucking crazy? She thinks this shit is a game. I really think she enjoys taunting me. So, I called her back and told her to leave me the fuck alone and to not call my phone. She had the nerve to text me back, trying to pull the crazy card, saying she's schizophrenic or psycho or whatever. But she's full of shit. Well, she is a psychopath, but what got me was when she said she deleted the videos of me, but told me it was in the clouds. And sent a bunch of cloud emojis. Trying to be funny. I didn't get it at first, but I think she is trying to say it was backed up in the cloud or something. She better delete them shits, that's all I know."

"She's not gonna do anything. Just relax."

"How do you know? You don't know. Look at what she was capable of. I'm gonna put the order of protection on her. I'm not putting nothing past that little bitch. She is going to be walking and driving soon." He leaned in and beat his chest so hard Ty heard it. "She knows where I fucking live, man."

"Well, do what you gotta do, Marlon. That will make her leave you alone."

"So, what happened when you saw her? Was she looking like herself?"

"It was really brief. No, she's a little lighter. She has short hair now from the surgery. She doesn't look how I imagined. She just seemed a little bit softer. I just wanted to make peace in case she tried to come for me, saying I pushed her or some bullshit. Do you know the cops are still looking at this? I have to cover my ass."

"Man, ain't nobody gonna say you pushed her. Too many people saw her jump. I don't know why you keep worrying about it."

Just then, Papa walked in slowly with no cane. He had on his pajamas and robe. He nodded respectfully. Ty knew he was being nosey to see what all the yelling was about. "Hola, Marlon."

Marlon slapped Ty on the shoulder with his mouth hanging open.

"See, you woke him up with your big mouth."

"Wait. Hold up. Hoooooold up just a minute. Look at you, player! What's going on, Papa?" He turned to Ty in disbelief. "What new drug is he on? What the fuck?"

"I told you between Elizabeth doing all her healing and Jocelyn dancing and singing, the old man is reverse aging over here."

"Man, this is great news. I never seen him without a cane or a walker. It's like a miracle."

Papa chuckled. "Gracias." He smiled and walked closer to them. "Be careful." He pointed to Marlon.

Marlon's head jerked back. "Why? What are you talking about?"

"Journey, she is berry, berry dangerous. She can't control it." He turned to Ty, and his gray eyes twinkled with intensity. "Sin control."

"Oh, you think I don't know that? That's what I'm trying to tell your stupid-ass, thickheaded grandson over here. He wanna play nice with her. We all need to just leave her alone."

Papa sent a message to Ty in his mind. *"Take it easy. She will fight back. She is stronger now. She doesn't have much control over her gifts yet. Let him know to just don't make her angry."*

Ty said to Marlon, "Yeah, Papa feels she really does have something wrong with her, so just take it easy."

"Oh, like we don't know that. I'm good. I'm not speaking to her again. If anything, our lawyer will."

Papa nodded and tapped on the wall. "Good night, Marlon. Tylercito."

"Papa, do you need something?"

"No, no, I'm good. I'm going to bed."

With lifted eyebrows, Marlon turned and watched Papa walking on his own in awe. "Yo, I never heard him speak English that good in my life. What the fuck kind of black magic did that little girl do?"

"He actually speaks English pretty well. He just prefers not to most of the time. But his speech has not been this good in years since he started declining. I'm telling you, that daughter of mine, Elizabeth, got some skills. It's Reiki. She said he had a lot of inflammation in his body. Reiki helped lessen the pain."

"Yeah, you might have to really start marketing her and make some money 'cause that shit is amazing."

They laughed.

Chapter 16

Journey

2 weeks later in Journey's home

Dominick made a fun little den to chill out in. He now lived downstairs in the back room that Natalia had once lived in. The plan was to stay only a month more to help Journey get back to herself. Because of rehab and his help, she'd been recovering well. Her mobility was much better; however, she was purposely dragging out her recovery, since she didn't want Dominick to go.

There were several floor pillows piled up in the living room, so Journey brought them downstairs with a few more comforters. They had the TV on YouTube playing the view of a beautiful aquarium with ambient music and crystal bowls in the background. A cloud of sandalwood incense swirled around them. Dominick stared up at the smoke and traced his finger around it to make it shape shift.

They were definitely feeling the effects of the mushrooms he brought after only forty minutes. The effect it had on Journey's body started off very calming. Journey felt so free, so alive, and extremely sensual. It definitely served as an aphrodisiac. She was so impressed by Dominick's knowledge about many healing plants that indigenous cultures used. His family practiced everything from ayahuasca, psychedelic mushrooms, to San Pedro in their shamanic rituals, so Journey felt safe with him. He called it the cosmic medicine, making it sound so cool and not like they were taking *drugs* just to get high, but for a purpose. He talked about the plants as medicine, something to help you heal. The plants help you sort things out. He said they really process your pain and trauma and help you get more enlightened. Journey really wanted that. She wanted to understand herself more, and maybe even her powers more. She knew she was getting stronger. She was changing, and she hoped it was for the better. She really did want to be a better person than she was before.

Journey stared at the ceiling and saw psychedelic patterns swirling to the sounds in her mind. The colors were luminous and some effervescent. When she closed her eyes, she saw and actually felt the mushrooms even more. "My limbs are vibrating. Is this normal? Are you sure we didn't take too much?" She giggled.

"No, I just gave you a moderate dose. It will help you step outside of yourself. It actually helps you connect with yourself more. When I do it, it really helps me expand my mind."

She laughed and tilted her head back with her eyes closed. "I've stepped out of myself all right. Yo, it's so crazy. I wish you could see what I see." She reached her hands out in the air and started making waving movements. "It's like I feel like I'm inside a lava lamp. You know those lamps from the sixties."

Dominick laughed. "Oh, wow. Maybe I did give you too much. You're in a lava lamp, Journey?"

"Yeessss."

He tapped her thigh. "For real?" He watched her and smiled. Dominick liked the effect it had on her. She was so relaxed.

"I'm tripping. This shit is wild." She opened her eyes and leaned on his shoulder. "I love this. I never met anybody like you before, Dominick. You're so spiritual. I'm so happy to have you in my life."

"Oh, thank you. I'm so happy I met you too."

Journey closed her eyes and laid on her back on the cushions. Dominick put a pillow under her knees to elevate her legs.

"You always in work mode. I'm fine. Come lay down."

He sat with his legs crossed, and his eyes seemed heavy. "I will soon. How are you feeling?"

"*So good,* so relaxed. But I'm a little sad too."

"Oh no, sad? Why?"

"Because no one likes me. Everyone is feeling sorry for me. The suicide girl. I don't know who is real anymore. My reputation is destroyed. It's me. I destroyed it. I know I can't even go back to my old job because of Helen." She started to sob. "Who knows what she told people about me? I remember before this all happened, I heard there were rumors. But now I know she started them probably. I fucking hate her."

"Don't worry. You'll find another studio."

"I have two others I can go to, but that one was my favorite. I had the most clients there."

"Well, you can have them follow you to this new one that you're going to be at. Don't let that lady stress you out."

"I hate her."

"I hate her too." He clenched his jaws. "I don't like to see you sad."

Journey's teeth chattered. "It is so cold. Aren't you cold?

"No, but do you want me to come warm you up a little bit?"

She pulled his arm back to urge him to the floor with her. Journey smiled. "Come under the covers with me."

"Sure. I'll keep you warm."

"Not with those work clothes. I want to feel the heat of your skin."

"Do you know what you're asking me?"

"Yessss, just take off your scrubs. I want to feel the heat." She moved her hips under the covers toward him, and it made his manhood rise. He quickly slid out of his blue scrubs and had on only his boxers and a tank top.

"Wow, you really have a nice body, Dominick."

"Thank you. I like to run and bike."

"It shows." Journey was turned on and so happy her mother wasn't home. The mushrooms were making her feel so free, so uninhibited.

He couldn't hide his happiness as he got under the covers with her. He cuddled in close to her but followed her lead. He didn't want to be too aggressive and scare her.

"You're so warm." Journey's hands rubbed all over his chest and legs. He was growing stronger like steel. Her hands ventured to his boxers. "Oh my God. Just touching you. You are like an electric blanket. You feel so good. You are so hard, Dominick." She rubbed on his dick, and he sighed. She pulled her hand away, and he put it back on it.

He whispered, "It felt good. It's okay. Don't stop."

She hugged on him and then got quiet. She sighed and wiped away a tear before it could fall. "Do you think my reputation is shot? Do you think I'm a ho? Be honest."

"Absolutely not." He pulled her closer to his chest. "You're a free spirit, not a ho. You can't let one person worry you. What we have is special. I would never call you that, Journey."

"That's just it. It is not just one person. It's Helen, it's Marlon, people that really wanted me to die. And now it could even be my great grandfather, but I don't know if that was just a part of the hallucination or not. I swear I heard his voice right before it all happened. Right before the jump. I don't know anymore. I just wish it would all go away. If I could blow up a car and push it into a ditch, I would put them all in it. Especially that bitch Helen. Helen is a fucking devil." A menacing laugh escaped her.

Dominick didn't laugh with her.

"I know, that was evil, right? Is this shit like a truth serum? I just can't shut up. I keep talking."

"No, no." He chuckled. "You are just expressing how you feel. It's helping you get things out. Things bottled up inside. It's a part of the healing. Just feeling."

"Shit, it's making me more angry. It's opening my throat chakra, I guess. I don't want to feel this."

"I'm so sorry that she hurt you. She's just a jealous old lady and pissed that her husband fell for you. But I don't know who wouldn't fall for you, Journey."

"Thank you." She caressed his goatee softly. "You're so sweet to me." She kissed him on the cheek.

He leaned in her ear, and she tingled from his warm breath. "But if you want me to take care of Helen and Marlon, just say the word. You know I was a sniper in the military?"

"Seriously? Get out of here. So you can shoot, shoot?" She pretended to hold a rifle and aimed for the window.

He nodded confidently.

"Like from really far away?"

"Sure."

"You look like you wouldn't hurt a fly. I can't believe it."

"Yeah, I don't really like to talk about it, but I've gotten people as far as a football field away."

"Holy shit! What do you mean, gotten people? You got bodies? Did you ever kill anyone?"

"Come on. I can't really talk about it, the things they had us do, but you're intuitive. You can read between the lines."

"Man, you did, Dominick. My sweet Dominick is a natural born killer. Holy shit."

"Hush, don't say that." He looked ashamed. "I was a trained sniper in the army, and let's leave it at that, okay? It's nothing I'm really proud of, and to be honest, it was a pretty traumatizing part of my life that I don't like to relive. But that's why I went to the other side of things to help people in healthcare. The army made us kill some folks who really didn't deserve it. That's what gave me PTSD. The 'shrooms helped me deal."

Journey tilted her head and blinked a few times. "Oh my God. Oh my Gaaawd."

"What? What's wrong?"

Journey pointed to his eyes. "They're turning colors. Your eyes. They were green and blue and purple. They are so beautiful. Do they always do that?"

"Oh, yeah, it's kicking in. I got a good batch. I guess I am used to it since I don't feel it as strong as you do. It's new for you still. Your body is adjusting to it. Sometimes you start to see things really bright."

"Tell me about it. It feels like I have on 5G goggles on my eyes. Everything seems so crisp and clear and beautiful."

"Imagine if we were outside in the mountains. It's really fun to do it in nature."

"Oh, I wanna try that next. I feel like all my life I was blind and just got a new set of eyes. Everything is so freakin' clear." She laughed. "I wish you could see what I see. It's so beautiful. You are so beautiful."

"Thank you, but I prefer handsome."

She giggled.

He gently stroked her cheek with the back of his hand. "You are the beautiful one. Inside and out."

She ached for him to make a move. She wanted to just do it, but she felt he might feel better if he did it. If he took much longer, she was going to have to hop on him. He was so sexy and didn't even seem to know it.

"You know my mom will be livid if she saw us in bed."

"Yeah, she would." He shook his head.

"But then again, I have a feeling she thinks that you're gay, because I doubt she would want you to be around me alone. She is so protective."

"Oh, boy! Why do I have to be gay?"

"Well, you're thirty-four with no kids, very handsome, very fit, and never been married. It's the typical stereotype of a gay man in the closet."

"So, I just got to be thrown in the gay box because I don't have kids and never been married? I know plenty of dudes just like me that are not gay. How about we are just not ready to be married and we know how to use a condom? That's a crazy stereotype." He was annoyed.

"Okay, I'm sorry. I am just telling you how my mom thinks."

"I don't think she believes that, but okay. Well, I can assure you that I'm not into men at all." His face was close enough to kiss her.

"Damn, you are going to make me want you."

"And what's wrong with that? I thought you already did. I see what you're doing. You are not slick."

Dominick's hands were under the covers and explored her thighs. They slide under her T-shirt and moved her bra up so he could fondle a nipple. Journey's mouth opened in pleasure as he pinched and twisted it, watching her reaction. Her legs opened slightly, and he started to caress in between them.

"Wow, it's so warm. You feeling good, huh?"

The music they had playing in the background seemed louder to Journey. The melodies enveloped them. "Oh my God, I could feel the music vibrating in my body. Everything is vibrating." She grabbed his hand and pushed it under her Spandex and panties.

"You are not making it easy, Journey." He began stimulating her clit, moving his finger faster as she scooted out of her Spandex.

"Damn, you're so wet." He kissed her, and his gaze was full of lust.

Journey sighed, loving how his tongue danced with hers. He sucked on her lips and neck. He slowly worked his way all over her body, and she sighed in delight. "Oh my God, everything feels sooooo good. I feel everything."

He plunged a finger inside of her, and she moaned in ecstasy. "Ohhhh . . . shit. This feels amazing."

He said in her ear, "That's because we are connected. Everything we have been waiting for is about to happen. Our energies have been craving one another."

"It's so tingly. All you have to do is touch me, and I feel like I'm going to cum. You make me feel so good."

His fingers caressed her like a delicate instrument. He whispered in her ear, and all of her senses and emotions were amplified.

She had a pleading look in her eyes. She wanted him inside of her, and he wanted her to beg him.

"Oh my God, oh my God."

"Say you want this."

Journey grabbed his dick out of his boxers.

He teased her and pulled back. "I want to hear you say it."

"I want it. I want you, Dominick. Stop playing." She realized she was getting a taste of her own medicine. He was doing to her what she did to her clients.

He got up and took off his tank top. His lean swimmer's physique turned her on even more. He had even more tats on his chest. It was of a phoenix rising from the earth. He was also very aroused and had a nice thick package to offer. She hadn't had sex since before the accident, so her hormones were roaring.

"I want you to be mine. I want you to say it."

She stood up and took off her top and kicked off her leggings. She was feeling more confident and sexier now that she had gained her weight back. She wanted to gain control, but Dominick seemed to be a good match for her.

"No, I'm not saying it. I want you to taste me."

He climbed on top of her and spread her legs open. He kissed her inner thighs and breathed deeply on her spot. He sucked and licked with such precision. It felt so familiar. It felt like they'd done this before.

She screamed, "Dominiiiiiick. You're so fucking good. Get the condom. Oh my God, I just can't take it anymore. I need you. My body feels so heavy, though."

"I'm not giving you what you want until you give me what I want. Say it. Are you mine?"

She didn't want to, but she knew if she wanted him, she would just say it. "Yesss, yesss. I'm yours."

He rubbed his hardness on her, teasing her, and she didn't even see when he got the condom off his dresser. He had it in his hand already. He kneeled while opening the wrapper. Journey was so excited watching him put it on.

"Are you sure you want to do this?"

She panted, "I'm absolutely positively sure. I want to feel you inside of me. Please be gentle. It's been months."

"Oh, don't worry, beautiful. I will."

She touched her nipples lightly and opened her legs, letting him get a good look at her.

"Yes, that's it. Damn, you are so fucking sexy."

Once he mounted her, Journey felt a rush go through her body.

"You're mine." He stroked her deeply. "Say it."

"Yes, I'm yours." She matched his rhythm and dug her hands into his butt, pulling him in deeper.

"Oh, I was going easy on you, baby. You want more?" He plunged deeper into her, and Journey screamed so loud.

"Fuuuuuck. Oh, this is soooo good. I needed this. I needed you. I feel so emotional." She started sobbing lightly.

He slowed down. "Are you okay? Do you want me to stop?"

"No. No, don't stop. I'm just so . . . so happy." He went slower, and they both sighed in ecstasy. The passion they had for each other was unreal.

"Oh my God. Your dick is so good."

"Oh, yeah?" He panted. "You feel amazing too. So amazing. Just how I dreamed it."

She whispered. "You are healing me."

"You are healing me too, Journey. You have no idea."

Her eyes were closed. "I feel like I am on a colorful rollercoaster."

"You're my rollercoaster."

They both giggled, and she embraced his back tighter as she sighed. Her body vibrated, and she trembled as he went deeper and deeper. He put both of her hands above her head and held them down while he penetrated her.

"I want to hear it again. Do you belong to me?"

"Yesssss."

"Say it."

"I belong to you. Fuck . . . I belong . . . Shit. I don't want this to end. This feels so incredible."

"Ah, ah . . . Wow, wow." He collapsed on his side, facing her.

"You knew what you were doing getting those mushrooms. Now I don't ever want you to leave. I am getting better, but I will play sick for as long as I can." She laughed and reached for the remote.

They lay together, watching Netflix.

She turned to him and kissed him. "Will you really protect me?"

"I will, Journey. I will hurt anyone that hurts you."

"You're really all that I have now. I have no best friends. No friends. My siblings haven't even reached out since I woke up. My mom and you.

Everyone hates me." She burst into spontaneous tears. "Why am I so emotional? I don't think I'm PMSing. Is this normal?"

"Yes, you're purging. You're releasing blocked energy."

"I feel like I'm in another dimension, especially after all of that loving you just gave me."

She slid her hand on his now limp dick.

"Careful now. You gonna wake him up again."

"I can do it again. In a little bit, though. My heart is beating so fast. It's kind of scaring me."

She put her hand on top of his and pulled it toward her heart. "Am I going to die? I feel like I might have taken too much. You can't die from 'shrooms, can you?"

"No, no. I know you're going to be fine. Just close your eyes and take some deep breaths."

"I'm just an asshole. That's why nobody loves me. I made a mistake. I let greed get a hold of me. I wanted what I wanted, and I didn't care who I hurt. I know now it was my great grandpa. I know it was him. He saw me do everything. He hates me now. I have to go apologize. I got to go there." She sat up, looking for her top, and was ready to put on her clothes.

He pushed her gently back down. "Relax. We can't go anywhere now. You're not thinking straight. It is thirty degrees outside, and I'm not taking you anywhere. You see what time it is?" He pointed to the digital clock that said 12:20 a.m.

"No, no, you don't understand. I can go there in my mind. I can travel. Astral projection. I was just going to get my crystals I like to meditate with."

He shook his head. "Just close your eyes and rest."

She knew he didn't believe her. Journey figured he thought she was just high and delusional.

"I just got the download. It's so clear now. It's something you helped with. I got it now. I have to apologize to Papa right now. That's all I know."

Dominick just held her tight, and she ended up falling asleep in his arms. Journey was way too high to astral project anyhow. She knew that she had to do it soon. She had to send the message to Papa.

"You are such a sweet person. I don't see how anyone would want to hurt you. There were so many nights that I stopped by your bedside and prayed for you to wake up. I prayed that when you did open your eyes again, you would have a normal life . . ." His voice trailed off. "And not have to suffer like the others."

"What others?"

"Most of all of my other patients. Some of them you met in your, your visions. Some of them you didn't. However, many of them I had to watch live out their last days in pain or as a vegetable."

"Do you mean like Francesca and Delilah?"

"Yes, there are many that were kept alive when there was no use of them living, since they were going to be brain dead. Just seems so selfish of the families to do that."

"Well, thank you for praying. It worked. I'm so happy I have you in my life, Dominick."

"I'm not going anywhere."

"The crazy shit is, I just met you, and I feel like you care more about me than my own father does. I feel that he can't give three shits that I'm alive, but I don't think he had anything to do with pushing me now. I just keep getting this nagging feeling like he's hiding something, like he knows something. I don't know, maybe Marlon has something up his sleeve. He was so nasty to me when I tried to make peace with him on the phone."

"Wait? You called him?"

"Yep, I really didn't want to call. My mother begged me to. She's afraid that he might—Oh, never mind. I think he's just mad that I exposed him that time. That I told Ty that we slept together. I don't know what the big deal is. It's not as if he took advantage of me, but I do know he was using his friendship with Ty to get closer to me."

Journey refused to tell him the whole story or the truth for that matter. What would he think of her? "You know, he knew I was young, and I knew he's in his early forties. I will admit things just got a little out of hand with the whole situation. He was drinking a lot, so most of what happened, he doesn't really remember. I was drinking too, but not as much as him."

Dominick has his eyes closed. Journey shook his shoulder.

"Are you awake?"

"Yes, yes, go on. I'm just feeling nice."

"Well, Marlon tells a whole 'nother story. He keeps lying and saying that I drugged him or something. Like, give me a break! Do I need to drug him to sleep with me? He wanted us to keep everything a secret, and I guess when I got so mad at Ty about other stuff, I told him I slept with his best friend. Marlon is now threatening me not to call him or he'll kill me."

"No, what? Are you fucking serious? That's going a bit far, Journey. Death threats? Why is he so angry with you? Just because you told on him? Did he become obsessed with you or something? That doesn't make sense."

It didn't seem like Dominick was buying the story. "Yes, that and well, because I have some photos of him. Some very damaging photos and videos. And I don't even know why I took them at the time. Maybe because I was drunk, or I guess I needed it for protection in case he tried to deny it, which he actually did. Maybe my higher self whispered in my ear that it would come in handy one day." She giggled.

"I support you and everything, but it sounds like you were playing with fire. You know these older guys can't handle young women. Shit, you already got my mouth watering for more."

"Dominick!" Journey blushed. "You aren't that old anyway, only like ten years older."

"That's old."

"No, not really. And I didn't think he was too old for me because quite frankly, I don't really deal with young guys, but I wasn't looking for a relationship. Call me crazy, but I like living on the wild side a little bit, because I knew it was wrong. I'm not an idiot, but the way he talks to me now is so disrespectful."

"Look, at the end of the day, just let me know if he threatens you again. Anyone that hurts you like that, let me know. Say the word." He tilted her face toward his and looked into her eyes. "You hear me?"

"I hear you. I know this is crazy, but what if they band together and figure out a way to take me out? They all have loads of money. Marlon and Helen are millionaires." Journey's eyes widened. Suddenly, she had a vision of running down the middle of an empty street in the city, then out of nowhere, a black SUV did a U-turn and skidded down the street toward her. She could smell the rubber burn. It came toward her and tried to run her down.

Dominick laughed. "Come on. Now it is definitely the mushrooms talking. No one is going to take you out or band together like we are in an action film."

"Yes, they can band together like a fucking gang!" She tried to laugh at her paranoia, hoping that that was all it was, pure paranoia.

"You've been binge watching too much true crime TV."

"Thanks to you!" She pointed at him. "Yeah, okay. They all got assassin money. They can put a hit out on me just like that." Journey snapped her fingers. "They hate me."

"I will get them before they get to you. Don't worry."

Journey still looked shaken up from her vision. He grabbed her face and kissed her lips to reassure her.

"When people have money, who knows what they're capable of, Dominick? Helen and Phil are filthy rich. I thought it was Phil's money, since he's a hotshot entertainment lawyer with a long celebrity client roster, but after further research, I found out his ugly wife is an heiress to a mustard company, one of the big ones."

His eyes were glassy, and he spoke slower. "Did you say a mustard company? That's fucking hilarious!" He laughed.

"Yeah, I know, right? She hasn't worked a day in her life from what I know. When I Googled her, she's just like a socialite that's on a lot of boards, donating money to charities. It made a lot of sense, since she was out of Phil's league."

"What? He's handsome, huh?"

"Yes, for an older man, and definitely for her. It makes sense that he probably married her for money and connections. She has so much money. She can really destroy me."

"And you never had an affair with this man?" He didn't seem too convinced by her story.

"Never. Like I said, I just did some things to keep him interested. It was more like teasing him. That shit backfired, when it truly was just yoga."

"So this ugly mustard queen has this vendetta because she thinks you and Phil slept together?"

Journey snickered. "Mustard queen. That's funny. And you're right, I never went there with him."

"But did you want to?"

Journey could feel Dominick's jealousy brewing, and it kind of turned her on in a strange way. She really did have a lusting feeling for Phil. He had a mature sex appeal about him. His confidence and power were what she liked the most. She realized how she felt about Phil was showing all over her face. Dominick was probing just a bit much.

"No, no. We are just good friends."

"I think you like him." He shrugged with a smirk. "You see, I know you're gifted, but I got a little bit of intuition myself."

"Oh, no, not like that. He was just very kind to me, and I love his money. He tips well, too. I can't lie." Journey twirled her short, curly hair and closed her eyes, smiling at how good she was feeling. Her body was buzzing.

In a stern voice, he said, "Why can't you look me in my eyes when I asked you that one question, Journey?

She spit out a laugh. "I'm sorry. My eyes feel sooooo good closed." She giggled. "I want to keep them shut. It is beautiful."

"What are you talking about?"

"When I close my eyes, I see little kaleidoscopes twirling."

"What?" He laughed.

"Dominick, if you could see what I was seeing. O.M.G., I'm tingling all over. I'm still feeling it. That sex was so good. Is it that good without the mushrooms?"

"I hope so. We'll have to try it again. Another time, mushroom free." Dominick's hand slid up her thigh, and he leaned on her. "That way we can compare." He kissed her neck then said slowly, "Soooo, what do you have on this other dude? The millionaire who's going to send assassins after you? Why are you so afraid of him? Or maybe why is he so afraid of you?"

Journey reached for her cell phone. She displayed a childlike grin, as if she were an eight-year-old little girl getting ready to show her doll collection. "Oh, you want to see? You won't get jealous, right?" A part of her wanted him to get jealous. She wanted him to see the type of men she attracted.

"No? I want to see. Show me what it is."

"I told Marlon that I deleted it, but actually, my Mom did. But you know shit is never really deleted. I'm still so sick that she went through my phone when I was in a coma. Totally violated me."

She pulled up a photo of Marlon standing with a rock-hard penis, and then another photo of Journey holding it in her hand.

"Whoa, whoa! Journey, what in the hell were you thinking? Claudia saw this?" He grabbed the phone out of her hand and swiped.

"No! You don't want to see the rest, Dominick." She slapped him on the shoulder. "I'm serious. You don't want to see the rest. Give it back."

He laughed while the video played. He watched Marlon say in a low, monotone voice, "You are the master. You are the master."

Then Journey's voice came in loud and clear, like a bossy commander. "Say it again. I can't hear *you*, Marlon."

Dominick's eyes widened in shock. Journey tried to pull the phone away, and he wouldn't let go of it.

She shouted in his mind.

"Give me the phone! I said now! LET GO OF IT NOW."

His hands went limp. The phone dropped onto the pillows, and she snatched it back.

"Not cool."

"What do you expect? I'm a man. How are you going to show me something like this? Damn, Journey, you sound like a dominatrix in this video. Like you do that shit on the regular. I don't know if I should be turned on or jealous. I might have to tie you up one day and see how you like being bossed around."

"Is that a threat or a promise?" She laughed.

He bit his bottom lip and moved closer to her. "Damn, you are so sexy. You little porn star, you. Now I can't unsee that. I don't want anybody to have you anymore. You can't do that to anybody else."

Journey was sure he was still in a mushroom fog, but what she was hearing loud and clear was his need for commitment.

"Chill. We're just starting out. Let's not go too fast. This is fun." She touched his chest softly. "I like you a lot. I don't want to ruin it."

"I don't think we'll ruin it, but it's cool. As long as you don't record me and put my goodies on display, I'm okay with taking it a little slow. We have to keep it a secret for now anyhow. At least until my job is over here." He pointed to her cell. "So, these photos and videos you have are pretty bad. Makes a lot of sense as to why he's terrified of you. You could really embarrass him or destroy him."

"Oh, we had a lot of wine that night. Way too much wine. I told you I like older men, so my ego got the best of me when I could get him to do what I wanted."

"Really? So you're just a regular party animal. You look really good in the video, though."

"Thanks. Hopefully I'll get back to that look soon."

"What are you talking about? You look beautiful. You're only a few pounds lighter."

"I'm sorry. I didn't really want you to see all of that. I don't know what I was thinking."

"No, it's okay. Now I can understand why he's so humiliated. Some young girl has a sex tape on him with him calling her a master. That's embarrassing as fuck." He rubbed her thigh. "I'm sorry for snooping. I gotta admit I was getting turned on by looking at it. I can see why he's probably so emotional about it. He probably still wants you. I'm sure of it."

"Whatever. He hates me. I just can't get over how evil he was to me, how he spoke to me."

"Yeah, the death threats were uncalled for. I might have to have a chat with him."

"No, no. I don't need you getting involved or to fight my battles. It's all good. I got something for him. I just have to do a little video editing."

"Oh, boy. I'm scared to know what you are planning."

"Don't worry. I'll show you soon. He won't even see it coming. Have you heard of that site that exposes men called dontdatethatdick.com? It usually showcases embarrassing videos or photos of married men, con artists, or gay men on the down low. It's a warning site, but it's kind of like a revenge site."

"No, I never heard of it. Thank God I behave myself, though. I doubt that I'm on it."

"Well, I might put his ass up there. Just for kicks."

"Oh, no, you're not gonna do that, because you'll be in it."

"I have photos of him alone and footage that I'm not in, and besides, there's ways to edit things. Did you forget I went to design school? I'm pretty handy in Photoshop." She laughed. "But I'm just playing. It's not worth the trouble. That would probably cause a lot of problems for him. I'm not gonna do it." Journey tossed the phone to the side and cuddled on Dominick. Her head was spinning, so she wanted to rest some more.

Chapter 17

Journey

After three days of playing house and being stoned for most of the time, they had to get back to reality. Dominick and Journey went back to their former roles as patient and medical assistant.

Dominick came back from picking Claudia up from the airport. Journey walked slowly to the door, holding onto the wall to greet them. She was a good actress. Her legs were working just fine now without support. She didn't need her cane or the wall.

"Mom!" Journey hugged her tightly.

"Hey, Nini. I missed you, baby." She hugged and kissed Journey on the forehead.

"So, how was your trip?"

"Oh, it was nice to see some of my colleagues and my presentation went really well."

"Did you meet anyone?"

"No, it's just business."

"Boo, so boring. You need to be working on my rich new stepdad already."

"Oh, stop it." She playfully slapped Journey on her back with a bundle of mail in her hand.

"Ouch." Journey laughed as they walked into the kitchen.

"My, my. It smells so good here. What is that smell? Candles? Incense?"

"Yes, it's both. Dominick mopped too." Journey winked at Dominick as her mother turned her back to put the mail on the counter.

"Ah, that's so nice. It's so good to come home to a clean house. Thank you, Dominick." She smiled warmly at him. If she only knew why he had to clean so thoroughly.

"We got a lot of mail. You forgot to check the box in three days, huh?"

"Oh, yeah. I'm sorry, Claudia. That's my bad," Dominick said and shrugged at Journey. The two of them had been having sex all around the house. The mail was the last thing on their minds. They were high off weed and 'shrooms the majority of the time. The undercover lovers were in a cleaning frenzy and spent the better half of the morning cleaning up. They had to mop, vacuum, and crack windows to air out the house, so that her mother wouldn't have a clue of the debauchery that went on while she was away.

"Hmmm. Would you look at this? You got something from the courts." She handed a card to

Journey. "Don't tell me you have tickets you didn't pay again? You need to handle your responsibilities now that you're back working."

"I don't think I have any tickets, and I'm only working two days a week. Let me see." Journey opened up a perforated postcard from the Atlanta County Clerk's office.

Her mother looked over her shoulder to see.

Journey turned and hid the paper from her. "Geez, Mom, why don't you go unpack? You are so nosy."

Dominick had just finished bringing her suitcase to her room and asked, "Claudia, do you want any tea or anything?"

"No, sweetie, that's okay. Thanks for picking me up. You've done enough. I'm probably gonna just order some food."

Journey read it over and over. She thought it was a mistake, but it wasn't. It was her name. The words jumped off of the notice and shook her to her core.

> *Your willful failure to obey this order may be subject to mandatory or criminal prosecution, which may result in your incarceration.*

She sat down, almost missing the chair.

Her mother laughed. "What happened? Is the bill that big? What happened? Do you have to go to court?" She grabbed the paper from Journey's weak hands as she sat there staring at the garden.

"Oh my God." Claudia read the paper and looked at Dominick to see if he was paying attention. He tried to act busy and put a pot of tea on for himself. He walked away for a moment, but he was really eavesdropping in the hallway.

Claudia pulled her aside and spoke softer. "What happened? Did something else happen? What made him do this?"

"I told you, Ma. I told you I shouldn't have called him. It was your fault. You made me call him. I should've just left it all alone. This is fucking terrible. This is all on my fucking record now. I can't believe this. Making me look like a crazy stalker!"

"Watch your mouth."

"Can you get it off? Please can you get it off like you did before? This is so embarrassing. It's gonna be on my background check when I've been trying to find a full-time job. Marlon is such a fucking asshole. I hate him. I hate him!"

Dominick came running down the hall. "What's wrong? Is everything okay? What's going on?"

Journey lifted up the restraining order court date and waved it in the air. "Do you know this jerk filed a restraining order against me? Like I'm really gonna come after him. I'm gonna stalk *him*? Give me a fucking break!"

"Nini, your mouth!"

"I'm sorry, I'm sorry, Mom. I'm just frustrated. I'm sick of it all. It's not even my fault."

"Journey, life has consequences. I saw the video." She pulled her aside and shot her a look to be quiet.

"He knows. You can talk about it. Dominick knows everything."

"Everything?"

"It's okay. I just, I can't believe he did this. He's so damn petty."

"Well, we will just follow the rules, and it won't be any problem. It's a temporary order, and we can most likely get it dismissed. Don't worry. I can help you handle it. Okay?"

"I don't want this on my record." She paced fast, almost forgetting to add a little limp when she walked. She held onto the counter to pretend she needed support.

"Just relax. We'll figure it out. I can help you."

Ty

"That's what I'm talking about," Ty mumbled to himself as he reviewed the company's latest numbers. The new building was almost sold out even before the official opening, and people were RSVPing in droves to the special launch date.

His office door was ajar, and he heard fast-paced steps coming toward him. Marlon knocked twice while walking in. There was a tightness in his eyes, and he was breathing hard.

"Hey, man, how are you? You look like shit. What happened to you?"

Marlon's suit was damp, and he held a cup of coffee in his hand. He closed the door behind him. "Thanks. I think I look pretty good after a really fucked up morning. For starters, I had to Uber here, because I had two flat tires."

Ty jerked back in disbelief.

"Yep, two." Held up two fingers.

"I'm sorry. Damn, that's crazy."

"Yeah, what's crazier is that it happened about three o'clock in the morning when I was in my bed sleeping." He sipped his coffee and pulled out a chair across from Ty. He tilted his head with raised brows.

Ty said, "Oh, come onnn. You don't think it was her, do you? She just started walking. Maybe you ran over something. I had a slow leak in two tires one time."

"Cameras don't lie."

"You got footage of her?" Ty leaned in.

"Well, someone came with all black on. They had gloves and a ski mask on, so I can't even see the skin tone. The shit was well planned out by a pro. They put a knife in my shit and were in and out within a minute."

"That's fucked up. You don't think it could be any of your exes?"

"Oh no, no. Hell no. I know I fucked over a few chicks in the past, but that was a long time ago, and they're too grown to be carrying on like this. It was her, man. If she didn't do it, she got somebody else to do it. And you know why, because I just filed the order of protection last week. We have a court date in a few weeks."

Ty had a hunch maybe she could be tied to it somehow, but he wasn't sure. "Let me see this video." He reached out his hand, and Marlon passed him the phone.

"It's grainy as fuck. It was raining outside."

"That's definitely not her. That's a man. You gotta go to the police. You need to put your car in the garage from now on until you figure this shit out."

"I'm getting more cameras and lights. I'm not fucking around. This shit really had me bugging. I almost ain't come in today, but I know we have a lot of things to tie up with the launch."

"You know, it could be one of our tenants we evicted. Who knows? Maybe it's an old employee we fired in the past?

"Come on, Ty. It's *her,* nigga." He slammed the desk. "Use your fucking super powers. Why do you want to cover for this bitch? She has something to do with it. I know it. The timing is too coincidental. She's doing it to spite me, right after filing the order of protection."

"So, are you going to go to the cops?"

"I don't know. I don't know yet. I didn't at first, since I didn't review the footage. I thought it was something I rode over in Midtown. I don't have enough proof. I'm thinking of handling it in another way." He took a sip of his coffee and shot Ty a sinister smile.

"I don't like the sound of that, man."

"The less you know, the better." Marlon stood up.

Ty pointed at him and shook his finger. "Don't do anything stupid, Marlon. Marlon! I'm serious. Especially with no proof."

"No, it's all good. I'ma catch whoever it was. They parked around the corner of my house. I think I'm going to investigate on my own and see if I can get some footage of that car." Marlon slapped the table. "Well, that was your update. Gotta run to my ten o'clock with IT. They want to talk about more things we need to spend a shitload of money on. Cyber security enhancement shit we touched on before. We'll talk later. I gotta clear my head." He rushed out, avoiding any more debate.

Ty had a bad feeling about what he was up to.

Journey

Journey wasn't sure how Natalia was going to react to her text, since the last time they saw

each other, she pretty much cut her off. She knew
that deep down, Natalia still cared about her. Her
mother said she did come to the hospital when
she was first admitted and called a few times to
see how she was doing. However, she hadn't seen
her since she woke up. Although Journey was nervous to reconnect, she missed her friend and
wanted to clear the air. She knew the reality was
that they would never be the same again. The lies
and betrayal were a bit much for Journey.

They met at a diner where they used to always
go after hanging out at a club or a lounge. It was
pretty busy and somewhat noisy with groups of
thirty-somethings sipping mimosas and laughing
loudly. The waitresses balanced several plates as
they hurried down the tight aisles of the happy
brunch crowd. Journey was always impressed with
their agility. Although there was a lot of upbeat
chaos going on around them, Journey was happy
for the distractions, in case she found herself at a
loss for words.

The sunlight glowed through the tall windows
and shone brightly over their table. Journey
noticed an extra glow on her friend's face. She
seemed content and happy.

"I'm glad you decided to meet with me after all
the bullshit I put you guys through."

Natalia looked shocked, since it was rare to ever
hear Journey apologize.

"Yeah, it was a lot, Journey, and you really did scare the hell out of us all. But I'm glad that you're okay now." She tilted her head, examining Journey. "You seem different."

"It's the hair."

"No, no, and I meant to tell you it's really cute, but it's not that."

"Well, after you almost die, it changes you." She held a smirk, trying to make light of it all. "I really had enough time to work on myself, or at least start. I thought about what I've done, and I'm actually quite embarrassed. But I really did almost die."

"No shit. Falling out of a building and surviving is miraculous."

"Well, thankfully it wasn't all the way to the ground floor. But I did almost cross over for a minute. I'm sure of it."

"What do you mean? Did you really flatline?"

"Yes, I saw my grandmother on Ty's side of the family, and it was wild, because I never met her."

Natalia leaned in with childlike wonder. "Really? What was it like?"

"The white light just envelops you. It pulls you in. It's like you don't want to leave. It's a calming feeling. It just feels like home. I saw people, not their faces, but I felt more of them. They were my ancestors for sure. But then, then . . . I remembered them pumping my chest, doing CPR. It was a violent shock. I guess they brought me back for a little while, then I just ended up in a coma for two months."

"Wow, that's incredible." She looked stunned with raised brows, but then Natalia said softly with a straight face, "*So,* no flames? No fire and brimstone?"

"You bitch!"

They cracked up. Journey missed her sick sense of humor that matched hers so well.

"I really wanted to meet with you for a couple of reasons." She took a deep breath. "One, obviously to tell you that I am sorry for my behavior."

Natalia bowed her head, acknowledging the gesture.

"I should have never acted that way. And two, I wanted to tell you that I absolutely did not try to kill myself. No one believes me, but I promise you I am not suicidal at all. Papa made me do it."

Natalia snickered. "Say what now? What do you mean? That little old man couldn't hurt a fly."

Journey spoke softer and looked directly into her eyes. "Look, I know it sounds crazy as fuck, but you have to believe me. There's a lot of things you don't know about my family. My family has gifts. Ty has it too. We can read minds. We can talk to each other without speaking, and that's just the start of it all."

"You know, somehow I believe that. Ty seems to really read me."

"That's because he does. Papa sent me messages in my dreams too. I've seen him. He wanted me out of the way. I was too much trouble, so I get it. I am not one hundred percent sure how he did it, but I recently remembered hearing his voice telling me there was a fire and to escape. I'm sure that's what happened. It goes way deeper than what you know. I feel we can impose even feelings on someone."

Natalia's mouth dropped as if her mind was recalling times with Ty. "That's wild."

"Oh yeah, so you got to be careful about Ty. I'm still learning a lot through trial and error. I don't think he really uses his abilities as much as I do. He's so stuck in the corporate world and doesn't make time to meditate and connect with his gift. At least from what I've observed. But maybe he's changed."

"I hope you know what you're doing, because what if it was a dark spirit just playing around with you, telling you to jump? You might have conjured up something evil for all you know."

"I highly doubt that, Nat. It doesn't work like that, at least not for me. Well, that's another reason I wanted to talk. How are you and Ty doing? He's actually acting cordial with me."

"He's been treating me better than I ever have been. I work full time now for him. He's been such a blessing."

"Are you a couple?"

"No, no. We just date for now."

"Well, that's good." Journey tried to smile through her jealousy. "It's still a little weird for me, but I see now I was being kind of selfish."

"Kinda?"

"Well, I don't know if I just got emotional about things. I just don't like being played for a fool. When it happened, I felt betrayed. It's like an obsession, and I couldn't stop thinking about it. I'm on some pills now for my anxiety and other shit."

"Oh, really?"

She didn't want to say what Dr. Brinson prescribed for her or what she was diagnosed with. "It's cool now, but I did have some wild shit just happen. Marlon filed a restraining order on me."

"Wow, really? Well, after what happened between you two, I guess."

"Yeah, but what did he think? That I was going to stalk him?"

"Journey, if I were you, I would just stay far, far away from him. He's a bit extreme, and I think he's still shaken up."

"What do you mean? He's shaken up that I'm still alive, I bet. He thinks I'm the fucking boogie man."

"I mean, he's super paranoid and high strung about everything since that incident. But I got to ask you, what made you do that? Take photos of him and *everything* else? Ty told me. That was cold blooded, Journey."

Journey knew 'everything else' meant the Devil's Breath and stealing money. She didn't have a good answer, though.

"Seriously, like what the fuck are you smoking, girl? I thought you had some laced weed or something that had you tripping."

"Yeah, I wish that's all it was. Look, I may be a little sick. The therapist is working with me to understand what's going on in my mind."

"Really? What is the therapist saying?"

"I don't really wanna get into it right now, but I don't know. I'm torn to believe it. I just get really emotional about things, and I can't stop thinking about something, then it just makes me a little crazy, I guess."

She didn't want to tell Natalia about all her demons. "Let's just say I'm working on myself, and let the past be the past, okay?" She looked up at the ceiling, hoping to push back the tears she felt coming. "Are we cool?"

"Yeah, we're good."

We're good just meant they were acquaintances. They could never be besties again. She got the message, but she was happy to at least have that connection with her.

"I'm glad you're doing better, Journey. I had a nice time catching up."

"I'm glad I could see you again. Thanks for accepting my apology. If things work out with you and Ty, just know I'm not calling you Mom, like ever. Fuck that."

They both laughed.

"You better respect your elders, bitch."

They gave each other a hug and kiss on the cheek goodbye. The tears she held back cascaded down her face. Journey quickly brushed them away.

She walked to her car, rushing to teach her yoga classes in person after such a long wait. One of the studios she worked in part-time took her back after her long hiatus. She had a long day ahead and was excited to be back.

Chapter 18

Ty

Ty woke up after a long night. He yawned as he sat up on the side of the bed to answer his phone. Marlon called him on FaceTime, and his face was full of anguish. He pointed to the screen aggressively.

"Just get my bail money ready now, nigga, 'cause I'm going to jail!" He panted and kicked a garbage pail to the ground as he paced around his house.

"What is wrong with you?" Ty shouted back at Marlon.

"Oh, you have no idea, man. This has been the worst day of my life! Why did my sister call me, telling me some wild shit about the people from the neighborhood, my old neighborhood in Brooklyn?" He paced up and down his hallway. "People calling her, asking if I'm single or did I turn gay yet, since I'm in Atlanta." He shrugged his shoulders. "And this is all because they saw me online . . . with my dick out."

Ty tried not to laugh. "What? What's wrong with that? Don't you promote yourself on those apps or send ladies pics with your dick out?" Ty smirked.

"No, now hold on, hold on! Let me finish this. I put myself out there for a date in suits. These pictures show my dick and my motherfucking face, Ty. Do you understand how embarrassing this is? Ain't no denying it. My face is in the picture," he said through gritted teeth. "You know how I feel about them pictures. I don't fucking do that. Only with someone I'm seeing. I don't do that. The only person that had them photos was Journey. These are the same photos she fucking took. She posted them!"

"Are you sure?"

"Yeah, I'm sure. One thousand percent sure," he muttered to himself. "That fucking little bitch. I know that's her way of retaliating, since we got a court date in less than thirty days."

"Marlon, is she in the picture? Are you sure it's the same pictures?"

"Ty, she posted a video of my hands in her purple panties. She posted a photo of me with a rock-hard dick, butt naked. The bitch is crazy." His voice went up an octave. Marlon was always bragging on his dick, so now when he finally got it on display, he was losing control.

Marlon kept looking at his incoming text messages. "Lord only knows who has seen these pictures and how many sites they're on. This is not the kinda fame I wanted, B. Yo, Ty, she's in one of the fucking pictures, but she blurred out her face, so I know it was her! First she comes for my tires, and now this shit?" Marlon paced back and forth. He punched the wall. "I told you it was fucking her. I told you she paid somebody to slash my tires. Now, my shit is all over the damn Internet. The girl is sick! Sick! Sick!"

"Damn. I don't know what to say. I'm sure it will blow over soon." Ty hoped it would, as long as the true story never got into the hands of his biggest fan/hater, Candace Overton, the reporter.

"Blow over. Blow over? No, we gotta do something about this. It's not just my photos. It's my rep. You know how this can hurt us? If you don't stop Journey, she's gonna keep coming for more."

"It doesn't seem to be working in her favor. Think about it. She was trying to ruin your rep. Seems like it did the opposite."

"Yep, she would hope that she was damaging me, when in reality, she is making all of my old bitches want to hit me up."

"But your fucking sister saw it, though? That's what would set me off." Ty covered his mouth, holding back a laugh.

"Yeah, man, the whole goddamn neighborhood saw it. Everybody's getting a good laugh out of it. The haters are thinking I've fallen on hard times and turned to the streets to make money. Like I got an Only Fans page and shit." His voice cracked. "This is so humiliating, man. But look, I'm just happy it's just a picture and one video. I don't know what I would do if she posted those other ones. That video of me calling her a master would ruin me."

"Damn, it was that bad?"

"That Devil's Breath drug ain't no joke. But I'm gonna put a stop to this shit."

Ty held the camera closer to his face. "Don't do anything stupid, man."

Journey

Journey sat in her car, primping. She was on a natural high, getting ready to be in her element once again. She put on eyeliner, mascara, and some pink lip gloss. This was her first time posting a reel on Instagram since the accident. A few days before, she had posted the flier announcing her new class, but she was dreading the response. She was nervous about people sending her messages about the accident, about the "suicide attempt," just all of it.

She recorded her Instagram reel.

"Hey, what's up, my loves. I'm baaaaaaack! I'm teaching a hot yoga class Mondays, Wednesdays, and Fridays at Sunset Yoga studios. I hope to see you there. Click the link to register. The first class is free. I can't wait to see you all."

There were just a few very concerned comments, but they kept it light. Journey knew it would die down eventually, and if she didn't like the comment or question someone posted, she could ignore, delete, or just block. It was time to move forward.

Journey had started back doing virtual classes, but she needed to be in person to feel the energy of the room. It was like her church. The students were her congregation, and she was the minister. Journey also had to admit that she loved the attention.

When she arrived, there was a nice surprise waiting for her. There was a dazzling bouquet of yellow, red, and orange roses. The receptionist looked up from her book and said, "Oh, hey. Journey, these came for you."

"Oh, thank you! What a nice surprise."

"Somebody came by like an hour ago and dropped them off. Word got out quick that you were back. I sent an email to our list."

"Thank you so much." She held the flowers and smelled them. "Wow, these are beautiful." The vibrant colors were arranged so elegantly. They were not cheap flowers from the supermarket. She looked at the card, and there was no name. It just said:

Welcome back. We missed you. I missed you.

"Do you remember who came by and brought them? Is it someone on the list for class?" Journey looked over her shoulder at the registrants. There was soft orange lighting in the room with about eight or nine people already lying on their yoga mats.

"No, I think it was a delivery guy. I had never seen him before. Older white guy. He didn't have a FedEx uniform, though, or make me sign for anything." She shrugged and glanced back down at her notes. She must have been a college student studying for a test or something.

Journey had a feeling that she knew who it was, but she wasn't quite sure. She was just glad the flowers were not black. She was not in the mood for Helen's evil tricks again. She felt grateful that people did miss her, even if they gossiped about what had really happened.

When she walked into the actual yoga room, she was met with huge applause. Out of the nine students, there were five of them from the other studio that she recognized. They all came up and hugged her. She felt so good as her eyes welled with tears.

"Welcome back."

"You look amazing."

"We prayed so hard for you, girl."

"You are a walking miracle."

"I love your short hairdo."

She was overjoyed by the reception and didn't realize people really cared. Maybe the rumors about her "arrangements" didn't spread as badly as she had imagined.

Her class was well received. It was fairly easy to get back into the groove of it, especially since she wasn't moving with them. She sat on a chair with a bottle of water nearby. Journey took them all through a slow vinyasa. The class was called Slow and Sexy. It was a hot yoga class, which she thought would be good for her body to detox and help her heal faster.

She taught three classes that day and was exhausted. When the day was over, Journey waited for the receptionist to lock up. They had a policy that no one closed up by themselves, especially since the area was pretty desolate after five o'clock. The neighboring stores were only a shoe store, a bank, and the post office.

Once Paula was safe and in her car, Journey waved to her, and Paula sped off. Journey began checking her phone, and before she knew it, she was scrolling on Instagram looking at all the comments, raving about the class. It was a bad habit she hadn't broken, since sometimes she could be in her car for fifteen minutes, looking at comments. She turned on her car and was about to pull out when she got a call that made her smile.

His familiar voice seemed a little nervous. "Hey there, beautiful. Did you get the flowers?"

"Oh my God, Phil, that was you? Thank you so much, but you are not supposed to be calling me. I don't need any more problems with your psycho wife."

"That's okay. She's calmed down. You have nothing to worry about. I'm just happy that you're back. Sorry I missed it today. I had to work."

"I appreciate it. Thank you so much. The flowers are beautiful, and the message was sweet. I miss you too, Phil."

"Maybe one day we can catch up."

"No, I don't want any trouble. I wish I was twenty years older."

"Oh, yeah, I don't. I like you just the way you are."

"That's because you're a dirty old man." She laughed.

"Hey, I was just gonna say we can meet for coffee to chat about your wellness center. Just to talk. I do want to invest and help you grow."

Phil knew exactly what he was doing. He knew A Place for Janet was a sweet spot for her, and talking about investing definitely got her attention.

"Before you say anything, my name doesn't have to be on anything. I can be an angel investor. Nobody needs to know, but I want to help you get back on your feet, and I know this is a big part of your dream."

"Thank you. You know, that sounds really good, Phil. Really good. I'm down. We should meet one day soon."

"All right, I'm gonna call you on Monday, and we'll figure it out. Have a good night, kiddo."

Still parked in her car, Journey went back to Instagram and posted a few selfies and group photos from the class. She was feeling confident.

Everything was going just the way she wanted. Soon she'd have a nice fat check to get started on her dream. She was posting away to show off just a little. This way, any of her haters could see she was back to normal. They could gossip all they wanted. She was going to get money either way.

Journey was shaken out of her social media trance when the loud roar of a car's engine startled her. A car pulled up behind her. She was the only one in the deserted parking lot. The huge black SUV turned their lights off and blocked her in so that she couldn't reverse. She got a bad vibe from it. It reminded her of the car chasing her in a nightmare she recently had. Her stomach churned from that warning. She looked out her window to see if she recognized the car. The windows were tinted. The passenger side window went down slowly.

"Heeey, Journey." The man wore a baseball cap and a dark scarf around his nose and mouth. She was terrified.

"Who are you? Why are you blocking me in? Can you please move?"

"We heard you were teaching yoga today. Word on the street is, you're *really* good." His eyes did not look familiar. She couldn't make out who the driver was and only saw his profile. The driver never looked her way and sat back in the shadows of the vehicle.

"Yes, class was over thirty minutes ago. Is this some kind of prank?"

"Oh, now, I don't play games or do pranks. Actually, we heard you think you're a comedian."

"Huh?"

"You know, doing some funny shit like slashing tires and putting naked photos and videos up. Not nice, Journey." He kissed his teeth. "Tsk tsk. Not nice at all."

"What are you talking about? I never did anything like that! Can you please get out of the way? I . . . I gotta. I gotta goooo home."

"Oh, you don't know what I'm talking about now? You putting niggas' sex tapes up on the Internet without their permission. Talk about violation. You gotta be punished, baby girl."

Her heart beat fast as beads of perspiration formed on her forehead. She fumbled with her phone, trying to record them, but her hands were too shaky. "I'm sorry, who are you? How do I know you? Are you friends with Marlon and Ty?" Her voice shook. "This isn't fucking funny."

"You're so right. It's not." He reached in his pocket, and the sparkle from a shiny gun reflected in the streetlight. "But don't worry about who I am. Just take that video and picture down ASAP." He pointed the gun and cocked it. "Don't fucking scream either."

Tears stung Journey's eyes. She felt her throat constrict. Journey instantly raised her hands in the air. She whimpered, "Oh my God, oh my God.

What are you doing? You have me mixed up. I didn't do anything. I swear! I don't know what you're talking about. I didn't slash anyone's tires. I don't know what video you're talking about. I didn't do anything, please! I didn't do anything."

The coldness in his eyes sent an icy chill to the marrow of her bones. "Take the motherfuckin' video down. We're gonna come back for you, and it's gonna be worse than what's happening to your car."

He pointed his gun. Journey screamed, ducked, and covered her ears from the gunshots.

Pop. Pop. Pop. Pop.

Her car jerked and lowered to one side. She continued to scream at the top of her lungs.

He shouted, "Didn't I say to not fucking scream? Tell the cops, and your home is next and everyone in it. That's not a threat. It's a promise, bitch," he said through gritted teeth.

She heard the car skid off, then a loud crash. Journey realized the only damage was to her tires, since her car was lopsided. She sat up slowly, realizing they were gone, but saw they had rammed into a pole before they drove off. "Oh my God. Did I do that?" Journey had been picturing the truck being squashed with everyone in it.

She was trembling so much that she had dropped her phone on the floor by the gas pedal. She frantically dialed 911, then hung up in fear that they would follow through with their threat. She gasped for breath. The shock took over. Her hands continued to tremble as she held them out and looked at them over the steering wheel. "What the fuck! Who the fuck was that? It's Marlon! I know it was him."

She called Dominick instead. "I need you to come get me. My car, it's got a flat. Can you hurry? I'm at the yoga studio."

"Okay, are you safe? You're not on the road, right?"

"No, I'm in the parking lot."

"Why do you sound like that?"

" I'm okay. Please just hurry."

"All right. I'll be there in fifteen. Please stay in your car. You're making me nervous, Journey."

"Just hurry."

Chapter 19

Ty

Earlier that morning

Ty realized Journey had really gone off the deep end and maybe he could help in some way. "Look, let me talk to her. Maybe I can find out—"

"No, no talking needed. It's handled. I'm not gonna come in tomorrow. I got to deal with this legal shit and get these pictures down somehow. I'm so pissed. She's gonna pay for my tires too. I'm so sick of her lies. What the hell did I do to deserve this shit? Nothing! She's trying to destroy my life, as if I did something to her. I gotta go. I'll hit you later." Marlon hung up.

A warm hand caressed Ty's back as he sat on the edge of the bed.

"You okay? What happened?" Jocelyn pulled herself up onto her elbows.

"Journey's at it again."

"What did she do now?"

"It's a long story, but apparently she's doing things to antagonize Marlon again. It seems to be some tit for tat craziness since he filed a restraining order against her. Now she's posting nude pictures of him on the internet. She's out of control."

"Shit, she's fucking crazy. Nude pictures? How does she even have them? Journey doesn't know how crazy Marlon is."

"He thinks that she slashed his tires or got someone to do it too, but he doesn't have any proof. There was a shadowy figure on video, but they couldn't make out a face. It looked like a dude to me."

"Could she do that, though? I thought she couldn't even walk without help."

"I honestly don't think it was her. Or even related to her, I told him it could be a disgruntled employee or an ex-tenant that we checked out. With Marlon, it could be anybody, some crazy ex-girlfriend. Who knows? But this naked picture shit is a whole other story, since she had to be the only one to share it."

"Well, that's what you get when you deal with little girls. She is too young for him."

"Don't you remember he was drugged? I honestly don't think he had intentions. Yeah, he's a flirt, but I don't think he would ever go through that unless he was really under the influence."

"That girl has been nothing but bad luck since she entered our lives."

"Yeah, and now she's diagnosed with some mental shit. I'm sure that's going to be a cop-out all the time. I'm really worried more about Marlon, because I know he has a temper, and he isn't wrapped too tight when people mess with him."

"What are you going to do? Are you going to try to squash it?"

"Honestly, I truly want to stay out of it."

"No, maybe you can talk some sense into her."

"I think I'm gonna have to go over there tomorrow, maybe, and involve her mother, since she doesn't listen to me anyway. I'm afraid it's going to escalate into something more serious. I just have a gut feeling."

Just then, Marlon sent a screenshot of the page dontdatethatdick.com. It included the video and the photo.

Name: Marlon C. from Brooklyn lives in Atlanta.

Beware! His New York swag will hook you in, and he is a good fuck if you like less than 5 mins. He's a selfish lover. He'll spend money on you in the beginning and then treat you like shit. Be careful of community penis. He's a class act dick. Run!

12,141 Likes

#Dontdatethatdick

"Oh, man, this can't be good. He just sent me a screenshot of what was posted."

"Lemme see?" She tried to peek over his shoulder.

"No, mind your business." Ty wasn't laughing, but Joycelyn was.

Marlon

Ty was furious and called Marlon back. "That's it. I'm going over there later."

"Hold up, man. Let me go with you."

"Fine. We need to come to a civilized conclusion of what the hell is going on."

"I don't want to be civilized." Marlon slammed something hard. "I'm sick of being fucking civilized."

"Look, you don't want to go to jail, man. So, if you're gonna come, you gotta act right."

"Whatever. Let's go there right after work."

Marlon showed up that evening.

"Wow, that post was wild. I'm so sorry, man."

"Let's get this handled already. My reputation is on the line all because I wanted a restraining order and she wants revenge. I don't know what the fuck made her so evil. All I can say is she made good on her threat. She told me the pictures and the videos were in the cloud, trying to be funny. She's full of shit. She posted this, no denying. You see how many likes that shit has? Over twelve thousand!

God only knows how many people forwarded this shit already."

"Yeah, this is really bad."

Journey opened the door slowly. She said to Marlon, "Oh, I see you brought a bodyguard. Are you violating a restraining order? How ironic, when you sent someone who almost killed me tonight."

Marlon held back a laugh, but the smirk on his face was hard to hide. He was happy that he had scared the shit out of her. That was just the start of what he would do if she didn't take those photos down.

Ty's eyes darted back and forth between Journey and Marlon, clueless.

Marlon really didn't want to hear Ty's shit and was gonna plead the Fifth till the cows came home. He didn't care if Ty could probe his mind with his magical powers. He was never going to admit it.

Marlon yelled, "I don't know what the hell you're talking about. You just need to take these pictures down!"

Ty ignored Marlon's request. He was more interested in what Journey had said.

"What is she talking about, Marlon?" Ty knew he had done something.

Claudia said, "Ty, did you know about this?"

"No, not at all. I'm trying to figure out what's really going on with you all before this gets out of hand."

"Oh, it's already out of hand!" Journey yelled. "Ty, he sent some thugs to come to my job and shoot at my car. I know he did it. Before he shot my tires, the guy yelled something about taking down the pictures. He threatened to shoot up my house and everyone in it."

"What? Really? Guns?" He turned to Marlon and shook his head. "You can't be serious."

Marlon shrugged nonchalantly. "Who else would post this?" He held up his phone to her face, displaying the photo. "You are the only one that had this photo!"

Dominick came to the front of the door. "So, you're not denying it? You sent those men to terrorize her?"

The wind whistled through the trees, and it started to rain. Claudia waved them inside. "Everyone come in before the neighbors call the cops on us. You're getting wet, and we don't need all this commotion."

They stood in the foyer, and the tension was building among them all.

Dominick spoke sternly. "We need to call the cops. This is bullshit. Why don't you tell them how you sent some thugs to shoot at Journey tonight? What kind of pussy does shit like that? I just came back from picking her up. She was terrified. Her car has two flat tires and needs to be towed now. We should have you arrested right now."

"My man, I don't know you from a motherfucking hole in the wall. You watch your mouth. Call me out my name again. I don't know anything about that." Marlon pointed in his face. "I don't have nothing to do with nothing. My hands are clean. I don't know what other people found out and took it upon themselves to do."

Journey started to cry. "What else do you want from me? I stayed away from you, Marlon. I haven't bothered you. I apologized."

"But you slashed my tires, or you got someone to do it." Marlon looked at Dominick's lengthy frame up and down. "Then to add insult to injury, you put up the very photos and video that you took. The ones you took when you drugged me." He turned to Dominick. "You know that part of the story? I bet not. Fucking drugged me to get fucked. You don't even know who you are defending so fearlessly, my guy. She's a whore." He pointed to Journey, and Ty held him back from going in her face. "You put my name up on that site, dontdatethatdick.com. Are you fucking happy? I got my own family calling me about it."

"What? I did not! It's on that site?" She looked at her mother and then Dominick. "You're insane. Why the hell would I put that up?" She wiped her tears.

Claudia held her chest in a panic. "But how could that be? Didn't I delete the pictures?"

"Apparently not all the way, because it seems as if I might have been hacked. They are backed up somewhere."

Journey turned to Marlon. "Somebody could have hacked you or me. I swear to you, I did not put them up. Why do you think I would put my body up there?"

"Oh, how convenient that you blurred yourself out. Nobody can tell that it is you, but my face and my dick is on full blast. Look, I don't got time for your games. Just take the fucking shit down. I'm not leaving until you do."

Dominick chimed in. "Yo, watch your mouth. She already told you she didn't put it up, so how can she take it down?"

Journey looked visibly shaken and confused. Claudia put her hand on Journey's shoulder, "Is this true? Did you do that?"

"No! No! Absolutely not. That's crazy."

Marlon said, "You owe me for two tires, and I'm still pressing charges on you, so I don't give a fuck."

"She doesn't owe you anything. She's either here at the house, the yoga studio, or a doctor's appointment," Dominick shouted.

Marlon's forehead tightened. "Come on now, I'm not an idiot. She didn't have to do it herself. She could have paid some soft nigga like you to do it."

"Yo, bro, you really trying to see how soft I am?"

"What, nigga? It probably was you. You look all pussy whipped. Ain't you supposed to be the nurse or something?" he asked with his finger pointing at Dominick. Then he poked him in the chest.

Dominick was about to hit Marlon before Ty got in between them. He put some more bass in his voice, and the commanding tone made Journey and Claudia jump. "Both of you, chill the fuck out." He pushed them both apart.

"Stop it. Please stop it!" Claudia yelled.

Marlon said, "She also previously threatened me about the photo, so that she can blame someone for hacking. There's no question. I know she did it."

"Marlon, please, I never shared that photo. Only to you. How do I know? Maybe someone in your network got a hold of your phone. You're in the public more than I am. I was in a coma for two months. Anything could have happened then."

"Please, stop the whining. I'm not buying it." Marlon rolled his eyes and waved her off, dismissing her pleas.

"Excuse us." Ty grabbed Journey's arm and started to walk toward the hallway.

She looked back. "No, no, I don't want them to be alone and start fighting."

"Let me talk to you for a minute please." He pointed at Marlon. "Hey, can you chill out?"

Claudia plastered on a fake smile and took a deep breath. "Actually, Marlon, I'd like to talk to you alone." Claudia turned to Dominick and gave him a gentle head nod as a sign to leave the room. Ty wasn't sure what she was up to, but it seemed as if she wanted to deescalate the situation.

Dominick crossed his arms. "And leave you alone with this hothead?"

Marlon looked him in the eyes and cracked his knuckles. "My man, you call me out my name one more time."

Claudia said softly, "Please, please stop yelling. Dominick, just leave us for a few minutes. I'll be fine."

"I'm right outside in the kitchen if you need me." Dominick slowly walked away.

Ty

Ty was exhausted from all of the drama. "Journey, you really don't know where this stuff happened? You really didn't do it, did you?"

Journey said, "God. You guys really think I'm that evil? First, I'm getting accused of slashing tires, and now this shit. Have you seen my new life? I don't have time to play games like this. And what would be the purpose?"

He tilted his head a few degrees in suggested disbelief. "Well, Journey, let's be real. You don't exactly have the best track record of making the best decisions. He assumed you were trying to get revenge on him since he filed the order of protection."

"Well, obviously I'm pissed about that. It was so fucking unnecessary, especially since I've reached out to him to apologize and nothing else. All I do is stay home and go to yoga and keep it to myself, so why would he even think that I'm coming after him? Give me a fucking break. His ego is out of this world. Last time I spoke to him, he just cussed me out and wouldn't even let me get a word in, so I left it alone. Now I'm being accused of some dumb shit."

She waved her hands toward the room Marlon was in. "I'm stressed out already. I can't do it anymore. This shit is exhausting. I'm trying to get my life together and make amends with my wrongs that I've done. Maybe he has other enemies, some chick he fucked over, but I swear it wasn't me. Read me, Ty! Can't you tell I'm not lying? I'm not lying." She got the vibe that Ty did believe her.

He patted her hand and said, "All right. We're going to figure this out."

Dominick had been eavesdropping in the next room. "Is everything okay in here?" He nodded to Ty.

"Hey, man."

"Yeah, the last time I saw you, you made Journey cry. Seems like you are upsetting her again." He shrugged.

"Look, this doesn't concern you."

Journey touched Ty's arm gently. "It kinda does, since he's with me most of the time. He came and got me when they shot my tires. Marlon's thugs threatened everyone in my house too. It was terrifying. You have no idea. They had a gun! Like, I didn't deserve any of this."

Ty put both his hands on her shoulders. He searched for a sign of deceit in her eyes but couldn't find any. "I actually feel that you're telling the truth, and I hope that you are."

"I am, and two can play his game. I will have to file an order of protection as well, if he doesn't stop accusing me and threatening me, especially when he has no solid proof. All this shit would never hold up in court at all."

"Well, there is a way. Maybe they'll be able to check the IP address of who posted that picture."

Ty wanted to get a reaction out of her, but Journey didn't flinch.

"Good. I want to do that. I want to show that I didn't do it."

Marlon

Marlon and Claudia walked into the living room. He stood by the entrance and observed the huge, elegantly designed space. The lady had class. Too bad her daughter didn't.

Claudia was calm and graceful. She sat down on the couch and crossed her legs. She pointed to the love seat across from her. "Sit, please."

He hesitantly sat down. He was shaking his leg and folded his arms like a bad kid in detention. He thought it was funny how she was trying to play a tough girl when she should have been doing it the entire time she was raising her demon.

"If everything they say is true and you are behind this, I'll let you know that this is harassment. Journey would have no reason to do any of these things to you. She apologized for her behavior in the past. I agree it was uncalled for. But what you did tonight was careless and downright dangerous. It would be considered attempted murder, not just a prank. Real bullets were shot at my child."

"You can't prove that I did anything. And I just find it pretty funny that the picture started going up on the internet right after I filed an order of protection against her. You know, I did some research, and her offense is something she can go to jail for. It's called revenge porn."

"Yeah, I have heard about that. But she didn't do it."

"You should know about it. You're an attorney, right?"

She scoffed, "I don't deal with that kind of law. Sounds like criminal law."

Marlon pulled out his phone and read a blurb. "Well, let me educate you. Revenge porn is a felony when the offender posts a photograph or video on a website that distributes sexually explicit conduct. In that case, a Georgia court may sentence an offender to a one-to-five-year prison sentence and/ or a fine of up to one hundred thousand dollars."

He was getting a kick out of seeing her squirm when she was trying to scare him at first. There was no way to tie him to the event. The guys who did the deed for him didn't even know who really paid them. Marlon was smarter than that. *It's always good to have some criminal friends,* he thought.

"Look, Miss Claudia, your daughter is what I like to call a good evil monster. She's calculating and charming. I know it's hard for you to believe it or admit it, but she is. Seems like you gave her passes all her life, so she feels like she can get away with whatever the hell she wants. I really hope you get her help before she does what she did to me to more men. The next person might not be as nice as I was. After what she did to me, I am actually disappointed she survived that fall."

Marlon leaned in, squinted his eyes, and clenched his jaw, thinking about all she had done to him. His voice was low and menacing, "She's a devious little whore. How can you defend her?"

Claudia jumped up. "That's it! Get the fuck out of my house. Get out! Get *out!*" Her shrill scream echoed down the hallway as she pointed toward the door.

Marlon laughed and walked slowly to the door. "The truth hurts, don't it?"

Dominick yelled, "You need to leave, *now.*"

Ty and Journey rushed into the living room.

"What happened? What's going on?" Ty said softly to Marlon at the door.

"I'm out. I'll be in the car. These broads are crazy. I see where she gets it from." He gave a head nod toward Claudia, standing behind Ty.

Claudia shook her head. "Please leave. You too, Ty. I'm sorry. I don't need this energy in my house. Journey has not done anything wrong."

Journey grabbed his arm. Her eyes were full of sorrow, not guilt. He tried to read her. Either she didn't do it, or she is an incredible actress.

She sent him a message to his mind. "*I swear I did not do anything, not this time. I want peace. I want this to be over.*"

Journey

Journey was exhausted from a long night of arguing. She felt sick after Ty and Marlon left, especially since she didn't know who to trust. She

watched how paranoid Dominick looked when
Marlon mentioned that website dontdatethatdick.
com. Journey couldn't remember for sure, but
she felt as if she had told him about that site. It
just wouldn't make any sense. There was no way
for him to get the photo. Her phone had so much
protection.

She lay in her bed, looking at the ceiling, trying
to recover. Her eyes were swollen from crying so
much. Then she got a call on her cell.

"Hey, hermana."

She sat up, feeling the energy shoot through the
phone. "Who is this? Elizabeth? Elizabeth?"

"Hey, hey! Yes, Journey, it's meeee."

"Wow, it's so good to hear your voice. I thought
you forgot about me. I heard you came to visit
when I was in another dimension."

"Oh, is that what we're calling it now?" She
laughed. "I've been calling you."

"Well, you never left a message."

"How was I supposed to know if maybe you
changed your number? I didn't want to bother you,
in case you were sleeping. I know you're getting
back to your old self. I wasn't sure if you were in
the mood to talk."

"Please, are you kidding me? I miss talking
and connecting so much. My social life has been
weaned down to teaching yoga three days a week,
going to the pharmacy to pick up new drugs, and
hanging with my mom or my nurse boo."

"Wait! Nurse boo? You gotta break that down for me."

"Well, he's not a nurse actually. Dominick is his name, and he's my medical assistant. Now that I'm getting better, he's more like a personal assistant and helps me with errands and things since I don't really need him anymore. I'm finally walking pretty good. I'm still teaching yoga from a chair, but I'll get there soon, and most importantly I can wash my own ass now." They laughed.

"So, if you don't need him, why are you keeping him around?"

Journey let out a hissing laugh. "Girl, if you see him, you will know why I need him."

"Wait, is this the same guy? I think I met him. Was he helping you since you were in a coma? It was this fine-ass Spanish nurse who had tats, nice body, and hazel eyes."

"Yep, that's him, honey, and girl, he's definitely more than just a medical assistant. He can fuck me back to good health." Journey cackled. "Plus, he's so sensual, and he totally gets 'our' worlds. He comes from a long line of shamans."

"Get out of here! You guys are doing it, huh?"

"Every chance we get. I get chills just thinking about him."

"Well, I'm glad somebody is getting chills. All I get is jealous, since the last penis encounter I had was an uneventful ninety seconds of whomp whomp."

"Oh, man. You're not getting some out there in college?"

"It's so not worth getting it here. Some college boys don't know what they are doing yet."

Journey felt like she was going to have to school her little sister. "See, that's the problem. That's why I love an older man. They take the time, and they know more about pleasure. They understand foreplay. They know they need to warm you up to make the experience extremely eventful."

"Well, I should have included that I was his first, soooo I guess I should have known."

"Oh Gawwwd. Who wants that? You have to show them everything."

"My dorm is located in Nerdville, so that's my circle, a lot of nerds. They've had their heads in the books and not in vaginas. To be fair, it wasn't that bad. At least he was a decent size."

"Well, maybe if you try again it will be better. I'm sure you're a good teacher."

"We'll see, but I got to say I'm really happy to hear you got someone nursing you back to life. You sound like your old self, full of energy and wisecracks. It was so hard to see you in that hospital bed."

"Girl, you have no idea. It has been pretty hard trying to recuperate and really face the music from everything that I did."

"Really? So, look, before we get into it, I should tell you that I'm here, because I know we have a lot to catch up on, and I'd rather do it in person."

"What? You're here in Atlanta?"

"Yes, I am here a little early for Ty's event at his new grand opening."

"Wow, you guys are really close now, huh? He invited you?" Journey regretted the jealous tone in her voice.

"Well, yes. I'm going to be working actually in the spa on the launch day, doing Reiki. They've had a lot of good results with Papa. I hear he's dancing, singing, and talking clearer now. He thinks that since having Reiki with me, he's improved. I feel so honored." She paused. "Um, I thought you guys were talking again. I thought you would be going."

"Nope, we're not that cool yet. It's been a lot of drama going on over here. There's still a lot of unanswered questions. I don't know who to trust. You know I can't wait to see you, because I need a reading. Like, bad. I will fill you in, but I don't want to tell you too much yet."

"What else is new?" She laughed. "You still owe me at least three readings."

"Shit, I do? I will do it when I get back to normal. I promise. I'm not there yet. Hello, I was in a fucking coma. Cut me some slack."

"Oh, boy. That's right. That's gonna be your new line. I was in a coma." Elizabeth laughed.

"Whatever. Where are you right now?"

"I just checked into my hotel a couple hours ago on Lenox Road, so I can Uber there. Give me the address. I can't wait to see you."

"Perfect! We can do lunch. Man, I miss you, sis. Can't wait!"

Chapter 20

Elizabeth

Journey looked so different. Her hair was no longer down her back with black curls and waves like Elizabeth's. Now she had a short pixie cut that really made her look even more beautiful, and her dimples were even more pronounced when she smiled. Elizabeth looked up to Journey. She was quick-witted, bold, and came full of advice when it came to dealing with men. Even though everybody was pretty much against Journey, Elizabeth still felt an allegiance toward her. They were sisters, after all, and they did have a bond.

Before the accident, the Fantastic Four was really starting to pull away from Journey. It came to light how she was hiding Ty from them and just being manipulative, trying to control them always. Elizabeth looked at her now, and she didn't seem as powerful as she once was. She literally had a fall from grace. Elizabeth hoped that the time in the hospital helped her look at her life more deeply.

After lunch, they went over to Journey's house to chill and to do Journey's reading. Elizabeth was curious to see just how much Journey had changed since the accident. She kept getting visions that Journey would need her and to stay close to her.

She wasn't sure why, but Elizabeth knew it was wise to follow her hunches. Journey was always cool but had higher energy. Today was a bit odd, since she was exceptionally calm now. It was weird to see her moving slower. It was almost as if she were high. She probably was. Something was definitely off. Elizabeth hoped she wasn't abusing her pain medications.

Journey wore sky blue jogging pants and a white tank top. Seeing her now compared to before she fell was like a new person had emerged. She had a different energy. Her light brown eyes were still beautiful, but they just had a little dim to them. Journey was moving slower as she sat on the floor, taking her time, looking like a little old lady. She gingerly adjusted her legs. One leg still kind of ached.

"Oh, don't worry I will do some Reiki on you. I love all of these pillows."

"Yeah, my mother has an addiction for floor pillows, and it's actually catching."

Elizabeth scanned the room and stretched out her legs and got comfortable on a huge floor pillow. "Your room is so cozy. The ambiance, the scents.

The whole vibe. I absolutely love the lavender decor. Are you a Prince fan?"

"Oh, no doubt, love Prince. But I've always had a thing for purple. Do you know what's amazing right now?"

"What's that?"

"That I'm even able to sit on the floor with you. I could barely sit down and get up by myself a few weeks ago. That physical therapy was no joke, but I made it through, and I'm so proud of myself."

"You should be!"

"That cane has been my best friend through it all." Journey pointed to her cane leaning in the corner of the room.

"It's beautiful." Elizabeth admired the tricolored bamboo cane with the engraved quote that read, *This too shall pass.*

"That's a beautiful work of art. Did your mom get it for you?"

"Nope, nurse boo did. He really looks out for me like no one else has in a long time. He cooks for me, makes my smoothies in the mornings, helps me with chores. He's amazing. Good dick. Did I mention the good dick?"

"Yes, you did." Elizabeth giggled. "This sounds serious. I want to meet this guy."

"You will. My mom doesn't even know yet. She just thinks he's my homie. He's not my usual type of guy." Journey shifted in her seat on the floor and added another pillow to her back. "I might need your help getting up when we're done."

They laughed.

"Don't worry. I'll do some more Reiki on you too. It'll help align you and get you feeling stress-free. Which leg is the bad leg?"

Journey pointed to her right hip and knee. "When I fell, that's the side that took the most of the impact. I take meds for it, but it's not always working. I end up sleeping more just to forget about the aches."

"Try doing a few deep breaths. In through your nose and out of your mouth. Now focus on the window and watch the pain leave your body every time you breathe out, and go out the window."

Elizabeth then put her hands together in a prayer position. She closed her eyes for a minute, then placed one of her hands on the knee and one on the hip. Elizabeth felt warm energy leaving her hands as if it were rays of light transferring to Journey's body.

"Wow, I feel a warm, pulsing sensation. Oh my God, your hands feel like a heated magnet. It's pulling the aching feeling away." She looked at Elizabeth in awe. Her jaw dropped.

"Focus. Breathe and stop talking."

They both giggled.

Journey sent her a message to her mind. "*Bitch, this ain't Reiki. This is something else you are doing, some witchy stuff. What are those, magic hands? It's got to be in our genes or something."*

Elizabeth laughed. "You still got it, sending me telepathic messages, you nut. We may have a bit more of an advantage then the next person because of our abilities, but I promise you Reiki can be learned."

"Well, teach me. I don't have any more pain. What the fuck? How'd you do that? That's some good hocus pocus you're doing."

"You got a lot of nerve. What about you?"

"What about me?"

"Rumor has it that you know how to freeze people in place."

Journey laughed. "Well, I didn't really know I could."

"Jocelyn told Ty that she couldn't move when you guys were fighting."

"I think I've been doing that a little bit more now. Do you think that's telekinesis?"

"Like moving shit with your mind?"

"It might be a combination of that and just mind control or something."

"Yeah, I told Jocelyn not to move. I do remember that. I didn't think it would work."

"Well, they said it worked. She had a temporary paralysis."

"They must really be scared of me now." She laughed. "You know, I felt bad about everything after the fact. I was really petty, and I did a lot of dumb shit. And to be honest, a part of me did feel as if I didn't have any control. It was as if I was being taken over something. Not possessed, but it has felt as if I had another personality or something. Because during the time I didn't have any guilt, I didn't have much good judgment. But now looking back on everything that I did, I'm really embarrassed. It was immature, and I got to get better. I got to get a hold of my powers too, because I noticed that when I get angry or emotional, bad things happen. We got to get the gang back together. I wanna practice again."

Elizabeth said, "Ooh, they are both so flaky lately, those boys."

It was hard for her to keep eye contact with Journey when she was hiding the truth. She did love that Journey seemed to be acknowledging her crazy behavior, and that was a good start. She would have to convince the rest of the Fantastic Four that maybe they could accept her back in.

Journey said in her head, *"There's something you're not telling me, Elizabeth. Spill the beans."*

Elizabeth looked at her and bit her bottom lip. "Oh my God, I heard you loud and clear. I hate that! Get out of my brain."

Journey laughed. "Well, that's what you get for holding back, bitch." Journey threw a pillow at her.

"Okay, promise not to say anything ever or get mad."

"I promise." She crossed her heart.

"Robbie discussed some new gifts he discovered, and I think he's a little freaked out. He won't even tell me what he can do, and he's been avoiding us. I'm dying to speak to him, but he barely responds now."

"So, it wasn't just me? I have a feeling there are a lot more things we can do if we just try it out and experiment."

"Well, that's why I think Robbie is ghosting us to be honest with you. He experimented too much, and now he's terrified. I will still try to get him to turn around some. He's hoping what happened to you wouldn't happen to him. They both think you well, kinda went crazy."

"Really? Well, I probably did. But I don't think it was the abilities. When we get to my reading, you'll see what I mean. What about Zack? What's his deal?"

"I mean, he's a bit of a pussy. He said he's had nightmares about everything and claims he doesn't wanna be a part of the group anymore. I think he's a little afraid of you. He thinks you have bad juju or something. He thinks that we experimented too much, and he just wants to be normal."

"Normal? That ship has sailed, bro." Journey shook her head and hugged a pillow.

"He may have it even stronger than us. Makes sense as to why he stays high all the time, so that he can't feel everything. Don't you remember? When we did stuff together, he was always the most laid back or the most quiet."

"Yeah, and the most nervous. I just wish we would really just get it together, because we could be so powerful if we join forces."

"Join forces? What are we going to be, a super-hero crew fighting battles being vigilantes?"

Journey shook her head. "No, crazy. I'm just saying, we could do so much more for the world and for ourselves if we understood who we really were."

"Funny you should say this. I didn't want to spoil it until we knew for sure, but I think Ty and Papa want to work on something for us. Kinda like a family meeting or something. Papa is talking now and feeling a lot better, and he wants to talk to us."

"I doubt that I'm invited. Papa doesn't like me after all that happened."

"Well, anything is possible. Maybe he had a change of heart. I feel that he might really want you there, because maybe that accident wouldn't have happened if you understood who you were."

"So, let's do this reading. Is it about nurse boo?"

"Yes, I need you to get in his brain and see what the hell is going on. It's been hard trying to read him or anyone lately. I swear, I just haven't been feeling myself. Just a little out of it."

"Yeah, I was gonna say you seem more relaxed. Less intense than I remember, even though we only met over the phone before. You were way bossier too."

"Oh, stop it."

"I just thought maybe you smoked some weed today or took some extra pain pills."

"No, not at all. But I have dabbled in some mushrooms."

"I really haven't tried that yet."

"All right, well, I won't tell you anymore, since I don't want to sway the reading, but I definitely wanna get into his head and find out what's going on with us."

Journey lit a candle and put it in between them. Elizabeth closed her eyes and meditated for a few minutes. A black woman's voice came on strongly in her ear.

It's all them damn drugs.

Elizabeth asked, "What?"

Journey replied, "Girl, I didn't say anything."

You so wet behind the ears. She can't hear me. She's all cloudy. It is the drugs. She needs to know that, Elizabeth. Tell her what I said.

She shook her head, as if she were shaking a bug off of her ear. "Um, there's a lady here. Maybe she's a spirit guide or something. I don't know, but her presence feels very intrusive. She's kind of sassy and demanding."

I'm her friend. Tell her it's me. She knows me. She knows who I am.

The voice was full of distress and sounded far away. Elizabeth couldn't see her face.

"She sounds like she is saying her name is Janice, Jean, Jana." Elizabeth rubbed her third eye so hard she was making a red mark over the bridge of her nose. She was straining to listen, as if that would help her get the message clearer. It almost felt as if she were translating a message from underwater.

Journey sat up straighter and slapped the pillow. "Oh, shit! I know who that is. That's Janet! Remember my friend that died, who taught me telepathy? The one I'm naming my lifestyle center after."

"Janet. Yes, that's it. A Place for Janet. That's the name. Boy, she is so aggressive."

"Yep, that's her."

Elizabeth tilted her head to the left as if she were adjusting her antenna. Her eyes were still shut, turned in that direction, as if Janet were right there in the room with them.

"Wow. Okay, okay. Slow down. This is a lot to remember." She turned back to Journey. "So, Journey, she's saying that the drugs you are taking are making you very sleepy and less psychic. She said he's taking your power away. She's screaming at me." She chuckled.

"Really?"

"Maybe the meds they have you on are too much?"

"I'm taking about six pills, several times a day."

"She's saying there's too much drugs in you and to watch that boy. Watch what he's giving you. She does not like him. She just keeps saying over and over, he's taking your power away. She sounds like a broken record. She's talking about nurse boo."

"Ask her."

"Yes, she said it's him. Don't take anything from him. Like, anything! He may be putting it in your food too. Didn't you say he makes your smoothies and stuff?"

Journey sat back. "Shit, it kinda makes sense. I thought it was just normal to feel like this from pain meds."

"She said to just try one day without taking anything from him to see how you feel, and you will understand. That it will click. Lord, what could he be giving you?"

"I don't think he would do anything to harm me. He knows I hate taking pills, so sometimes he puts them in my smoothie. Janet just wasn't a fan of doctors, so she could be a little paranoid when it comes to the medical profession. He might be here soon, so we have to be careful." Journey looked toward her room door, which was cracked.

Elizabeth felt tension in her body, and it didn't feel good. Chills ran down her back and crawled up her arms. It was a warning. "Give me his full name, so that I can read him. That's who you wanted to read anyhow, right?"

"Yeah, then Janet barged her way in."

"For real. She really is worried about you."

"I know. I miss her so much. Okay, his name is Dominick Bustamante, and he is thirty-four."

She started to breathe in and out deeply. Elizabeth saw him meditating inside of a hot sauna. He was thinking about Journey, fantasizing about her. "He's in a spa or something like a sauna."

"Damn, you're right. He's at the gym. They have a steam room and sauna."

"He sees you as someone he has to protect. It's weird. It's like you were his little sister or something, but there's definitely a sexual energy there. He's obsessed with you. A very hot and steamy energy I'm picking up." She rolled her neck around to stretch. "He is nervous about you finding out something. Do you know if he has a secretive past?"

"Yes. I think he's been hiding something from me. Ask him what it is."

"My guides keep showing me shotguns and many flags. It's weird, like little awards. Emblems? I think they're medals or something."

"He was in the military. Maybe that's what you are seeing."

"Ah, yes, that makes sense. Like the ones on their uniforms. He's showing me that he knows how to shine a gun. He's very proud of his collection.

The flags are telling me about places that he's traveled to while he was in the military. Okay, Mr. show-off." Elizabeth snapped her fingers in the air. "Wow, aren't we braggadocious."

"Yes, he was in the army or marines. I'm not quite sure, one of those. I never really got the details. Seems like a touchy subject. I know he has PTSD from it."

"Has he . . . wow. Man, you like this guy?"

"Has he what?"

"Killed before?"

"Possibly. He was in the military. I don't know."

"Yes, I'm getting he has, and he's sort of good at it. Sounds sick, but he did it for sport. Journey, you might not like this, but bro is a little messed up in the head. He's pretty dark in some ways. His ego is out of control. I get the savior complex with him. Does he act like he has to fix your problems or something?"

"Just really protective. I wasn't trying to marry him. I just really love how he treats me. I feel so good when I am with him. He gets me. He isn't judgmental."

Elizabeth shrugged. "Yeah, he seems to think you are the center of his world. It's not going to end well if you cut him off. All I'm saying, once you start getting back to your old normal self, he's gonna want to keep you under his wing. He likes you fragile."

"Really, I don't see it at all. We did mention that we would check out what our past lives were. We feel so connected."

"Oh, boy. He got you with that? Journey, even I know that's all men do is use certain buzz words when they know you are into spirituality. Soon he'll text you at exactly 1:11, at 111."

"Shut up!"

They laughed.

"I did have some serious drama happen, and I'm hoping he wasn't the cause of it. Can you ask him if he had anything to do with Marlon's tires or photos? I'll tell you the rest later. It's fucking crazy. Just ask him that."

His higher self said to Elizabeth, "*I will do what I can to protect her. It's my duty.*"

"He won't give me any more details. He just folded his arms and walked away. That's real suspect. I'm gonna guess and say he did. He's acting too guilty, but I am not getting any details. He's kind of hard to probe. Is he pretty spiritual?"

"Yeah, he comes from a long line of shamans. Or so he says. I don't know what to believe now."

"Lord, you better watch out. He might have an altar made up for you."

Janet jumped in. "*I told her to watch that boy. She don't listen. He's trouble. A whole lot of trouble.*"

"Journey, Janet won't leave. I don't know, Janet is persistent. She said you really need to stop eating anything or drinking like right away. She even said you're so stubborn and you should understand that's why you haven't seen her in a while, because he's blocking your third eye. You can do some things, but not as good as before."

"I had a feeling. I guess I didn't want to believe it. That motherfucker! It makes sense. No wonder I feel so groggy, and I can't get my messages like I used to. She definitely might be onto something."

"You have to be careful. That's pretty scary, and I'm telling you his energy feels very intense when I asked him about you. His higher self is definitely enamored by you."

"If all this is true, he's causing me way more harm than good."

"Do you really need him anymore? I mean, you seem okay."

"No, I just really like him, so this is hard, but if he's manipulating me, he has to go. He has to go."

Chapter 21

Journey

Journey's mind was collapsing in on her, and everything started to make more sense. After her reading with Elizabeth, she finally started to see things for what they were. She had been more tired than usual. She felt groggy, and her thoughts weren't as clear. She wasn't sure if it was related to her diagnosis, or if she was just having a bad reaction to the medicine.

Flashback memories came to her with Dominick lying on the pillows and laughing. It was when they took the mushrooms for the first time. She was talking about what she would do for revenge. Did she really mention that website? No one else knew about that besides Dominick. He had to have taken the photo from her phone and posted it. She didn't know how, but she was going to find out today. After Elizabeth left, she was convinced she had to end it. She had to listen to Janet.

Journey waited a full day and a half and didn't eat anything he gave her. She didn't take any of her meds either and just ordered Japanese food for lunch. That morning, she dumped her smoothie in the sink when he wasn't looking. She couldn't believe how alive she felt, how clear she was. It was proof, just like Janet said. Proof that he was doing something.

Dominick was just coming back from the gym, and Claudia was at her office downtown. It was the perfect time to confront him. Journey did not want to believe it, but Dominick being involved was the only logical answer for Marlon's nudes being posted and for the tires being slashed. It had to be him. He swore to protect her, and at this point she knew he really hated Marlon. Before she thought he made her feel safe. She knew he was falling in love with her, but this shit was not helping. He was making it worse. Everything was pointing back to her as if she were the culprit behind everything.

"Hey, beautiful." He was cheerfully unpacking groceries and putting things away. He was really making himself at home. She was suddenly disgusted that she had even let him get this close to her. As her legs dragged slowly toward him, her mind raced. The betrayal was hitting her like a landslide that took you under. She could not believe how manipulative he really was, how he weaseled his way into her life so naturally.

"Are you feeling okay? Why the doom and gloom face?"

"Oh, I think you know, Dominick." She studied his face and let the silence linger.

He laughed nervously as he folded a paper bag and put it in the recycling drawer.

"No, I don't. What's going on? You're acting weird."

"What's going on? What's going on is I realize I've been in denial and living with a stranger. Are you the one behind tormenting Marlon?"

His stare was blank. He looked down and continued putting things away to avoid eye contact.

Her hands shook in anger, and she folded her arms to hide her fear. "What's wrong with you? How could you?"

"Don't yell at me. I'm not a child. He was hurting you, Journey, and all you did was talk about him as if it bothered you."

"It wasn't your place. What the fuck is wrong with you? They could have killed me. They had guns. Guns! He sent real gangsters. Why would you do something so fucking stupid?" As he caved in, Journey's stance became strong. She looked at him square in the eyes. "What I want to know is how did you get into my phone? Where did you get that picture? Have you been snooping through my shit when I'm asleep?"

He held his hands up to tell her to stop. "No, no, can you give me a minute, so I can answer your questions? If you would just take a breath, calm down, and let me speak."

"Calm down! You almost got me killed. Don't tell me to calm down!"

"I didn't break into your phone. I just took a picture of what you had on your phone. You kept your phone open that night and fell asleep. It was the night we took the 'shrooms."

"Did you plan that, to get me so high I wouldn't know what you were doing? How dare you invade my fucking privacy? His knees seemed to collapse beneath him. His eyes began to water, and he came in close as if to hug her.

She pointed her finger at him. "Do not touch me." Her hand was visibly shaking. "Do not fucking touch me. Who the fuck are you? Are you even anything that you said you are?"

"I just wanted to protect you, Journey." His words were filled with shame.

Journey backed away, and her voice cracked in pain. "I trusted you. I confided in you. I invited you into my home like you were family. I can't believe how much I told you. I was alone, and I needed somebody. I thought everybody hated me, and now you just made it fucking worse, making me out to look like a villain. What would make you want to do something like this? I thought I was falling in . . . I can't even believe I fucked you!"

"Don't talk like that. Don't talk like that. That's because you do love me. I love you."

"You're acting crazy. Have you been drugging me? You do know my entire family is psychic, right? You can't be that full of yourself to not think someone would figure it out. I need to know what you have been putting in my food. If I go get my blood tested and find out something, I will get you arrested."

"Relax. It was just 'shrooms. I was just mi-cro-dosing. You liked it."

"I haven't been having my visions. I haven't been as intuitive lately."

"That's a good thing, isn't it? You were sort of going crazy, Journey."

"You are unbelievable. I could have been driving high."

"It wasn't that much. You were fine, right?"

"Everything you've done just got the finger pointed at me. I can't believe you."

"They will never know it was me or think of you. I took precautions."

"Right, like what? Blurring out my naked body? Thanks for that. Made me look more guilty. Then you put all the shit up about him on that site, and it could get me arrested. I know you thought you were having fun. Even when he already has a restraining order out on me, he thinks I'm doing all of this crazy shit. Like, it was so unnecessary,

Dominick. When I said I would put him up on dontdatethatdick.com, I was just joking. You took it too far. We were fucking high, for chrissakes."

"As long as I am around, nothing's gonna happen to you. That guy Marlon is just a thug in a suit, but nothing is going to happen to you."

"Do you realize he would've never took it that far if you didn't fucking provoke him?"

"Let me protect you. I can protect you. If anyone is bothering you, I am on to them. You don't really have anyone to help you but me."

"Look, at this point, do not worry about my family or protecting me."

He paced back-and-forth as if thinking.

"I don't know if I want you here anymore. I don't know if this is going to work anymore.

"No, nooo." He tried to grab her shoulders, and she shook him off. "Please, can we talk about this? Please, I'm begging you." His hands went toward his chest to surrender to her verbal blows that hurt his heart. "Don't yell at me. It's time you took your medicine. I think that's what's going on right now. You're acting erratic. I think it's giving you a temper, and you may be having an episode."

"No, I'm not taking shit. Nothing that you're giving me. I haven't been clearer in weeks, as a matter fact, ever since you moved in."

"Please, please calm down. I really love you, Journey. Everything I did, I've done for you. I don't wanna fight. I don't." He cried.

He grabbed her and held her tightly in a bear hug and she screamed, "Get off of me!"

Dominick grabbed her tighter around her waist and kissed her neck. She pounded his back like a meat tenderizer. "I'm serious. Get off of me. Leave me alone. I need you to leave now, or I'll call the cops."

"Claudia doesn't want me to leave."

"Well, Claudia will see my miraculous improvement today. Your services are no longer needed."

"You don't mean that."

"Oh, yes the fuck I do!"

Her breath was clogging in her throat. She strained to send him a mental message.

"Get the fuck off of me now!"

"What's that noise? It's so loud. Stop it please, Journey."

"There's a dark energy around you. You are evil."

She penetrated his thoughts, making his skull ring as if a siren were going off in his brain. His eyes widened, filled with fear the entire time. It shocked him into a stumble, and he fell backward onto the pantry floor. He held his head and screamed.

Journey started to panic, and she sat down. He was moaning and holding his head. She was afraid she might have killed him or given him an aneurysm or something. She closed the door behind him. Journey felt dizzy and a light drip of blood came out of her nose.

She looked up and saw Francesca standing in front of her. This time, she wasn't in her gown from the hospital. She had on jeans, white Converse, and an oversized pink sweatshirt that hung off of her shoulders. She looked good now. Not sickly anymore. It kind of spooked Journey at first, and she backed away.

"It's me, sugar! Girl, why are you acting crazy? Don't you know I ain't gonna hurt you? I'm glad you got the message from Janet. Your sister Elizabeth is pretty good."

"You met Janet?"

"Oh, yeah, that's the auntie right there. We are all rooting for you, girl. I told her all about Dominick. I told her to tell you to be careful. Clearly it worked, 'cause you see and hear me now."

She nodded.

"I know your ass ain't worried about him. Don't worry. You didn't kill him. He's in there suffering like he should. But I will thank him for crossing me over. He did one thang good, that bastard. Oh, I think he's waking up now."

"Stop it. Make it stop. It hurts," he moaned through the door.

"You're fired." Journey wiped a small droplet of blood. She was proud of her work.

He collapsed onto the floor, whimpering. He pounded on the door profusely. She put a chair under the door to trap him in there while she figured out what her next step was.

"You're going to clear my name today. You're going to confess. You're fucking up my life, and you need to mind your damn business."

He whimpered through the door, "Make it stop. Please, make it stop."

"Only if you admit to doing it all. Did you flatten Marlon's tires and steal the photo from my phone?"

"Yes, I did. I'm sorry. I did."

"Why did you do it?"

"To protect you, Journey."

"Okay. Good. Now, I'll let you out."

She frantically called Ty on the video phone.

"Hi, Journey, are you okay? What happened? You look like you've been crying."

"I'm okay. I know who did it. Dominick did it all. I got him to admit it. I just need you as my witness because he is getting out right now. I just kicked him out. He's fired."

He got up from the floor, and she put the camera on him.

"Oh, man. What did you do to him?"

"I just locked him in the closet until he told me the truth."

She shouted to Dominick, "Please leave and go back to your family now. You can get the rest of your things when my mother is here. I need you to leave. I don't feel safe."

"I'm calling Claudia."

"You do that on your way out." She shooed him away as if he were a stray dog.

He walked out slowly, since he knew she was on the phone with Ty.

"Good. He's gone. I'll send you the recording now of his confession. He was batshit crazy. Can you believe this shit?"

"Wow, I'm glad you found out. Now he's gonna be in a lot of trouble. Marlon is not one to play with."

"I gotta go. Gotta call my mom so she knows we have to change the locks and alarm code asap.

"Good idea."

Journey

Even though he did what he did, she still missed Dominick and felt lonely. However, she also felt very betrayed and knew she had to keep her guard up. He was still trying to apologize, but Journey would just ignore him, not block him. Meanwhile, Phil had been checking on her daily, texting her to say good morning and see how she was doing. She really liked the attention. He offered to help her get her business set up and wanted to discuss how he could be an investor. She figured it would give her something to take her mind off of Dominick and his obsession with her. She agreed to meet with him.

They sat in the hotel lobby's lounge. The lighting was dim, but it still highlighted his smile. She admired how handsome he was. He looked so sexy in a suit. She was so used to seeing him in yoga clothes. He wore a dark green shirt with a blazer. Phil's salt-and-pepper hair was cropped shorter than usual. He definitely had a Richard Gere/ George Clooney kind of swag about him. The old man was winning today.

He greeted her with a warm hug, and she smelled a light scent of cologne.

She teased him, "So, what happened today? Why are you here at a hotel? She finally threw you out?"

"Ha ha, very funny. No, I was at a conference as a speaker. It's been grueling long fourteen-hour days. I didn't wanna have to keep going home and coming back. You know, in the entertainment industry, there's a lot of activities, movie screenings, live music sessions, and more. Since I was a speaker, they gave me a free room, so I figured I'd take advantage of it. Ya know, get some alone time in. Because you know Helen doesn't give me a break anymore."

"Oh, that's right. I'm sure you needed it."

"So, let's get down to business. What are you in need of?"

She was surprised by his take-charge attitude. He was really taking her seriously.

"You look good, kiddo. You really do look good after all you've been through. Are you doing okay?"

She probably didn't look her best. Her eyes were swollen from yesterday's tears, so she had put a lot of eyeliner on, but her energy was lower than normal beside him. Maybe him thinking that she was depressed might just help with his investment.

Journey pulled out her laptop to show Phil the blueprint of A Place for Janet that she had designed.

"This is it. This is my vision. It's going to be sustainable, certified all green, so we can help save the environment. I need to buy land or buy a property like a warehouse that we can turn into a wellness center. I already have an amazing team in mind."

"This is really impressive. You did this by yourself?"

"I guess you forgot I was an interior design major at SCAD. Everything I do is not all yoga. I'm not namaste all day, you know?"

"Tell me about it. We know you sure are one heck of a businesswoman. A shrewd one at that."

"That's why I have goals. I'm about getting my paper."

"So what's the next step?"

"I would love to pay someone to help me with the business plan, and then I'd like to start looking for spaces and more investors."

"Okay, I can loan you maybe up to ten thousand for starters. I'd like to be a partner and be on the board."

"That sounds risky. For you, at least."

"No, not at all. I can be a silent partner. It's not sweat off my back, but I'd like to be an advisor behind the scenes to help you. You're gonna need a lot of legal help."

"Well, thank you, Phil. That's a generous offer. How much time do I have to pay it back?"

"You may not have to." He winked.

"Well, you know my mom is probably going to want that title as a legal advisor."

"Oh, she could have it. That's fine. But is your mom giving you ten thousand dollars?"

"This sounds like a bribe."

"No, no, it's not. Remember, I don't need my name in lights. Okay, listen up. To make you feel that it's official, I'll give you up to three years to pay it back, no interest. After three years, five percent interest. Fair?"

"Sure."

"I can have my team draw the papers by next week."

"Oh my God." She leaned in and hugged him.

"You're welcome, sweetie. Anything for you, kiddo. You've been through a lot, and I want to help you get back on your feet."

"You are definitely one of my favorite clients."

When he leaned back, she heard a pop from the side of his back. "Phil, so what's going on with you? You sound like the freaking tin man."

"I'm just tight. Sitting in that conference for hours today, and yesterday was thirteen hours of running around different workshops. And my yoga girl kicked me to the curb."

"Oh no, don't put that on me. Your crazy-ass wife did that."

They laughed.

He put his hand on top of hers. "I could sure use a little stretch, though. My room is upstairs. Can we do a few yoga moves? Ya know, for old times' sake?" His gaze couldn't hide his true intentions. His eye penetrated her soul, as if he were the mind reader. "I promise I'll behave." He stroked her chin. "Only if you want me too."

"So, what would you like? Just a quick yoga session?"

"Yes, that'll be nice. You did promise me a little more."

Ever since he became her client when they had her special arrangements of pleasure and yoga, she did tease him with promises of one day fulfilling his needs all the way. She was attracted to him for some reason, now more than ever.

Journey had used the gift of telepathy to seduce him every time. Journey had no idea she was finally going to give in to his advances. She really wanted to see what he was able to do, since he definitely was driving Helen so crazy. Truth be told, part of her just wanted to fuck him out of spite. Another part of her just wanted to thank him for helping her. She also was in need of a good release after the Dominick fiasco. Her stress needed more than yoga to fix.

When they walked into the room, he took off his suit jacket and hung it over the chair.

"You're looking really good, Phil." His back was more defined. Even his arms looked more buff. "Damn, Phil! You've been working out, huh?"

"Well, I had to do something when you were in the hospital, Sleeping Beauty. I cheated on you just a little. I got a trainer."

"Oh, really now? Well, I'm not the jealous type. The gym and yoga are a nice balance. You look really fit. I'm so proud of you. But that's probably why you're so tight. You haven't been stretching. So, where do you want me to stretch you?"

"Shit, Journey, I'm missing your classes, and I know, but it's not like I don't remember some of the moves you taught me." He sat down in the chair across from her on the couch. "You were so sexy when you used to do it."

"*Were* sexy?"

"I mean, you are still very sexy. Come on, don't give me a hard time. You know what I mean. It's just the way you taught me, you kept my attention. I love the way you would stretch me and hold me. Can we do *that* again?"

"Well, maybe. If you're really going to help me with my business, I guess I can give you a freebie, because you know my private classes are not free."

"See, there you go, shrewd businesswoman. I'd write you a check tonight, but we just gotta do the official paperwork before we move forward. I just want you to do what you used to do to me." He gazed into her eyes, and his voice went lower. "I need that. Can you help me?"

Journey felt so aroused just from the tone of his voice. His masculine energy was magnetic, pulling her back in.

"You really used to heal me. Just by your voice, your touch."

Her ego was being stroked, and she enjoyed every minute of it. Journey said in a very sultry voice, "You're gonna have to remove those slacks, sir. I can't stretch you good in those."

He stood up quickly and started unbuckling his pants. "Oh, *no* problem. I follow instructions." His smile was filled with anticipation.

He had on purple satin boxers. "Oh, nice." She giggled. "That's my favorite color." She was really looking at his imprint that was swelling. She wanted to touch it.

"I don't have my yoga mat."

"Oh, it's okay. I'll give you something to do."

"Should we be on the bed maybe?"

"I'm sure you'd want that." She smirked. "No, Phil, we can do some standing stretches or with you sitting in the chair. What hurts? Your neck or your back?"

"It's really my lower back that hurts the most."

"Let's try this." Journey showed him the position, bending all the way down and then allowing her hands to hang low to the ground. "Do that for me, Phil." She maintained her sexy voice and enjoyed watching him get harder and harder.

"Let me take off my shirt too."

"Okay, you want to show me your new muscles? I see you."

"Hey, I'm proud of this body." He removed his shirt and tank top, showing his defined abs. "Not bad for an old man, right?"

Journey admired the definition in his body and how much he had sculpted since she last saw him. She was really impressed. He looked as if he were twenty-five, even though he was really closer to sixty.

She stood close behind him. "Spread your legs more, grasp your elbows, bend lower, and let them hang.

"Oh my God."

She rubbed his lower back and kneaded her hands into him. She glided up and down with slow, deep strokes.

"Oh, how I missed you."

Journey giggled. She loved how much he adored her.

"Wow, that feels *so* good. You could've been a masseuse with those hands. You know that, kiddo?" he moaned.

"Thank you, Phil. Okay, now rock slowly side to side." She stood close behind him and held his hips.

He mumbled. "I think we should switch. I need to have you bent over like this." He laughed.

She sent him a message to his mind.

"I'm really horny as hell. Do you want me to-night? It's time."

She wanted to see if he got the message. "Okay, slowly come up. Breathe. Remember to breathe."

He was extremely hard when he stood and turned around. He looked down and looked back up her. He knew it was turning her on, and he smiled. "Ya see whatcha always do to me. You see why I can't go to a regular class anymore. This is embarrassing."

"It's human nature. You shouldn't be embarrassed." She looked down at his hardness and licked her lips.

"Any other stretches that we can do tonight?"

"Possibly." She lightly touched the tip of his dick imprint.

"Oh, I think you're finally going to get fucked. It's the message I'm getting."

"Yes, you are getting the right message." Journey moved in closer to him. "I'm ready."

"Did you really say that, or am I hallucinating?" He smiled and pulled her closer.

"Oh, no, I think you heard me. I'm dead serious." His arousal grew and was now peeking out of his boxers, letting its presence be known. She put her hand on it softly and grabbed around the neck with the other hand.

He started to kiss her, and she mumbled, "Damn, Phil. You deserve all of this pussy."

"Shit, don't talk like that. I don't wanna cum yet."

They both giggled.

All of the buildup of her teasing him for months paid off. Now she wanted him just as much as he wanted her.

"Are you sure?" He slowly started to pull off her leggings. "Fuck. Journey. You're so fucking soft."

She helped him peel off her leggings and helped him get out of his boxers.

"I'm sure. You're not dreaming anymore, papi."

"There is a fucking God."

Chapter 22

Journey

Their lovemaking was slow, deep, sweaty, and passionate. She realized why she always went for an older man. They really knew how to please and understood it was not all about them. However, she wasn't ready for just how talented he was. He really knew what he was doing, and those years of experience helped. She guessed it was true what they said about Italians being amazing lovers. He kept kissing her on her face and neck after it was over. He was so passionate, so loving.

His hands cupped her ass while he slept. He was snoring lightly, and she just smiled, looking at him. Journey slowly released his grasp and started to get dressed.

He opened one eye and stretched out an arm to pull her back to bed. "Whoa, whoa, where are you going, kiddo? You're not leaving me already, are you?"

"I've got to get home, Phil. I didn't even tell my mom I'd be gone so long. It's after two a.m. I had a great time. I mean, a really great time."

She only had her bra on, and he gave her a light tap on her ass. "That was really amazing. You're so beautiful. You made my dreams come true. You got me for however long you want me. It was so worth the wait."

She bent down and kissed him on the lips. She mumbled, "Phil, please don't call me kiddo anymore. It sounds really pedo since you just fucked the shit out of me."

They laughed so hard.

"Really, I think YOU fucked the shit out of me, all the way back into my 20s."

"Text me when you get home, okay, so I know you're safe." He pulled the sheet back over his naked body.

"Okay, I will. Sleep tight."

Journey smiled all the way home.

Two days later

After coming in from a long day at this yoga studio, Journey opened the door and saw her mom sitting in the living room with someone. They were talking low, and the other woman's back was to the door.

"Hi, Mom."

"Hey, Ni-ni, look who's here from yoga class."

When the woman turned around, Journey's yoga bag fell from her limp hand. It was Phil's wife, Helen.

"Well, hello there. Surprise, surprise," Helen said as she crossed her arms.

"What the hell are you doing in my house?"

"Journey!" Claudia screamed. "What's wrong with you? That is so rude."

"Mom, what you don't know is that she is crazy as hell. She's a psycho." She stood by the door and pointed to it. "Get out of my house, Helen."

"I thought you were friends!" Journey's mom yelled.

"Is it your house, or don't you just live here? You're still a child." Helen stood up. "I'll leave once you tell me where my husband is."

"Are you for real? You're still on that shit?"

Helen dramatically threw her Gucci shawl around her. Her designer khakis and Gucci loafers helped give her the look of class when she was truly unhinged. Journey looked at her mother.

"I didn't wanna worry you, but this crazy woman came to the hospital threatening me when I had just come out of a coma. I mean, I couldn't even talk, then she sent black roses with a threat to stay away from her husband. Who does that?" Journey's arms waved in the air. "I don't even want your husband. He's a client."

Claudia turned to Helen. "Is this true? I thought you were really trying to connect as a friend."

"I was, but yes, partly true, but there's much more to the story. Your daughter forgot to tell you that she sleeps with married men, and now she's a yogi prostitute."

Journey screamed, "Oh my Gaaaawd."

"I'm sure she left that part out, Claudia." She started to walk slowly toward the door.

"Bitch, get out of my house."

"Where is he, Journey? He was with you last. I saw the text messages of you telling him you got home safe and had a nice time. We have a shared plan. I see it all. You were the last person in contact with him. He also had emailed a team member about a contract for ten thousand dollars. Where you trying to extort my husband?"

"No, no, we had a meeting, and he wants to invest in my wellness spa, if you must know. We met, but it was a business meeting. That's pretty much it, but that was like two days ago."

"Oh, you mean with the business of your filthy pussy? That's your money maker, isn't it?"

"Mom, call the cops before I beat this woman up."

"Don't you lay a fucking finger on me. I'll have your ass locked up so quick you won't even see it coming."

Claudia jumped in between the two of them. "Okay, you get the fuck out, Helen. That's enough."

"If you have something to do with my husband missing, I'll make sure that you will pay for it. Believe me, sweetie. I have the money and the connections to find out. So, if you know something, you need to spill it. There will be detectives here knocking on your door. I promise you that."

"Do you know where he went, Journey?"

"No, Mom. He hasn't even returned my calls. His team was supposed to send a contract."

"Well, you can consider that deal null and void. I'll be damned if he gives you another cent."

"Get ooooout!" Journey opened the door and held it for her. As soon she did that, Dominick was walking down the pathway. He looked back at Helen getting into her car.

"What's she doing here?"

"Don't worry about it. What are *you* doing here?" Journey was furious and now had to deal with him.

"I got most of my stuff when you weren't here, but I forgot my juicer and blender in the kitchen."

"Fine. You can wait outside, and I'll get it."

"Journey! Don't be so rude. Hi, Dominick. Come in."

Journey walked off and cut her eyes at him as her mother walked up to him and gave him a hug.

"I have my reasons," Journey said.

"Well, um . . . it looks like I came just in time. You guys were having a little problem, huh? I heard the yelling."

Claudia laughed nervously. "You could hear it from outside? Aye dios mio."

"Some crazy lady was here," Journey said.

"Wasn't that Helen? The one that came to the hospital that you told me about?"

Journey asked, "How did you know? You never saw her."

He grabbed his jawline and said, "Cruella de Vil."

Journey laughed then remembered she was supposed to be mad at him. He had a five o'clock shadow and looked tired, but he was still so fine it made her sick to look at him. But she knew she had to stay far away from him.

She bagged up his appliances and handed them to him. "Here you go."

He caressed her hand slowly. "Oh, you know, I forgot I have a few more things to clean up downstairs. I think I left a bag and some sneakers." He scratched the back of his head.

"Can you come back when my mom is here, alone? I have a lot to deal with right now. You really should have called first."

"I know. I was in the neighborhood, so I—"

"I have a lot to deal with. Call my mom tomorrow."

"It was good to see you both," he said sheepishly, trying to drag out his visit.

Journey said softly, "You too. Goodbye," while closing the door slowly in his face. Her heart ached remembering the times they shared. But she also remembered the betrayal.

"All right now, take care." Claudia waved. "Nini, that was so rude. That man nursed you for months back to good health."

"Yeah, and he also crossed the line and took advantage of me. Leave it to you and you'd invite him back for tea and cookies. He is just too obsessed with me, Mom. There was a lot of stuff going on, and I didn't want to worry you. Dominick is just . . ." She sighed. "He's not right in the head. Don't let him come back here when I'm around. Let him get his stuff for the last time stepping through that door. You don't have to feel guilty. You paid him well. He'll be just fine. I'm glad you at least listened to me about the locks. I don't want to wake up in the middle of the night with him standing over my bed."

"Oh, stop it. He won't. I miss him. He really helped you so much. He just went a little overboard. Deep down he was such a nice gentleman."

"Well, looks can be deceiving. Don't be so gullible. He's trying to work his way back in. I don't want him near me. As a matter of fact, I will bag up his stuff now and just mail it to him."

"Where is he staying?"

"Back at his brother's in Dunwoody. They were roommates. Can you text him for the address? I'm not dealing with him anymore." Journey headed to the basement. She started to feel uneasy about Phil being missing. What if all of that lovemaking gave him a heart attack? She really had not heard from him since that night, and that was so strange.

Her mother was lying on the couch with her book and light jazz playing in the back. She grabbed the remote to mute the music. "Wait, Nini. So, are we not going to talk about what just happened here with Helen?"

"What's there to talk about? Look at her and look at me. She's jealous and deranged and thinks everyone wants her man. What does she really think? Phil and I have a getaway bungalow on a lake and I'm hiding him there? He probably just wanted to get away from her for a little bit I'm sure. When I last saw him, he was at a conference at a hotel. That was two nights ago. He was talking about how he stayed there to get alone time."

"Two nights ago you got in around three a.m."

"Yes, there you go, trying to be a private eye. Jeez, Ma. You're still clocking me like a warden. I'm twenty-three."

"You're still my little girl. I worry about you."

"Well, they had a banging after party for the conference, so after our meeting, we hung out there for a while."

Her mom shot her a distrusting glare. She was not convinced. Journey wasn't as good a liar as she thought.

"Really, Mom! Phil is like sixty or something. I like older men, but not that old."

"Excuse *you*. Sixty is not old. Stop the age shaming. He's younger than me." She laughed. "So, did you meet someone there? I do remember you had a big smile on your face the next morning."

"No, no. It was pure networking. I was mingling with more investors and trying to get more private clients. On the hunt for money is all."

Claudia took a deep breath. "You love money too much. Well, let's just pray he's okay. She seemed very worried. Especially if she went through all of that acting to be chummy with me. I really hope what she said about you is not true."

"Please don't believe that psychopath. I pray he's okay too. Lemme go clear out Dominick's crap."

Heart palpitations took over. Journey's mind raced. Guilt took her under. She jogged downstairs to the basement. What if their encounter led him to realize how miserable he was with Helen? What if he was planning to leave her? Maybe he left town to clear his head? She really was hoping he wasn't sick or had a stroke or something. It could be anything. She felt he really was a good man, so kind and generous. She admired him. Journey never thought that Philip Esposito would also be one of the best lovers she ever had. She tried calling him again, and it went straight to voicemail. Her stomach churned in fear. It didn't feel good.

She closed the door to Dominick's room and started going through what he had left in the closet and the drawers. As she rummaged through his items, she wasn't even sure what she was looking for, but her instincts told her to keep on digging.

In his gym duffle bag, she saw something sparkling in the bottom. Then she heard a voice behind her speak softly.

"Hey, that's mine." She jumped and looked behind her. It was Delilah, now in a red jumpsuit and heels. She looked so mature with a full face of makeup. Her locks fell to one side over her shoulder.

Journey was thrilled that her skills were coming back, but still shaken by the intrusion. "Hey, Delilah, you scared the shit outta me."

"*I'm so sorry, honey. Well, Francesca and I have been trying to reach you for weeks. It's good you stopped doing those drugs.*"

Journey pulled out the gold belt and held it up in awe. "*Holy shit, this is yours!*"

"*I know.*"

"*It's what you had on your hospital gown.*"

Delilah giggled. "*Yeah, I know.*"

"*Why the hell would he keep this? Didn't you die over a year ago?*"

"*Memories, I guess. We kinda had a thing.*" Delilah did a little wind of her waist and stuck out her tongue like she was dancing. Typical teenager.

"*What? You were so young.*"

"*Well, let him tell it, he wanted to remember the girl he thought he saved. He had a bit of a hero thing.*"

"*Saved, but you . . .*"

"*Yes, thanks to him. He took me out of my pain. Glad you survived.*"

"*What do you mean, took you out of your pain? He didn't, like, pull the plug on you or anything?*"

"*No, no, not at all.*" She came closer and leaned against the dresser. "*You know, at first I loved all the attention. My family was around a lot in the beginning. But as months went on, I wasn't getting any better. Surgery after surgery, and nothing was helping. I just felt so happy being around Dominick. Truth be told, he was grooming me. I know he was too old for me, but he knew how to act young. You know, just be fun and shit. I'm no dummy, I knew what he was doing, but I just wanted to feel love. Feel a man's touch. Be told I was pretty. And it felt good. He was massaging me the same way he did you, gurl. I just thought I was the only one.*"

"*My God, he's a fucking predator.*"

She put her hands up in surrender. "*But I let him fuck me. I was too weak to stand up for myself, and I honestly didn't want to. I wanted him. He had me so high all the time. I don't know what drugs they were giving me, but I know he added*

more. *You know, our little relationship started
off nice and romantic. He would kiss my hands,
play in my hair, watch movies with me, buy me
little gifts. Just loving up on me all the time. But
then . . . then there were times I would wake up
with his dick on my lips, or see him jerking off to
porn on his phone. He was nasty, chile. A certified
freak. Anything to get his dick wet.*"

"What the hell. I'm so sorry. I can't believe he
did that!"

"*I really thought he did love me, so I just let him.
I didn't want him to get in trouble, but he's just
sick.*"

"Oh, please don't make excuses for him."

Her voice boomed in Journey's head. "*No, he is
sick, I know he is. That's why we been trying to
get to you before something bad happened. I've
seen what he did to other girls after I died. He
wasn't as sweet to them as he was to me and you.
They were touched and even fucked when they
were out cold. Like, who wants to have sex with
a damn near dead body? He would take them out
the same way he did me, so no one could tell on
him.*"

Journey jumped up. "A mentally disturbed fuck,
that's who. Delilah, this is making me wanna kill
him! I can't believe I slept with a damn pervert
who was raping young girls."

"Journey, I don't know how he got away with it. I was beginning to think all of them people in the hospital was in on it or something, 'cause when I turned up pregnant, no one even suspected him. But it was his baby."

"Lord, how many months were you?"

"Only two, but they found out during my autopsy, and everyone just assumed it was my boyfriend. I ain't gonna lie. I was kinda fast. Already had an abortion when I was fifteen years old. I think he knew that about me." Delilah pointed to Journey's eyes. "Well damn, you got murder in your eyes. Dominick done messed up now." She laughed. "I'm so happy you finally woke up. That Dominick be putting his love spells on us. He really be having the girls going crazy in the hospital. It's not just the young ones. You see how Dr. Alexander look like she wanna fuck him? Lord have mercy!"

"Wow, I did see they had a little chemistry going."

"She clueless too, though. Just like us, she fell for the smile, the tats, and the muscles. That dick was working too. I ain't gonna lie, I needed it. I was so lonely in the hospital. He made me feel so beautiful."

She sighed. "I know the feeling." Journey folded the golden belt and put it aside.

"You wanna keep it?"

"Yes, I want it to remember you. I'm so sorry, Delilah. How did you die? Did he do something to you?"

"I wasn't getting any better, so he put some insulin in my IV, and it took me right on out of here." She clapped her hands together and imitated a plane taking off with her hands. *"Don't look so sad, gurl. It's okay, I've seen my baby already."*

Journey's eyes widened. *"You did?"*

"Yup, she here. We good. You gonna be good when it's your time too. But until then, you got work to do, Miss Journey. I got work to do on this side. They keeping a sister busy."

She walked out of the room and waved, then she vanished into the staircase.

"Delilah, wait. Delilah?" Journey rushed up the stairs and saw no sign of her. "Damn it! She's gone. He was raping those girls. Taking advantage of the weak. She was so young. Dominick was a wolf in sheep's clothing," Journey mumbled to herself. He preyed on young girls at their weakest and most vulnerable moments. She was angry at herself for falling under his spell too, but there was no way she was going to let him get way with that. She had to get revenge, not just for herself, but for the many girls he took advantage of. Journey had the perfect plan, but knew she couldn't do it alone.

Journey didn't find anything else in the bag but socks and T-shirts. Then she remembered to check the desk drawer. She saw receipts from Publix, Chipotle, Amazon, and then the Hilton. The Amazon receipt was for a key finder, which she knew was also used as tracking device. It was ordered over two weeks ago. That was around the time she started driving again and working.

The Hilton receipt was dated the same night she had met with Phil at the very same bar. Dominick had two drinks. Her skin crawled as she envisioned him watching them the whole time. Did he see them go up to the room?

Her heart plummeted in her chest, and her hands shook. She didn't want to believe it. This motherfucker was following her, tracking her like a piece of property.

There was a crumpled sticky note in the drawer next to it that read:

1. Phil Esposito
2. Helen Esposito
   561 Peachtree Court
3. Marlon - C&C CFO
   542 Sycamore Lane

"Oh, no!" She took the paper and ran upstairs. "Mom, I'll be back. Please do not let Dominick back in here. I think he did something to Phil."

"What? How? Where are you going?"

"I'll be back soon. I'll explain later. Dominick is dangerous." She started to panic, realizing there may be a tracking device on her car, so she took her mother's car instead. "I'm going to use your car. I'll be back soon. Please trust me on this, Mom."

As she got in her car, she called Elizabeth. "Girl, can you meet me at the coffee shop? It's urgent. No, better yet, can I come to your hotel? I don't want to talk on the phone about it."

Chapter 23

Elizabeth

When she opened the door, Journey's face was drenched in disbelief.

"This asshole played me. He was controlling me this entire time. Following me. I think he hurt Phil. I just have a feeling. My client Phil is missing. I am so afraid he has a tracking device on my car, so I used my mom's car to come here. I saw receipts that he bought one."

"Come in, sit down. Breathe. What happened to Phil?"

Journey just started crying. "I don't know. I don't know. It feels bad. So bad, and it's my fault. We had a meeting, and then he invited me to his room to do yoga, and things got a little heated. And . . ." She lowered her eyes.

"*No*, Journey, you slept with him? Couldn't he be your grandpa?"

"Yes, I know. I know. It was just so much build-up, and he just knows how to make me feel good. I was lonely."

"He's old and married."

"Girl, he was the best lover. Like he was a twenty-nine-year-old. I need you to read him please. Can you maybe find out where he is? If he's hiding? Or maybe someone has him for ransom. I don't know." Terror smothered her thoughts, and tears glistened in her eyes. "I just have a bad feeling, and I want to be wrong."

"Okay, okay, give me a minute."

"Philip Esposito, fifty-nine." Elizabeth went in quickly, and then her breathing became labored.

"What's wrong? What's wrong?"

"I'm just feeling like I am having a hard time breathing. His throat." She touched her neck. "It feels constricted." Elizabeth rubbed the back of her neck.

"Do you think he's . . . alive?" Journey wrung her hands nervously, searching for answers in Elizabeth's face.

Her eyes were closed, and she said calmly, "I, I am not sure. I don't feel good."

"Is Dominick involved?"

"I'm not sure. This is kind of new to me, reading a crime. I don't want to give you the wrong info. Maybe you should call the cops."

"With what proof?"

"Those receipts. The notes."

"Yes, but that doesn't prove anything. We have to do something. He's dangerous. I have a better plan."

"We should tell Ty and Marlon too. What if they are being targeted? You never know."

"I need you to help me."

"I will, sis."

Journey

Phil Missing -DAY 3

Journey saw that her old yoga studio had posted a missing person's alert on their page. It was for Helen. She wasn't answering her phone, and no one seemed to know where she was. Her throat tightened. Journey shared the graphic with Elizabeth, then called her.

"It's him. I know it's him."

"It's time, Journey."

An hour later, Journey sent Dominick a text.
Journey: I'm so sorry.
Dominick: For what?
Journey: For how I treated you.
Dominick: It's okay. I really didn't mean any harm. I just wanted to help you. You know it was all love. I just might be a little passionate about it.

Journey: Can you come over? I want to talk in person.

Dominick: Sure. I'm leaving work and can be there in thirty.

When he entered the house, she realized this was going to be harder than she thought. All the feelings rushed back to how he was before. She really knew the truth about her stalker, and now was the time to get him to confess. He walked in slowly. They hugged, and it felt so good to her.

"I missed you," she confessed in her softest voice.

"Journey, you don't know how long I've been waiting to hear you say that. I'm just so sorry about everything. I just want justice for you. I—"

"It's okay. You don't have to explain." She thought she would have to brace herself to kiss him, but it was easy. She couldn't lie to herself. She missed Dominick when she knew she shouldn't. She missed the pampering and the affection he gave her, especially when her mom wasn't around. They hid their secret love pretty well. She knew now that came with a heavy price.

He held her chin gently. "There's so much I wanted to say to you today, and now just looking into your eyes . . . I'm speechless."

"Me too."

He pushed her against the wall and ran his hands down her body slowly and seductively. "When does she come home tonight?"

"Not until later." Journey wasn't thinking. This was not the next step, but she was actually considering having sex with him, until she heard a shout penetrate her skull.

It was Elizabeth.

"Stick to the script! Stick to the script!"

She rubbed his crotch and said softly, "Is there anything you want to tell me? I feel like you held onto too many secrets."

He sat in a big chair and pulled her onto his lap. He started kissing an earlobe, her neck, behind her neck, and rubbing his hands through her hair.

"If you're a good girl, I might tell you later. I like to keep some things as a surprise. Let me feel you again." He slid his hands slowly down the center of her legs. Journey didn't resist and let him venture deep inside her panties. He maneuvered his finger with precision. He remembered every inch of her. He knew exactly what to do to make her quiver. She was so close to just saying abort mission, but she couldn't let her thirst for pleasure take over.

"Shit, Dominick. This feels *so* good."

"Let me put it in. I want to feel you again."

Journey reached down and grabbed his dick. She slowly pulled it out of his scrubs and started to jerk him off.

"Wait. Oh, shit. Damn. Journey, waaaait. I want you. Ah, shit." He came all over her hand, and some of it went on her leggings. It was barely two minutes.

"We can always do it later. Don't look so sad."
She laughed. "Someone was horny. I want to talk
first about everything. This is important." She
went to the bathroom to rinse off and brought him
a towel. He sat there looking dumbfounded by
what she had done.

She sat down on the edge of the bed, facing him
in the chair. "So, I started to pack up your stuff and
found Delilah's belt."

His lusty gaze turned into a wrinkled brow. He
raised his voice. "What? You went through my bag,
through my stuff?"

"I was just trying to consolidate everything. I
remembered seeing that gold belt from visions
when the girls would come talk to me. I thought it
was so funny to have a belt on a hospital gown.
It was just so odd to know you held onto her stuff
and didn't give it to her family."

"I, I don't know. It was just a cute and funny
memory. I wanted to remember it and her."

"You know, since you left, my third eye is turned
all the way back on."

His lips pressed flat. "But you need to take your
meds, Journey. I don't want another incident to
happen like what brought you to the hospital."

"No, I'm good. I couldn't see Francesa and
Delilah on those drugs, and I think that was in-
tentional. I wondered why you were so concerned
about what they told me about you."

"Oh, see, it's already started, mama. The para-noia."

"Dominick, do not try to paint me as insane. I'm just gonna come out and say it. Did you sleep with those little girls?"

"What?" Guilt was plastered all over his face.

"That's a yes or a no question."

"They had crushes on me. They probably wished." He pushed out a fake chuckle.

"Really? I spoke to Delilah, and she said you did."

Francesca appeared on the arm of the chair he sat in. Journey was trying not to laugh. He couldn't see or feel her. Francesca was making funny faces and sticking out her tongue.

"You know, I can hear messages, read energy, and sometimes even read minds. I'm very tele-pathic. So be careful. Francesca is right here."

"Oh, is she now?" He laughed, trying to down-play his nervousness.

"Well, my little friend spilled all the beans."

"Uh oh, so I'm being ambushed by ghosts?" He kept laughing, and it made Journey want to really go in on him.

"How did Francesca die?"

He squinted, shocked by the question. "I thought I told you. Her lungs gave out,"

"How did Delilah die?"

"Her tumor. She had a brain tumor. Her body shut down from it. Wait, why are you asking me this shit? What are you implying?"

"Oh, I'm not implying anything. I know what you did. You killed those innocent girls, and I'm sure there were more. Oh, wait. And Francesca said you raped Delilah consistently, even when she was unconscious and couldn't tell. You kept her drugged up. She died with your child in her belly. No one ever knew since she had boyfriend. They blamed him for the rape, and you just watched it all unfold."

"Wow, wow. You really sound crazy now. I think your wild imagination has gotten the best of you. We need you to book another session with Dr. Brinson."

Francesca said, "*He's laughing now, but he finna go right to jail. They are gonna love his pretty ass in there. You know how he killed us, Journey? He put insulin in our IV. Just injected it with not a care in the world.*"

"You killed those girls by overdosing them with insulin. That's how you did it, right?"

His face was drained of color. His laughter came to a halt as he watched Journey with sheer terror. She was on to him, and he knew it.

"You killed innocent girls after you had your way with them. God only knows what the fuck you were doing to me in those two months I was in a coma."

"That's sick. I would never do anything to you without your consent. I didn't need to. I helped you feel again, love again. I protected you, Journey.

This is how you treat me? Attacking me with these ghost stories. This is how you repay me? This is what you invited me over for? I'm your only friend," he shouted.

Journey's eyes watered. "It all makes sense. They say serial killers save things from their kills. That belt was a sign. Your little souvenirs. No wonder you loved watching so many true crime and murder shows. They were teaching you how to get away with murder for real."

"Oh, great. Now I'm a serial killer. I never murdered anybody. I wouldn't call it murder. I just quieted them. I took them out of their misery."

"I regret even letting you back here."

"Don't play victim now after you just kissed me and stroked me. You want me still. Admit it." He got up, and his crotch was eye level to her while she sat on the edge of bed. "You still want me. Admit it. I'm just as intuitive as you. I see your energy craving mine."

"You know, that's what hurts the most, Dominick. I truly had feelings for you, and now I wonder if it was all a lie."

"Come on, you know that's not the truth."

"You just wanted to control me. I was your little project."

"Journey, you know that's not true." He caressed her face and tilted her chin up towards him.

Her eyes were glassy. She was holding back something. She was hurting. "Where's Phil? Did you do anything to him?"

"Who?"

"Philip Esposito. Helen was here looking for him the other day when you were over here."

"How the hell should I know?"

"I find it very strange that right after I kick you out, Phil turns up missing. Was it a coincidence that you were at the hotel the same exact night I was there for a meeting with him?"

Journey invaded his mind and heard, *She knows. Shit. She knows.*

She shot him a loud message.

"That's right. I know what you did. Don't play dumb."

"How do you know where I was?"

"I have the receipts, that's how." She went in her pocket and held them up. He snatched them out of her hand.

"Oh, come on. You really think I didn't make a copy of the evidence already?"

His voice was slow and deliberate. He sounded sinister. "You know, Journey, you really tried to play me for a fool. You think I wouldn't find out?"

"Find out what?"

"That you were fucking him?"

"Wow, really? Is that what you think? What's it to you if I did? You were never my man."

That stung. His face went sour, and he clenched his jaws. "I was the best thing that you had in your life, and you threw it away to whore yourself off. You are better than that. I was trying to help you to honor your temple. I worshiped you."

"What the fuck are you talking about? Whoring myself out?"

"I know you were selling yourself. You went to his room to have sex. I heard it all. Room 546 right? I was right there."

She felt his rage building, and fear started to take over. Journey got up from the bed, and he followed her.

"What? What did you do?"

He walked closer to her, and she walked backwards until he was right on her in the corner of the room.

"He was pretty much pimping you out, and you didn't even know it. I know about the clients. I know about the payments. Some of them were referred to you by him, you know? I researched a few of them, and they are in his little entertainment circle. You were their little amusement park."

"What are you talking about?" Journey's stomach churned, realizing he may be right. Some of her "special arrangement" clients never wanted to say who referred them, but most were in the spotlight somehow.

"I was on your phone just like your mother. I had access to learn all about you for months. I got you. I studied you. I saw the messages, the photos, the videos. I knew about all of it. I wanted to help you. I wanted us to help each other. You are just as obsessed with sex and control like me. That's why we are perfect for one another. Don't you get it yet? Like attracts like. You are my soulmate, my twin flame."

Her voice was shaking. "Dominick, where is Philip Esposito? You followed me. You went to the room?"

"Yes, yes. I know it all. I saw when you left too. You need to look around more. Watch your surroundings."

"You had a tracking device on me, didn't you?"

"Yes, but it was only for your safety. Look at you, you little private investigator." He tickled under her chin.

"What is wrong with you? How could you do this? They did nothing to you."

"That's where you're wrong. They hurt you, and that's hurting me. I have been with you the entire time. You want to run to an old man for help, and he just used you like an exotic doll." He shook his head in disgust.

"What? What are you talking about? Are you speaking about Phil?

"Yes, absolutely. What a fine gentleman. Definitely old enough to be your sugar daddy or grandpa."

"What did you do to him? Please tell me."

"Oh, nothing. We had a nice drink at the bar together. After I pulled the fire alarm to make everyone get up. Everyone was relieved it was a false alarm. I just did it to bring him out of his room. I actually treated him at the bar. He's a friendly guy. I think he thought I was coming on to him, and he wanted to fuck me too. You know a lot of those entertainment dudes are freaks."

"Stop it. Stop it."

"But I think his yoga session with you wore him out. I'm not gay anyway, but I do think I know how to use my charm and good looks to get answers."

"Where is he, Dominick?"

"What do you mean where is he? Haven't you spoken to him? When I saw him, he was drinking. I only bought him a shot, but he seemed to want me. He's fine, I'm sure. Last time I saw him, was just at the hotel bar."

"You need help! Did you hurt him?"

"He's with his wife. They are together. They deserve each other. You needed to leave married men alone."

She screamed in his head so loud it was like a thumping migraine.

"WHAT THE FUCK DID YOU DO TO PHIL?"

Her voice quivered. "Did you hurt him?"

"I'm not having this conversation with you. Why are you out to get me today? What's with all the drama? This interrogation? I'm thinking you invited me over so that I could make passionate love to you." He fondled her breast.

She slapped it away, and he grabbed her hand tightly. He said in her ear, "I know you still want me, Journey. I felt how wet that pussy was. The body doesn't lie." He grabbed her face and shoved his other hand in between her legs.

"You are a sick fuck. Stop it." She squirmed in the corner like a trapped animal.

"Your mouth is too pretty to be talking like that. Come here and let me show you how sick I am. I know you like it rough. You want me to fuck good, right? Is that what this is? Get me all worked up and angry so I can fuck you hard? Just thinking about you fucking all of those guys." He sighed. He grabbed her closer, and she moved her face away from his.

"Seeing all those nasty pictures you took for them and of them. Just sucking and fucking random dudes. You are such a freak, and I loved that about you. So free spirited. So uninhibited. I just want you more right now, because you are finally all mine now. Philip won't be calling you anymore. He was in the way. Marlon is next, because he is threatening me now. I guess you told them."

Journey froze at the realization that he did do something. He killed him. He might kill Marlon and her next.

He pulled down his scrubs. "You should have just taken your medicine." He slapped her butt. "Come on. Let's do it right here. I know you aren't ovulating now, so we should be safe."

She let him pull her pants down and whimpered. "Pleeeeease. I don't want to. Stop it."

"Look at how sexy you are. You have me so turned on. Damn, I love you, mama."

Journey balled her fist and pushed him off. "I said no! Elizabeth! Elizabeth!" Her anger sent a forceful jolt to Dominick's body that pushed him to the ground. He was on the floor with his erection in the air and pants to his thighs.

Footsteps charged down the stairs.

"That's it. That's enough." It was a police officer.

He pulled up his pants quickly and stood up. "What's going on? Who's this?"

He pointed to the cop and Elizabeth behind him. Another cop followed behind her.

Journey pointed at him. "He assaulted me. He tried to rape me. He forced me to touch him." She started crying. "Look!" She pointed to the semen on her leg and on the towel.

"What? Are you kidding me? Officer, this is my girlfriend. She's just playing. We were just role playing. Elizabeth, you called the cops?"

She ignored him and shouted, "She's not his girlfriend! He was trying to rape her! He was fired as her home care attendant."

"So, this is not a lover's quarrel with his girl?" the officer asked.

"No, officer, I am not his girl. I was his patient. He used to rape me. Drug me and rape me. I think he killed two people. I have his confession. I have everything." She pointed to the camera.

"What the fuck are you talking about, Journey? What confession?"

She pointed to a red light on the bookshelf. "I recorded you for my safety."

His face was flushed. "She's lying. Can't you see they set me up?"

"Hands behind your back. You're under arrest. You have the right to remain silent."

Elizabeth chimed in, "She was screaming for help. That's why I called the cops."

"Bravo. Bravo. You ladies set me up." He started to cry as reality sunk in when they put the handcuffs on him. "Journey, how could you do this? I did it for you. I did it for us." Spittle sprayed everywhere as the officer led him out of the apartment. Two cop cars were outside, and more policemen came to put him in the car.

"You're a monster!" Journey screamed. She was crying because of Phil, but even more so because she had believed Dominick could be her someone, her soul mate, but he was just a sick, controlling fuck. She was crying because she was hoping he was wrong about them. They were not the same. She was nothing like him. She had changed for the better.

Janet, Delilah and Francesca all stood on the curb by the police car. They clapped and waved as the car drove off to the precinct.

Elizabeth and Journey hugged and cried. "We did it. Thank you, sis. We did it." Journey cried.

The ambulance arrived to check Journey out while the cops took her statement. She had his DNA all over her yoga pants and towel. That was a part of the plan as well. Watching true crime shows had come in handy. She was going to make sure he never got out of prison.

Chapter 24

Journey

The next day

Claudia said, "I'm so sorry, Journey. I just heard the news."

"What news?"

She handed her the phone. Journey saw an article from the local gossip blog. Journey collapsed to the ground with the phone and sobbed. "No! No! He's gone?"

Her mother bent down and hugged her. "I know, baby. I'm so sorry."

Double Homicide Rocks Buckhead, ATL Area

The Black Rose Murders:

ENTERTAINMENT COMMUNITY MOURNS AS A PROMINENT ATTORNEY'S BODY WAS FOUND in Lake Lanier. Wife murdered execution style.

Philip Esposito, ESQ, 59 years old, was found on the shore in Lake Lanier by a local fisherman two days ago. His body was just identified. Esposito was an entertainment lawyer who was Italian-American and hailed from Brooklyn, NY. He was an attorney to some of Atlanta and LA's top rappers, actors, and comedians. The community is in mourning and in total shock to learn of his sudden passing. It is deemed as foul play, due to the fact he was found shirtless but with black rose petals stuffed down his pants and his pockets. The witness said he had rope markings around his throat and a possible bullet wound. However, he figured it was overkill due to the strangulation.

A day later, the mysterious clue of black rose petals were also sprinkled around Mrs. Helen Esposito's torso. She was discovered by their maid in their Buckhead mansion. The cryptic message has not been solved yet. Black roses represent either death and mourning or power and strength, so it's up to

the detectives to put that puzzle together. A
suspect is now in custody.

Ty

The last week had been a whirlwind. Journey
and Elizabeth actually came together to solve two
murders and open up cases on two more. Ty really
couldn't believe all that they did to get Dominick
arrested.

Ty read the blog article online and said to Papa,
"That Dominick was a piece of work. What a twisted
individual who was acting as if he was truly sup-
porting others. He's going to jail for a long time."

"Yes, he was evil."

"His trial isn't set yet, but based on everything
we heard so far, they're probably going to put him
in jail for life. The news is calling him the Black
Rose Murderer."

"Journey did good." Papa shook his head.

Ty was surprised by his comment, since he knew
she was not one of Papa's favorite people. Journey
wasn't going to be trusted one hundred percent yet
by any of them, but they had seen that she was on
the road to recovery.

Marlon dropped his order of protection against
her. Everyone was thrilled that they got Dominick
off the street. Ty knew that a family meeting was

finally going to happen later that day after the Sweetwater building launch.

"Papa, what do you think about inviting Journey?"

He grunted. He did the sign of the cross and laughed. "She should come. They all must know the truth about our family. I'm afraid more bad things will happen as their powers progress. They need to learn early how to control them. They need to understand their gifts. I've seen it all. I remember my visions from the future and the past when I travel in my sleep."

"Will you be okay with her around?"

"Yes, I just want them all here."

"You know Elizabeth found one more child from the sibling registry?"

"Yes, yes. I am very pleased. He is the one I wanted to meet next."

Epilogue

The Meeting

Ty had everyone in the living room sit in a circle. Papa sat in his chair and smiled proudly. He had given Jocelyn the day off since he wanted this gathering to be private for family only.

"It is very nice to meet you all. Three months ago, I could barely speak and couldn't remember much English. I could not walk unassisted." He pointed at Elizabeth. "Your sister doesn't know just how grateful I am to her for healing me with her gifts. Because of her, she made it possible for us to come together. I tried to reach you all in your dreams, but most of you thought they were just dreams. Now, I can share with you in person some important things you must know. The truth. My heart has been aching, because you have all been living your lives in the dark. These things pertain to our own heritage, our bloodline, and things that must not leave this room." He slowly made eye contact with everyone seated in the circle. "Do you agree?"

They all nodded.

Incense danced around the room, and candles were lit around them for a calm ambience; however, the room was tense. Everyone was nervous and unsure of what was to come. It was an awkward situation for them since they didn't all know each other that well yet. They could see their features in each other's faces. The Garcia genes were very strong. That made Papa proud. They might not all come from the same places around the world, but they were indeed family.

Zack tapped his foot nervously and twirled one of his yarn-like golden locks. Elizabeth slapped his leg to stop it. Robbie covered his mouth, trying not to laugh. Siblings. They truly acted like it.

Ty cleared his throat. "This is serious, guys. Please listen and pay attention."

Papa continued, "In all of my years of silence, I was confined to this very chair, but I traveled. Oh, how I traveled." He chuckled as if reliving a memory. "How is that possible, you may ask? It's one of my skills. I enhanced it tremendously with practice. I was able to visit other regions of the world and other dimensions, other planets, and other times."

His storytelling was music to everyone's ears, especially Ty's. Just to see his abuelo command the attention of the crowd again made his heart soar.

"I know we are all capable of it. Some of these gifts we may call a superpower can also cause instant death and destruction when not handled properly. I really want you to take this seriously." He looked at Journey, and she sat up straight up, realizing all eyes were on her.

Ty stood behind him and said, "So, are you going to share with everyone about their special gifts that they have?"

"Yes, you are the artist, eh, Roberto?"

"Yes." Robbie smiled at the Spanish version of his name. He wasn't going to correct him either. "Well, kinda. I do illustrations."

"You will be able to draw the future, meaning what you draw is a prediction. But you can also make things you draw come to life. You are also a very talented medium."

"I kinda thought that was something happening, so I stopped drawing. It made me afraid."

"No, no. You must not stop. There's nothing to be afraid of. You just have to learn how to guide your thoughts better for positive outcomes. You must not abuse it either."

Elizabeth shook her head. "Papa, he's also a very good psychic. So talented."

Robbie held his head down. He was embarrassed by the attention. "I'm . . . I'm still figuring it all out. Thank you for doing this to help us. We need it."

They all mumbled in unison, "Yes." A few chuckled too.

Papa pointed to Elizabeth. "You are the medicine woman with healing hands. You see or feel chakras. You heal illness, but you mustn't let your ego get in the way. You must be careful, because if you do too much, you will be watched. Draw too much attention to yourself."

Zack said, "Maybe even captured by the government to study under the guise of working for them as a scientist."

"That part!" Journey said, pointing.

"Say less," Robbie said, and they all laughed.

Papa wasn't really getting the joke, but he got the gist of it.

"Yes, you see, everyone must not know what you can do, because they will try to coerce you with fancy titles and money, and then you will turn into a lab rat instead."

He pointed to Zack. "Oh, you, you float through the cosmos, eh?"

Everyone started laughing.

"Sounds about right." Zack nodded and laughed.

"You are not here on Earth much, no?"

Robbie cackled.

"Meaning, you . . . you travel to different planes similar to me. I do my travel mostly in my sleep. You do it in your waking hours."

Journey laughed. "Oh my God. Nailed it. That's right, you got him."

He rolled his eyes at Journey. He didn't seem happy about the wise cracks.

"Zack, you mustn't be afraid of your gift. You can travel within dreams like me and time travel."

"Wow, I haven't done that yet, but that sounds so cool. I want to learn."

"Journey!"

She jumped.

"Journey, you can move objects with their mind. You can travel as well, and you're a very good psychic medium. Ah, and you all have the gift of telepathy. We all have it, but I see Ty and Journey might have it stronger than most. It can be dangerous if you use it wrong."

Ty agreed. "Yes, it can be abused. Guilty." He raised his hand, and everyone smiled.

"But the telekinesis and the mind control is a dangerous combo gift, and they have it," Papa said.

Ty said to Journey, "Let's try something together." He tapped his temple. He was sending her a message. Everyone in the room started to gently tap their toes unconsciously.

Elizabeth looked down at her feet. "Oh my God. I'm not doing this, Robbie!"

"Neither am I. What the fuck?"

Papa's feet tapped too, and he laughed.

"Sorry, Papa. I didn't mean to cuss."

"It's okay."

They all started laughing, and the feet tapping stopped.

"Okay, we get the picture." Elizabeth was amazed.

"Do you see why this is dangerous?"

They all nodded in unison.

"We have one more sibling coming, yes?" Papa took a sip of his water.

Elizabeth checked her phone. "Yes, he's running late. His flight got delayed. He's coming from Guyana."

"How cool. The family is growing," Journey said. "What's his name?"

"It's Steven Amar Singh, but he likes to go by Amar. I looked it up, and guess what it means? Immortal." Elizabeth whispered it dramatically.

"Do you think he's going to make it?" Zack asked.

"Yep. He should be in a Uber right now."

"So, what can Big Papa do?" Robbie asked.

"Same things," Ty said. "Read minds, barely telekinesis, but I haven't really practiced it. And out-of-body traveling. I'm just as amazed myself at all of these gifts we have. I am looking forward to practicing more. And like Papa, I can visit people in their dreams, but I haven't done it in a long time."

Robbie said quietly to Ty, "Wow, kind of like Freddy Krueger, right?" They all giggled.

Papa said, "I want you all to know there are some dangerous energies around us and in our bloodline. We have to focus on the positive side of our gifts and not abuse them. When you let ego get in the way, it causes great damage. Be careful of manipulating people. It will come back to haunt you.

"I'm a perfect example. Your grandmother tried her hardest to tame me. Sometimes what she thought might have been good for me caused more damage. She played around with magic, and it ended up crippling my body and my mind instead of helping me."

"Whoa, really, papa? I never knew that." Ty looked at him with raised brows and leaned in more.

"There are a lot of things you didn't know about, Tylercito. I was a gambler, a womanizer. I manipulated people on many, many levels. Even stocks and bonds and things in the marketplace were shifted by my doing. Your grandmother saw me spiraling out of control and tried everything she could. Our marriage became a marriage of bondage and not so much love. She tried to control me, and I tried to control her. It got worse each year, and I was a danger to myself and her."

He continued his story. "In Cuba, I worked with the mob. I was a hitman without a weapon."

"No weapon? What did you do to kill people with your bare hands? You know karate?"

"Yeah, how?" Elizabeth asked.

"Make them have an accident in their mind."

No one wanted to look at Journey, but Ty noticed Journey shifting in her seat. She knew.

Papa pulled his hand out and made a squeezing motion. "I would squeeze their hearts in their sleep until it exploded."

"Ahhh! Damn!" Robbie slapped his leg. "That's cool as hell."

"They would just be written off as having a heart attack or natural death." Papa seemed to revel in their excitement listening to his stories. "One day, I will share more, but I don't want you to learn any of my wicked ways. I want to teach you self-control. If you don't have control of yourself, these gifts will become curses and will take you to hell and back. I don't want that for you. I didn't really have many teachers. I want you to help each other, look after each other. I don't want to have to control you myself." He stared everyone in their eyes as if in warning. They all looked at each other in fear, wondering if he had almost killed Journey for acting out and abusing her gift.

Elizabeth said, "How do we manage it or develop it more?"

"With dedication, daily work, daily meditation, practice with one another. I know you were doing it before, but you need more guidance from me."

"Can we meet weekly like on video or something, but with you, Papa, and Ty?"

"Yes. I have nothing else to do." He chuckled. "I'm an old man, and I want to pass this on. I thought I didn't have much time left, but thanks to Elizabeth, she may have prolonged my life five or ten more years.

Robbie rocked in his seat excitedly. "Yo. bruh, this is really dope. It's like the X-Men for real." He gave Zack a pound, and they giggled.

Elizabeth said, "Now we have to change the group to the Fantastic Six. No, Seven, since one more is coming."

Robbie said, "Nah, that's wack. How about the 1544 Alliance?"

Zack covered his mouth. "Ohhhhh, yeah, that's it right there."

"I likes. I likes," Journey said. "That sounds official."

"Will we be able to learn each other's skills?" Elizabeth asked.

"I'm sure with practice and intention anything is attainable. It's in our blood. You just need to own your power. My other reason for bringing us together is about a vision I had. It's a recurring dream. I think it's a message, but pray it's not going to happen. I had a vision of one child that is in this group causing major destruction to a city, the planet even, and the cause of a rippling effect. I don't know if it can be stopped, but I'm hoping it can. I don't see who has this gift yet, but this child will know how to manipulate the elements."

Ty asked, "Wow, you mean like the weather?"

"Yes. Air, water, metals. I saw earthquakes, mudslides, tornadoes, great destruction."

"I doubt if it's any of us," Robbie said.

"Not now. It doesn't happen in my lifetime, and it might not be orchestrated on purpose. The biggest thing we have to watch for are our human impulses. The need to control, to be right. Manage our jealousy, wanting revenge. Those are all of our weaknesses."

Elizabeth said softly, "It's like we might have a tendency for being quite narcissistic."

Ty said, "Sounds like it."

Papa sighed as if remembering the harm he had caused in his life. "People will hurt you. You will be disappointed, betrayed, and lied to. But if you don't understand your gifts, you won't allow these moments take over you. It's a part of life."

They all stared at Papa with newfound wonderment, taking it all in. It was a lot of pressure for these twenty-somethings. They weren't ready for the responsibility, Ty thought.

Ty said, "So, to be clear, this stays between us. No texting, no social media posts about it. Don't start making a logo for the 1544 Alliance." He pointed to Robbie, and they laughed.

"We're keeping a low profile. Understood," Robbie said, zipping his lips.

The doorbell rang, and everyone sat up with anticipation.

Elizabeth jumped up. "I'll get him."

Once the doors opened, everyone's eyes fixed on a strong, regal presence that walked in. He was a handsome, tall, lean man. He had clay brown skin like Ty's with a full, shiny beard. He was close in height with Ty. He almost floated in the room with a white African headwrap, white linen tunic, blue jeans, white sneakers, and a Gucci backpack. He had a clean yet classy look for a young man.

"Hello everyone! I'm Amar. So nice to meet you all!" His innocent smile lit up the room.

Elizabeth said, "He's our baby brother, everybody. He's the youngest at only nineteen. Robbie, sorry. You're not the baby anymore."

Everyone said, "Ahhh," in unison.

He walked around the circle and shook everybody's hands. Amar bowed with his right hand on his heart to Papa and Ty. "My pleasure, my pleasure. So nice to meet you all."

He looked like a young Indian guru, but spoke like a proper British boy. There was a splash of an island accent. He seemed very interesting to them all.

"This is so surreal. I look just like you!" Amar said to Ty.

Ty laughed. "Yes, you do. That you do." They hugged.

"I'm so happy to have an extended family. Thank you for having me. For many years, I felt a part of me was missing. Today you have blessed me with that part."

Ty felt his energy was pure and inspiring.

Papa extended his hand. "We covered a lot already, but we're just beginning. We will do more this weekend. Today, we have a big day of celebration for Ty's new building opening."

They all clapped.

"Yay, Ty. Congrats!" Elizabeth cheered.

Papa said, "Welcome to our new family. We have lots to cover. Let's do a few exercises before we leave for the event. You will all learn to protect the legacy."

Journey said, "1544 Alliance."

"Yes, that's us!" Ty's eyes felt moist as he blinked, trying to hold back his tears. He was buzzing with excitement to see everything come together. Even with Journey back in the circle, he felt it was somehow going to all work out. They would all learn from one another to protect the family's legacy.

The End

Author Bio

Simone Kelly is an author, filmmaker, and the CEO of Own Your Power® Communications, Inc. where she assists many as a Holistic Business and Intuitive Life Coach. She's the author of six books, her most recent being the Amazon bestseller titled *#1544*. Originally from the Bronx, NY, Simone currently resides in Atlanta, Georgia.